Elysium

A Black Diamond Vacation Romance

DL White

BOOKS

Welcome back to Black Diamond...

FINDING THE GREATEST LOVE REQUIRES TAKING THE GREATEST risks...

Athena Wilcox leads a solitary life as a travel nurse, committed to her work and her only child. When entrepreneur Vance Griffin sends a flirty private message, she's intrigued...but conflicted. Casual flirtation soon blossoms into late-night conversations that bring a yearning for more.

A tempting invitation and sensual first meeting sparks hope that the fantasy they've been creating could become reality. Both know this is no casual fling, but could an online relationship translate to a perfect real world love affair?

The emerald waters and white sands of Black Diamond will sweep you away with pulse-pounding romance, sensuality, and emotional depth as two lovers begin the second chapter of their lives while discovering what it means to wander together. What started with a flirty message could become a love that stands the test of time.

Author's note

Hello again. We're doing this thing where the people pop into my head and tell me stories. Then you buy them and tell me how much you enjoyed the stories the people in my head told me. I'm so happy to be back here with you.

This book is...*fun*. That's the word I want to use. It is fun, sexy and decadent. I had a ball bringing Vance and Athena, a seasoned Black couple who are ready to fall in love, to life. I know you will also enjoy this couple.

I have a few words to prepare you for this book:

There is sex in it. *GASP.* There are several scenes, both virtual and in person that use toys, cameras, adult language and situations.

You will not see our fave couple from BEACH THING, Wade and Ameenah, in this novel. There is a mention of Tikis & Cream, Ameenah's shop. You will see them in the next Black Diamond book. Hang in until then! ;)

There is no mention of condoms, birth control, or methods to prevent sexually transmitted infections in this novel. I realized I hadn't written them when I was already in deep and I simply did not feel like going back to write them in. Assume they're there and that Vance and Athena are sexually and biologically healthy. In addition, my characters are near fifty and *grown*, grown. There will be no surprise babies. The lack of condoms in this novel is not a hint to any story twists.

I *love* to hear how much people are enjoying my books. Please send any "GIRL, HE DID WHAT?!" to me on any social media site or to my **email**. Post any criticism to your review at your fave retail or review site.

I appreciate your time and good opinion and truly hope you adore this novel.

XOXO,

DL White

WAN·DER·LUST: (NOUN)

a strong desire to travel.

ATHENA

Started with a DM. Now we're here.

In a private chat room under cover of darkness, doing things I never imagined myself doing. And enjoying the hell out of it.

On the screen of my iPad, a long-legged, pecan-toned man lay in the middle of a king-sized bed on black satin sheets, knees wide and both hands...*occupied*. He glistened with the sheen of lubrication and a light coating of sweat.

On my end of the connection, I was naked, in view of a camera mounted on a tripod across the room. Vance, my long-distance, online—boy toy? Plaything? Temporary dalliance? —watched my hips undulate while a silicone rosebud toy sent alternating puffs of air and suction to my clit. In the absence of a man between my thighs, it was the next best thing, and it was sending me into orbit.

Some women used porn as a sleep aid to de-stress and take the edge off, then they were asleep before they could log out. At the end of a day, the only dick I wanted to be looking at, masturbating to, or imagining stroking in and out of me belonged to Vance Griffin. Nothing helped me relax like the view of him erect for me, his limbs poised for action, the sound of his palms massaging his shaft while he described erotic fantasies of us together.

Evenings with Vance, affectionately dubbed my night cap, were the best part of my day.

"I can't see your face, baby." His voice rode the tips of my nerve endings. It was a gruff and raspy whisper, like his throat was dry, but he didn't want to waste the seconds it would take to quench his thirst. "I need to see your face. I want to see you when you come."

"My bad. I got too comfortable. Let me sit up so you can see all this goodness."

I released the nipple I'd been twisting and sat up, then moved to my knees and spread them, a pillow shoved under my body for balance. In my peripheral vision, the iPad tipped precariously atop the blankets and sheets I'd thrown back. I picked it up and reset in my eye line. I didn't want to miss a moment of watching him pleasure himself while watching me.

"Can you see me now?"

"Mmmhmm, I see you," Vance answered. "I see *everything* —them titties, that sexy belly you be whining about, that pussy that's so wet it's shining, and I can hear it from here. *Fuck*, woman. You make me hard as shit!"

I snickered but kept it low. "You say the sweetest things."

I went back to kneading and massaging my breasts with one hand and rolling the rose over my throbbing clit. I would not last long in this position, but I didn't need to. Vance was so close, I heard the tremble in his voice. I just needed a few minutes to take him over the edge.

"I wish I was there with you, Vance."

"I wish you were here, too. Then you could do all this yankin'. What you thinking about doing for me?"

"I have..." I chuckled, rolling my eyes before letting the

lids close. "...so many thoughts right now. I'd take you in my hands and stroke you, nice and slow. Firm. Just like you're doing now. Tight grip, warm and wet. Until you're right on the edge and begging me to finish."

"Uh-huh..."

"And then, just when you think you might lose it, I'd take you into my mouth." I sent a lusty gaze to the camera. "All of you."

"Ooh, shit. You chokin' on it?"

I had to work to not roll my eyes. Vance had a swagger about him. He made me laugh, was sweet and thoughtful and generous and handsome, which was what made him sexy to me. His dick was an untested benefit that didn't figure into the equation. From my vantage point, he was an average length and girth. And I had a big mouth. I would hardly choke, but the imagery mattered.

"*Choking* on it, baby."

"I like that," he said, panting. "I want that. All of that. All of you. I wish I was deep inside you, with your wet pussy milking my dick."

"Oooh," I purred. "My skin is tingling, thinking about how it would feel if you were fucking me. Can you feel how tight I am? How I'm gripping you?"

He groaned, his movements growing faster. "Shit...feels so good!"

"You're so hard for me." I whimpered, my orgasm beginning to swirl. His breath hitched as I hunched into the rose. "You're...so..." I gasped. "..deep! Oh, God, Vance!"

His breathing had become erratic the faster he pumped. Judging from the volume of his groans and the juices seeping, he could climax at any moment, but he always waited to make sure I'd be right behind him. He had let his attention to the camera waver, but he remembered he wanted to watch me. He tipped his head up again and caught my eye.

"Thena…where you at, baby?"

I bit my bottom lip and rolled my hips in a steady rhythm, pressing the vibrating nub against my clit and pinching a nipple. The thrill of driving Vance to the brink, to bring him close to climax, then tip him over, was like nothing else.

"I'm ready when you are, handsome. Let's go together."

Vance

Athena and I had perfect synchrony, a frenzied rhythm where one of us spun us up, then relinquished power for the other to take us to paradise. Athena had led the charge. Now she wanted me to finish.

Don't mind if I do.

A rumble of pleasure rolled from me as I feverishly pumped. My breaths were heavy, loud in my ears, self-control slipping fast. My body begged for the release that I would give it in due time. I had to make sure that Athena was getting hers, too.

"Use your fingers," I told her. "Match me like I'm fucking you."

Athena moved a hand from her breast to the warm, wet junction of her thighs. She inserted two fingers and worked them in and out. Slow. Tempting. Sensual, then speeding up.

I wanted to close my eyes and imagine myself buried deep inside her, but I also wanted to watch her reach the peak and fall over. These moments made our sessions the most difficult. If we were together, I wouldn't have to choose.

"Shit...I want to come," Athena whimpered, her hips beginning a sexy rock.

"Tell me what you want, baby…"

"Open me wide. Fuck me hard, Vance!"

"*Yessss*," I growled. My balls tightened, the muscles in my body beginning to pulse.

She pushed out a stuttered, "Fuck, I-I-I'm c-coming!"

I watched her convulse in full-body shudders that began at her pelvis and radiated up and out across the airwaves to me. The sight and sounds of her climax sent me over the edge, her moans of bliss and pleasure-filled cries drawing out my orgasm. With a last stroke, I joined the chorus of loud enjoyment, marinating in the mood we had created with words and visions without even being in the same room.

Athena heaved a deep sigh and tipped back, unfolding her legs, stretching out on the bed. She flexed her calves, pointing her toes, caressing her body through the aftershocks.

Her breathing slowed, growing quieter as the minutes ticked by.

"You fall asleep on me?"

"I'm awake," I heard, but she sounded sleepy as fuck. "That was amazing, baby. Thank you."

"Nah, thank *you*. I enjoyed you tonight. Get up and cut that light off so you can sleep. 5AM comes early."

"Um-hmmm," she mumbled. "G'night."

I shut down the Zoom connection and slid the iPad to my nightstand. I lay there for a few minutes watching the ceiling fan rotate in the shadows, letting the aftereffects work their magic. The exhale I pushed out released pent up energy and was almost better than the orgasm.

My eyes slid closed, but that never shut out the thoughts, wants, and desires that had become more frequent as of late. Sex with Athena—actual sex, with no screens between us, my body connecting with hers, communicating more than base lust.

The craving to feel her breath on my skin, to watch her come.

The knowledge that she was lying next to me while we basked in the afterglow.

The entire experience that was Athena Wilcox had become a need that burned deep inside me and begged to be satisfied.

Someday.

ATHENA

Thena W: Morning handsome. Hopping in the shower. Room is open.

Vance-Wanderlust Travel: Good morning, gorgeous. Headed to Zoom in a few.

THE SOUNDS OF ESPN'S MORNING SHOW BLARED FROM VANCE'S TV as I emerged from the shower. I moved the iPad from the sheets where I'd left it the night before to the dresser so I could see him. Then I stepped into view of the webcam and tugged the towel from where it I had tucked it under my arm.

After a dramatic pause, I let it drop to the carpet.

"Jigglin' jigglin'...how that song go?"

Vance's teasing chuckle carried through the Bluetooth speakers, sending a ribbon of warmth through me.

"Ass be wigglin'..."

I kicked one leg out, then the other, twerking and crouching low to the beat of a song I only heard in my head.

"Get it, girl! Throw it in a circle!"

I snorted a laugh, then had to stop before I ran out of breath, bending to snatch the towel up off the floor so I could put it in the hamper. I planned to do a load of laundry that evening as soon as I got home.

"I'm defeating the purpose of taking a shower. I hate sweating before I even get dressed."

"You could just not get dressed," Vance suggested.

"And go to work naked? In Minnesota? In the winter?"

"Are you sure you have to go?"

"To work? Yeah, I'm pretty sure."

Vance lounged on the light comforter that always covered his bed against two large pillows, keeping his moisturized, nude form in view. "I've never seen you do that dance before."

"There's a lot you've never seen me do before."

"There's more stuff you've never done? Do tell."

I smoothed body oil into my skin, rubbing down my arms, then across my chest and belly. I poured another palm of the fragrant oil before I moved to my thighs, then bent to coat my legs and feet.

"The young nurses are always doing TikTok videos in the break room. Probably picked it up from them."

"The young nurses, huh?" I heard the smirk in his voice. "It's ok to admit you practice TikTok dances in the mirror, Thena."

I giggled. "Hush up, Van." I pulled open a drawer, back on task now that I was moisturized and dewy. I was not used to dry winter air, and it was hell on my skin, so I worked hard to protect it. "What color are we on today?"

"*Mmmph!*" I didn't even glance up at him. I knew he was ogling my full, pendulous breasts and dark brown nipples hardening in the cool air of my bedroom. "We gotta go with purple."

"Of course. It's your favorite color." I pulled a few sets of panties and bras from the drawer and held them up. "These are our options. I'm doing laundry tonight."

He pretended to consider the pairs in my hands, but I

knew which set he would pick. He clicked his tongue and shook his head. "I don't even know why you're asking. The deep purple ones with the lace and matching drawls."

"This lingerie is too expensive for you to be calling them drawls."

"I bought them just so I could see you in them. I can call them what I want."

I stepped into the deep eggplant-colored panties, pulling them up thick thighs and smoothing a palm over the fabric covering a soft belly that I was always complaining about. Then I wrestled my breasts into the supportive matching bra and turned so he could check me out.

Another growl unfurled. I watched him wrap a hand around himself, already growing hard.

"Everything is sitting real pretty. You sure you don't have time for a round?"

"I'm sure I don't. I wish I could stay online with you all day, but duty calls."

Vance frowned. "Fuck duty."

"Alright, grumpy. I see you didn't get enough sleep. Did we play too hard last night?"

A smile cracked the frown he was trying to hold. "Nah, baby. Last night was good. I want to play with the real thing, though. I'm ready to rip those purple drawls off of you and get personal."

"I'm sorry, ripping what? Not the Fenty!"

He frowned again, so hard a single dimple indented his left cheek. "Don't think I don't notice you change the subject every time I bring up meeting you."

"Don't think I don't notice you bring it up every day."

"That should tell you something."

"It tells me something, alright," I answered, chuckling.

"I said I would come up there if going away was too much pressure."

"And I appreciate that, but Big Fork, Minnesota is not a romantic destination."

"I don't plan to see much of it."

"You wouldn't even fit in this bed," I said, pointing to the bed shoved into the small room. There was barely room for a dresser and the closet was shameful. It was a good thing the house was cute.

"Come on out to Texas. We both fit in mine."

"You and a small army can fit in that big ass bed." I smirked at the camera because I was always shading Vance's large, manly bedroom.

"I told you I have a work trip coming up. You fly here, we spend a few hours on the road, then you play on the beach while I do my thing. Doesn't that sound nice?"

"Flying me out for a vacation in paradise sounds serious."

"Hell, yeah it's serious. We've been hanging out every day for months. I know you; you know me. It won't be any different when we're in person. It'll still be my name on your lips when you come. We'll just be in the same room."

Something about the words *in the same room* made my heart skip a beat and then gallop forward double-time.

"What happened to taking it slow? Messing around, having fun because, and I quote, *'it's not like we'll ever meet,'* hmmm?"

Vance's soft laughter floated through the speaker. "That horse left the barn the first time I saw that pussy. It's been real slow and a long while."

"It has been *nine* months. That's not a long while."

I was sure he'd have something to say to that, but no rebuttal came. When I checked the iPad, Vance was staring off-camera. The veins in his temple popped as he worked his jaw back and forth.

"I know you're not trying to hold back on me. Come on with it."

17

"Maybe I'm reading the wrong room," he said after a few moments of tense silence. "That shit you say at night doesn't apply during the day, does it? Is it just words that sound good because it gets me off? Like when you roll your eyes when I joke about how big my dick is? All of that, I wish '*I was there, I'd suck the black off—*'"

I shouted a laugh. "I have never said those words."

"Shit, that's what it sounds like. And it sounds damn good to me. I'm interested in making it a reality, but maybe you don't want to see if this thing is more than some Instagram flirting."

"I didn't say I don't want that."

"You're not saying you do, either."

I crossed the room to the closet, grabbed my last pair of clean scrubs, and sat on the bed to put on a lavender top with a bright pink flower print and two deep pockets in the front. The matching drawstring pants, compression socks, and non-slip sneakers followed.

"If this online, long-distance situation is never moving offline and up close, I need to manage expectations. Either we're doing something, or you're playing. Tell me which way we're going because I like you, but I'm not about to waste my time."

"Don't get an attitude with me, Vance. I wouldn't be online with you all day and night if I was. Our expectations aren't different; we're moving at different speeds."

I recalled clearly the first time I let him see me...*really* see me with the lights on, in frilly, lacy, pretty things he sent me because he wanted to see them on my body. I remembered his appreciation for the deep bronze tone of my skin, how he talked me through stroking in proxy for him. He'd surprised me with the rose toy and wanted to watch me writhe in pleasure while using it.

Mere months after he'd joked that we'd probably never meet, he'd been pushing for us to do just that.

"You don't want to meet up? You don't want to travel with me? You don't want to be all hugged up with me in real life? You like for me to live inside your computer and in your text messages and be nasty with you after 9, but not any other time—is that what you're trying to tell me?"

I stood at the mirror and untied a large multicolored scarf from my hair. While we talked, I dabbed styling gel along my edges and used a small brush to lay them down.

"You know that's not what I'm saying."

"Give me a sign, then. Yes? No? Shut the fuck up?" He bit out a laugh, but I knew he wasn't playing. "I'll do whatever I need to do for you to be comfortable. I'm trying to hear what you have to say. I hear you not saying no, but not saying yes, either."

I glanced at the clock in the mirror and went into a mild panic. Vance was about to make me late. I hated being late. My supervisor and I were two of the few Black nurses on staff. Everything I did reflected on her.

I swept thick blonde goddess braids into a low ponytail, securing it with an elastic band. "I know this is an important conversation, but I want to stop for coffee before I go in, so I need to get out of here. Do you want me to call you when I get in the car?"

"Nah," Vance grunted. "You're just gonna keep ducking me."

"I'm not, I promise. Does your offer have an expiration date?"

"Kind of," he answered. When I whipped around, brows hiked, he rushed to complete his thought. "Remember, I told you my college roommate is the general manager of a new hotel on that island off the coast of Texas? He'll comp me a few days to come down, tour the property, put together some packages to attract tourists. I'll be working, so I won't be in your face all day. You'll get the red carpet treatment at a nice resort. You keep saying you want to travel more. I'm saying I want to take you where I'm going, Thena."

I reached for my makeup bag and dug out a tube of tinted moisturizer, applied it liberally to my skin, then applied a coat of mascara and a layer of soft pink lip gloss to my lips. I pressed them together and leaned back to take in my look for the day.

I packed my work bag with extra head covers, socks, wallet, and keys. I slung it over my shoulder, then picked up my iPad and set it next to the tripod. It would live there until we connected that night.

"I forgot it's Nurses Week, so people will pay attention. I can't be late. Are you getting up or are you going to sit there naked all day?"

He smirked. "Why you clockin' me?"

"I'm not clocking you," I teased, taking the edge out of my voice, lowering my register to something more friendly. "You know your East Coast clients start calling as soon as their eyes open."

"I'm getting up." He picked up his tablet, which was propped on a pile of pillows, and rolled sideways off the bed.

"I'll text you later. Save energy for a nightcap."

"I'm about to cut you off until you answer me."

I smirked, seeing right through that lie. "You better not. Have a good day, handsome."

"Have a good day, gorgeous," he said. "We'll pick this up later."

We never said goodbye when we disconnected because it was never goodbye. We texted back and forth most of the day, and we'd see each other again in about twelve hours. My days were more intense than his, but we both experienced our own brands of stress. It was rare to find someone who understood the demands of my lifestyle—early mornings and late nights, the long spans of time when I had no more to give because the job took all I had. In the short time that I'd known

Vance, he had never failed to support me, no matter what was happening in my life.

I hadn't always had that.

I picked up my purse and lunch and packed a few items into my bag before heaving it over my shoulder and stepping out into the frigid late winter air.

VANCE

> Vance-Wanderlust Travel: Just checked the weather for Minnesota. 19 degrees! Brr! Hope you bundled up.

> Vance-Wanderlust Travel: Houston is supposed to hit 79 today. I might work poolside.

> Thena W: Fuck you, Vance Griffin. Fuck you, your 79-degree day, and your comfy chair poolside.

> Vance-Wanderlust Travel: Could be us, but you playin!

AFTER LOCKING MY PHONE, I TOSSED IT ONTO THE KITCHEN counter, the sounds of the TV from my bedroom grabbing my attention. While I wasn't a huge sports enthusiast, I found it made for good small talk with my clients.

I inserted a green tea pod into my brewer, poured in water, then pressed the power button, leaning against the counter while I listened to the machine hum. A thin stream of opaque liquid poured into a clear glass mug.

Though 5AM was too early to be awake and functioning, Athena was awake and getting ready for work, so I was up. I could take a nap; Athena could not. I could sacrifice to start the day off right.

My days started and ended the same way by design. I wasn't so much a creature of habit as I liked to have my comforts around. More quickly than I'd planned, Athena had become a comfort that I needed to have around. Seeing her face first thing in the morning put me in a good frame of mind, in a mood that carried throughout the day.

We'd fallen into a nice rhythm. Texts back and forth, Instagram private messages, then evening FaceTime or Zoom sessions. We shared a calendar, so she'd know when I was traveling or would otherwise be outside our norms. I knew her work schedule, when she'd be up early or out late, no matter where she was working. Her location changed every few months, and her schedule shifted on a whim. We had to be agile and open communication was key.

I removed the used pod from the brewer and disposed of it in the garbage, then carried my mug of tea back to the bedroom. I picked through my wardrobe options, settling on one of my new branded t-shirts. Made from a soft and breathable cotton, the shirt featured screen print images of various destinations and my company name, *Wanderlust Travel,* in bold typeface.

I pulled on a pair of shorts, then headed to the bathroom to brush my teeth and my hair, and apply oil to my beard, ensuring that I was ready for consultations. While I followed up with written details, I liked to connect with clients face-to-face, or as close as I could get to it. There was great value in hearing people describe their dream travel plans.

My clients did indeed start calling, emailing, and texting

early. If I wasn't confirming plans, I was researching options, gathering information, and resolving conflicts. I loved the work, especially when I'd crafted such a perfect trip from departure to return that clients came back again and again with bigger and bigger plans. My favorite travelers provided a budget with few constraints and let me cook. Whether the trip was business or pleasure, I could be creative and inspire memories.

I snapped off the TV, returning my spacious bedroom to its normal peaceful state. Athena liked to call it a black hole—large, dark, masculine. I didn't argue. I bought the biggest bed I could find so I could spread out when I slept...or someone could spread out with me. I had a comfortable seating area and two French doors led to a patio where I could enjoy my tea with a view of the pool.

I moved down the hall to my office and settled into the leather chair behind my desk. I booted up my laptop, woke up the monitors that flanked it, and dove into the digital world that made Wanderlust thrive. I opened WhatsApp for team chats, Trello for checklists, and Zoom for virtual huddles. Then I logged into Google Drive to access shared documents and Amadeus, our travel management software. WhatsApp was already jumping with messages.

Throughout my years in the travel industry, I had assembled a small but powerful team, each skilled in planning and executing the most luxurious experiences money could buy. We had a standing morning meeting, and I wanted to flip through the pending requests before I logged in.

There were several emails in the general mailbox. Some were seeking rough estimates, which I couldn't provide without more details. However, a few potential clients were eager to kick-start the process for their upcoming travels: a couple planning a destination wedding and group honeymoon, a family seeking a location for a reunion, and a group of friends ready for adventure.

My mind churned, making a note to bring them up in our

staff meeting so we could assign coordinators, reach out to potential clients and begin crafting the trip of a lifetime.

While I was quick to throw some clothes and a passport into a bag and jet off to an exciting location, my life was quiet when I was home. I liked it that way, but I also needed to shake things up as I approached my fifties. I had a lot of life left to live and, if I was honest with myself, I missed sharing good times with someone special. Someone to support me through challenges, to spoil, to curl around at night, a neck to nuzzle when the mood struck me.

When I met Athena, I wasn't looking for a sexy, sweet, full-figured, bronze-skinned woman. I had no intention of steering the boat to where it had ended up, but I was so damn glad we had drifted here.

A reminder to log into my staff meeting popped up, bringing my computer to life. I clicked the link to log into our meeting and turned my camera on.

"Morning, Vance!" Whitney, our California based consultant, cupped a mug of coffee as she greeted me. Though it was early for her, she was always the first to log into the meeting and the last one logged in at night. If I thought I loved the job, Whitney had my enthusiasm beat by a mile.

"Hey, Whit," I replied. "How's Stinson Beach?"

"It'll be beautiful as ever, once the sun is all the way up." She grinned, leaning to the side so I could see the view out of the window behind her. She and her husband, a retired private pilot, had a home with a view of one of the most sought-after beaches in the country. From my single-story brick rancher in Sugar Land, Texas, I envied her beachfront home and the lifestyle that seemed to be a perpetual vacation.

"I say it every day, Whit, I'm jealous of that view."

"I thought you were planning to sell your house and get yourself a nice view?"

"I am. I just have to figure some things out first."

"I get it. Moving was hard for the first few months, but..."

She sighed, taking a sidelong glance out of the window. "I wouldn't give it up now. Completely worth the work. And you know we'd cover Wanderlust while you do what you need to do."

Will, based in Tennessee, popped on just then. "We're still talking Vance into moving?"

"So, yeah, let's get started…"

"Uh-huh." He laughed. "As soon as I log in, we have to get down to business. I see how it is."

"Eh, I'm at an impasse. No reason you should have to watch me flounder about where I want to go."

"We just want you to be happy, man. That's all."

"I want that too." I shot a shy smile into the camera. "I'll keep you both posted. I appreciate the flexibility when I make my move."

I sighed, moving my notepad so I could see it. "Let's get going. I pulled the potentials from the mailbox and from the looks of it, we'll have a full day between us. As far as pending files are concerned, I'm still ironing out the details for the Mariano family reunion in Hawaii. I'm finalizing accommodations and their event schedules. I feel like they're over-booked, but we'll see. The Findlay group yoga retreat is on my radar too; I need to respond to a few more questions regarding their itinerary. The sorority cruise departing next week is almost wrapped up. I'll meet with their planner this afternoon to go over instructions."

"Their custom luggage tags arrived," said Whitney. "I shipped those out to their point person to hand out. Do you need any more help with them, or are they set?"

"They'll be set today," I replied. "But I'll reach out if anything pops up. Will, you're working on the Baker's golden anniversary celebration trip to Europe. Were you able to hook them up on a tour of the Louvre?"

The sound of pages flipping was followed by, "Yep. We

can do a guided, skip-the-line tour for their group if we can squeeze it between two other events they have planned."

"Oh, great. That'll turn out nice." I picked up my nearly empty mug of tea and sat back. "What's the progress on the Athens and Greek Islands tour we talked about last Friday?"

ATHENA

I RENTED A HOUSE THAT WAS ONLY SLIGHTLY BIGGER THAN A TINY home across from a rambling five-bedroom farmhouse. Ronnie and Marian Singer were a sweet couple who offered their guest house as a rental for the contract nurses who worked at Valley Hospital.

It was cute, furnished, and well-kept. The Singers were generous and treated their guests like family. The door was open whenever I didn't feel like cooking, and often left a care package when I worked long shifts. It meant the world to have family away from home.

Ronnie was out behind the house, pushing a wheel-barrow toward the shed at the rear of their property as I left for work. I waved as I walked to the garage and waited for the door to roll up. Once it was up, I dumped my bag on the passenger seat of my BMW and ducked into the driver's seat, started the car and turned the heater up high.

Though it was late spring, it had snowed overnight. We were lucky to only get a little over an inch, and the salt trucks had already come through. I backed out of the garage, Sirius XM radio blaring through the speakers, pressed the key fob to lower the garage door and pointed the car toward my second home, Valley Hospital.

After years as a staff nurse at a regional hospital, I was in a rut. I was newly single and tired of sitting alone at the dinner table since my son was rarely home. I needed a change of scenery and found it in travel nursing.

For the past seven years, I had worked a 12 to 16-week stint in a different hospital, then returned home for a few weeks before I was off to another destination. It wasn't always a perfect assignment; it was hard being the new employee and an outsider, but the job paid well and allowed me to travel the country. I was halfway through my time in Minnesota and beginning to crave a new adventure—one with temperatures above freezing.

Traffic was light as I bobbed my head to the radio, singing along to the only words I knew, and moved lanes to exit the highway. "You can keep that n—"

A call broke into my car concert. "Always messin' up my solo," I grumbled. A glance at the display revealed it was Valerie Kennedy, Nurse Supervisor.

"Hey, Valerie. How's it going?"

"Too early to tell." Her distinctive gravelly tone filled the car's interior. "I was hoping you were on your way and stopping for coffee."

I laughed because I had just pulled into a strip mall, then got in line at Moose Tracks, our favorite coffee shop. "I just pulled into the line. Are you already in?"

"Yeah. My husband is on the way to a conference. All the

other surgeons are riding to Duluth together, so I had to get him here. No time for Moose Tracks."

"I got you. You want your usual?"

"Please. And can you get me a muffin? Like lemon poppy-seed, or if they have a raspberry Danish, I'll take that. I've got a taste for something that isn't here or in my lunch bag."

"I'll pick you up something. This line is long, though."

"Don't worry about it. You're on an angel's mission." When she paused, I knew what was coming. "So. Did Vance ask again today?"

I pushed out a hard breath. I hadn't meant for that to be my answer, but she took it as one.

"We can talk about all that sighing you're doing when you get here," she said, then hung up.

I met Vance when he laughed at a comment I made on a Shade Room Instagram post. We had a funny back and forth over a series of photos. A few days later, he commented on a photo I had posted on my account.

You one of those 'I don't talk to men in my DMs' women?

I replied with a question mark because...*what*? He said he'd sent me a message days ago, and I never responded. *I'm about to take it personally*, he'd written.

I tapped the icon to view his profile. My brows rose.

He had a stocky, solid build, and brown, expressive almond-shaped eyes. His salt and pepper beard added character, framing his full face perfectly. His profile photo captured him at the bow of a fishing boat, rod in one hand, cigar in the other, and a Texas-sized grin on his face. Fittingly, his profile listed Houston, Texas as his home. I scrolled through the photos on his page, each one a snapshot from some far-flung corner of the world. They were captivating— vivid scenes from Brazil, Portugal, Jamaica, and even Iceland.

Okay, Vance Griffin. You can get some attention.

I'm so sorry, I replied, returning to his comment. *I didn't get a message from you, but I'll check the spam folder.* Nestled between several messages from brands that thought I wanted to wear their ugly platform nursing shoes was a message from him. Before I could reply, I got a notification: **Vance Griffin is following you. Follow back?**

Dig me outta that spam box. Respectfully, he'd said in a private message that now rolled to my main message inbox. I laughed out loud and hit the follow button so hard, I almost sprained a finger.

I'm Athena. Nice to meet you, Vance.

Our conversations gradually evolved from occasional messages to frequent emails. One night, he talked me into calling him. He claimed to be so captivated by my voice that he wanted more—he wanted to see me, hear me, making FaceTime our regular communication channel. We made a habit of talking late into the night and early in the morning, discussing everything from the mundane to the meaningful. We shared stories of our past relationships and spoke about our grown or nearly grown children.

We talked a lot about our love lives that were empty and left us longing.

"I feel like I've known you forever," he said one night. I said that sounded like a line. He said that didn't make the line any less valid.

So...we kept talking. Until it was more than talking.

I had picked up an ER shift at my home hospital, and honestly, it was a mistake. Those hours had been the most harrowing of my career and hit me hard. As I drove home in tears, Vance called because he hadn't heard from me. When he realized I was sobbing, he talked to me all the way home. I logged into Zoom so we could see each other on a larger screen, poured a glass of wine and, without thinking, started pulling off my scrubs.

Before I realized it, I was standing in my bedroom in a bra and panty set. It was purple, and that was all the encouragement Vance needed.

The chemistry between us was undeniable, sparking with an electric intensity. The more we talked, with the door to the more sensual side of me now open, the steamier our conversations became. I had never dated anyone I met online. I had just *barely* dated any I met offline. I'd wasted 20 years with Kane, my son's father.

Vance was the constant, the comfort, the raft in the storm. Now he wanted to capsize the raft by meeting *in person*.

I parked in the employee deck at Valley, rushed through the automatic sliding doors, and badged through the secure area, flush from below freezing temperatures. I took the elevator up to Obstetrics, where my unit provided antepartum and postpartum care. A giant banner that read *Happy Nurses Week* in a cartoonish bubble font was wrapped around the front desk.

"Hey, Thena. Did you bring enough Moose Tracks for everybody?" Easton, a fellow nurse, asked as I passed him. He wore dark indigo scrubs and sturdy black Clarks. A surgical cap obscured a mop of curly brown hair.

"Sure didn't," I quipped. "I grabbed something for Valerie since I was already there. I'm surprised we aren't overflowing with muffins and coffee."

"Suck-up." He grinned as he pulled a fresh surgical mask from a box. "You haven't seen the lounge yet. Looks like Panera threw up in there."

Valerie turned out of a high walled cubicle we referred to as her office, which was the only way she got any privacy to do work that was not patient-facing. She wore a pristine white lab coat over her scrubs.

"Coffee's here," I said, presenting her with the tan, lidded cup and a small bag containing her muffin.

"Oooh, thank you, lifesaver. I've been up since 3 AM, and that weak sauce they're serving in the lounge is not it." She took a timid sip of her usual order, a mocha with a double shot of espresso. "Walk with me, talk with me."

I groaned, about to make an excuse. I had planned to text my son before he left for work and scroll through my phone until it was time to clock in.

"You have time. Come on," said Valerie, calling over her shoulder and darting down the hall toward the lounge.

The spacious room, usually stocked with coffee, a cooler of beverages, a vending machine full of snacks and a wall of lockers, was, as reported, overflowing with a variety of food options. I tried to pick something people hadn't breathed on or touched. I found a slice of banana bread wrapped in plastic wrap and took my chances.

Valerie dove right in. "So...spill."

I pulled the combination lock from my bag and chose the first locker available. I stuffed my bag inside after pulling out my head covering and tools. "There's nothing to spill. We talked like we talk every night and every morning."

"And every night and every morning, a man you've been talking to for months on end asks you to fly somewhere to meet him." Valerie settled into a chair at a round table and tore open the bag containing her muffin. "How have you not met this man yet? I was a resident when I met Miller, but you couldn't keep me from that fine ass man."

"I think you're living a little too vicariously, Valerie. You might be more invested than I am."

"You don't fool me, girl. You're trying not to sound sprung over that man. You chickened out again."

"I did not *chicken out*," I said, rolling my ponytail into a bun, then adjusting the cap over my head and tightening the straps so it was snug.

"Bullshit. So you said yes, like you should have weeks ago?" I grunted in reply, and I wanted her to take it as my response this time. "I thought you liked Vance. What happened?"

"I do like Vance," I argued. "A lot. That's the problem."

"That's not a problem, Thena. You're thinking too hard for

your answer to be no, so you must *want* to say yes. It's a free trip to somewhere that is not Minneapolis, where the temperature is above freezing and it's not still snowing in May. What's stopping the word *yes* from flying out of your mouth?"

I tucked my phone into a pocket of my scrub top and settled into a seat across from Valerie, then pulled my cup of coffee toward me. The slice of banana bread was still warm as I unwrapped it.

"My son said, and I quote, *that whole situation is cringe.*" I recalled his words from our phone call a few nights ago. He was not a fan of…whatever I was doing with Vance.

Valerie squinted, twisting her lips to the side. "What does *cringe* mean?"

I hunched a shoulder in a shrug. "Hell if I know. It seems silly. I'm not a hot young thing, trying to get something free off some man I met online. And I'm not trying to get clowned. I don't *do* stuff like this—"

"Baby, Vance has seen more of you than your gynecologist. He knows what he's getting. You sound scared, Thena."

I squirmed under her intense scrutiny. "Flying somewhere to meet a man I met on Instagram isn't silly to you? That's a sound, mature decision that a woman damn near fifty should make?"

"Chile, who cares about decisions a fifty-year-old should make? Take it from a woman who is lighting the path to the fifties for you—the best part about being our age is that it comes with a deficit of fucks."

She paused, piercing me with sable brown eyes. "You have already lived a full life. You've had a long career as a staff nurse, you raised a child into adulthood, your house is almost paid off. And there is a man on your phone that would eat you up if you let him. You're a fool if you let him get away."

She stopped long enough to refresh herself with a sip of coffee.

"If the rest of your days look silly, as you put it...so *what*? You can't base your life on what people will say. They're just mad it ain't them. Shit, at least you gave it a chance." She leaned over, muttering, "And gave yourself a gift, too. When's the last time you...you know, rode that ride?"

"Valerie, please!" I whispered, shushing her. I was thankful the lounge was still empty. Then I leaned in. "It *has* been a minute since I had the real deal, though."

"See now, that's what we call a benefit," she replied. "And it'll be attached to a man who has been asking to take you somewhere warm so he can give you said benefit in myriad positions. Don't make me take you off the schedule to force you to go."

Valerie unwrapped her muffin and bit into it, demolishing half of it. She shrugged and chewed, then took a long swallow of coffee.

"You would not do that."

"I might if you don't get it together. Do what you want to do, Thena. I know you're used to your triflin' ass ex, but make no mistake, honey. Vance is not Kane. And men like Vance don't come around often. Would you rather regret taking that step or *not* taking it?"

"HEY, ATHENA..."

One of my favorite patients shuffled off of the elevator, a handbag hanging off of the crook of her elbow and a Stanley cup clutched in one hand. She heaved the most long-suffering sigh that I'd heard in a long time.

"Robin!" I brightened, slipping into the nearest chair and waking up the computer to open the patient intake system.

"Good morning. Is your husband coming, or is it just you, today?"

She grunted, lowering her heavily pregnant body into the nearest chair. A few months earlier, she reported an episode of swelling and a headache that seemed more pronounced than usual. Robin's blood pressure and pregnancy at thirty-seven meant she was at risk for complications, so her team required her to come in for monthly check-ups.

"You know your friend is here. He's parking the car." She rolled her eyes, then added, "He's been getting on my nerves. Won't let me do a damn thing. He took today off to bring me here. I can drive myself to an appointment."

"You know you like being a passenger princess. Brian is just showing that he cares."

"He needs to care about ten steps away from me. He knows how I get when I'm pregnant—I can't get comfortable to sleep well, I have heartburn, I'm cranky as hell. That man stays up my ass."

I bit back a chuckle. "Let's get you checked in so you can get back home and take a nap. I'm going to tell Brian to get you one of those belly pillows that I see on the internet all the time."

"They don't do a thing for me," she said, taking a long drag off of the straw protruding from her cup. "He's already bought me four of 'em."

A few hours later, I had burned through my patients and all of that banana bread and coffee. I was running on fumes and chocolate, so I headed to the lounge to warm up my lunch. LaTasha, one of the nurses I'd become friends with, clutched a vase in her arms and was headed right for me. It was stuffed with wine-red roses and sprays of baby's breath.

"Oh, who got roses? Those are gorgeous?"

"Just the woman I was looking for! These are for you, Athena."

I froze, my eyes wide. "For *me*?!"

"Your name is Athena Wilcox, right? Then yep, for you."

"What in the world?" My jaw was almost on the floor as I took the thick crystal vase. I plucked the card from the plastic holder, then flipped it open.

Happy Nurses Week to one of the best nurses I know, it read. *I will wait as long as I have to wait to say it in person. Talk later, Vance.*

"Alright, alright. Uncle," I muttered to myself but grinned at his sweet gesture. It probably cost him an arm and a leg to get same-day delivery.

"Are they from him?" She asked, one brow cocked in curiousity.

"Mmmhmm," I hummed. I handed the vase back to LaTasha and told her to put it at the front desk. "For ambience," I told her when she protested. "I don't even have a desk. What am I supposed to do with flowers?"

I detoured to Valerie's cubicle on the way to the lounge. She was, as usual, buried in folders, charts and paperwork while her fingers flew over a keyboard centered on an old wooden desk. I paused in the doorway and leaned against the makeshift wall.

She stopped typing and pulled a pair of gold-rimmed frames from her eyes. "Thena? What's up?"

I sighed, then shoved my hands in the big pockets of my scrub top. "Vance sent flowers."

"Ohhh." She rolled her chair back from the desk. "Flowers at work? Pulling out the big guns."

"Mmhmm. Happy Nurses Week. Can't wait to say it in person, et cetera. He said he'd wait as long as I needed him to."

"Uh-huh," she replied. "And how long are you going to make him wait, Athena?"

I huffed, transferring my balance from one foot to the other—stall tactics to avoid admitting that I was coming around. I stirred up every bit of bravado I could muster to push out, "Not much longer. I think I'm going to say yes."

"Honey, you've *been* thinking. You think, or you are?"

"I...am. I am going to say yes to Vance."

"Alright now!" She squealed, slapping her palms together, and stood, then rounded the desk and grabbed me by the elbow. "I'm holding you to it. And you know I need all the details. The itinerary, the pictures—we need to shop! I can't send you on a romantic ass baecation in whatever you have in your closet."

"I hope I don't regret this," I groaned.

As nervous as I was, I was more than curious to feel his skin under my fingertips, to breathe in the musk of his natural scent, to hear his baritone so close to my ear that his breath stirred the hair on the back of my neck. I'd been harboring a recurring daydream of those lips on mine...and everywhere else.

A wave of heat rolled over me as I thought about his mouth, his tongue, his hands on every inch of my body. I was ready to do more things I had never done.

The rest of my shift rolled by in a blur. The sun had sunk below the horizon, and I was turning my patients over to the next shift. I spent the drive home thinking about what I might end up doing with a handsome man on an island with nothing but between us but time.

The anticipation made my stomach flutter.

I waved to my landlords, who were out for an evening walk with their dogs as I turned into the garage, but I didn't stop to chat once I had parked. I didn't want to get caught up in conversation, and I knew they'd be generous and ask me in for dinner.

I stripped out of my scrubs, socks, and cap and tossed them to a basket in front of the stacked washer and dryer. I added the purple undergarments to a lingerie bag and dumped them into the open machine, poured in detergent and pressed the start button. Then I unpacked my work bag, loaded my dishes into the dishwasher, and started that up too. I was always ravenous after a session with Vance, so I would eat something later.

I pulled up my VIP list and sent a text to the most frequently dialed number on my phone.

VANCE

My phone chimed a notification from its perch on the charger across the desk. I fought myself to not snatch it up. If everything went as scheduled during her day, it was time for Athena's evening text to tell me she was home and comfortable. I'd sent her flowers at work, hoping the gesture would prod her to come to Black Diamond with me. If nothing, she'd texted to say thank you for the flowers.

"Do you need to get that?"

The woman on the other end of the video call interrupted the thorough pre-travel lecture I gave to all my clients. She and a group of ladies were taking a cruise to celebrate their sorority's milestone anniversary.

I glanced at the phone, then back to the screen and shook my head. "We're on a roll. Let's finish up."

She nodded, so I continued. "Alright. So, your group will fly into Miami on Saturday. I sent you a file with the confirmation numbers for the flights and the rooms at your hotel. I've arranged for transportation to the port on Sunday morning. Your driver's name and phone number are in the file. I need everyone to understand that there's very little room for error here, okay?"

"What...what do you mean by very little room for error?"

"If you're not at the port and haven't checked in by the appointed time, I'll be booking you a flight home. Be ready to go to the port, be prepared to board the ship: ID, passports, ticket info. Check the packing list to ensure you don't have anything that you can't bring on the ship. They depart at noon, and they will not wait for you."

Her eyes widened, and she appeared alarmed. Good. I liked to scare them a little, so they took the arrangements more seriously.

"I sent over the full eight-day cruise itinerary—excursions, off-ship needs, etc. Use all of the benefits and amenities; you're paying for them. After 5PM tomorrow, barring emergencies, this plan is locked in. As we agreed, any changes after that will cost extra for my time and expertise. Any questions?"

"None," she replied. "We have a meeting tonight. I'll distribute all of the documents. I run our trips, and I'm real bossy with travel. Though..." She frowned, pulling a corner of her lip between her teeth and raking her fingers through a long ponytail. "I'm nervous about getting on a boat. Are you sure it's safe?"

"Remember, you're as safe as the precautions you take. Be aware, and don't be too cool for PPE. You heard me?"

She smiled. I felt her relax across the airwaves. "Heard, Vance."

"Good. It's all over but the packing. Have a great time, and don't forget to leave me a fat five-star review when you get back."

"Thanks, Vance!"

The screen went dark as my client disconnected. I closed

the Zoom app, made a few notes in Amadeus and saved everything before I logged out.

I sent a message to the other agents at Wanderlust to let them know I was logging out for the night. Whitney replied she would be on for a while.

I stretched, letting out a satisfied sigh. Turning around in my chair, I surveyed the controlled chaos of my office. A few boxes, neatly labeled, sat in one corner, but mounds of paperwork, binders, acrylic plaques, and files still needed attention. I'd been toying with the idea of selling my house, so I'd packed in fits and starts, but with no place to go, I wasn't motivated.

I grabbed the phone and shuffled out of the office. The living room, dining room, and kitchen were bathed in late afternoon sunlight. Alexis and I bought the house right after we got engaged. We were young and naïve, with stars in our eyes and a little money in the bank, thanks to a generous down payment from her parents.

We went to the same high school and continued to the University of Houston. We were comfortable with each other, so we figured we should get married and settled in to make a life together. I worked for a series of mortgage and insurance companies as an underwriter. My wife was in telecom sales, working her way up the ladder until she hit the pinnacle— President of software sales at M6 Telecom with offices in Houston, Austin, and Baton Rouge.

By the time she made her mark, I had become disillusioned with corporate life. The 9-to-5 existence was boring and uninspiring. I turned a rarely used home office into my headquarters and gave in to a yearning.

Wanderlust Travel was a source of pride. I built a profitable business helping travelers plan and execute dream vacations and group events.

The divorce wasn't a surprise. When I didn't seem interested in playing husband to a high-powered executive, Alexis found a man that matched her energy. They moved to Austin, where she and her new man were already buying an ostentatious residence. I supposed she thought it more worthy of her. They lived in an upscale enclave, in a big house with too many windows, a three-car garage, and an Olympic-sized pool. Alexis couldn't even swim.

I started seeing a therapist after the divorce because I was a little *too* resolved about the demise of my marriage. I was also having a rough go of reconnecting with our daughter Kareema, who went to work for her mother in the Houston office right out of college. While the boys, Sedrick and Alex, adjusted to the divorce, Kareema didn't take the split well.

Years later, it was a struggle to relate to a person who used to be my shadow. At an age where I watched bitterness eat away at the soul of so many people, I was committed to not living that kind of life, and I didn't want it for my children. I wanted to be happy.

Quietly, judging by the number of times Alexis called to *check in* and *get my perspective*, I wasn't sure she was happy. Ah, well. That bell couldn't be unrung.

I pulled my phone from my pocket and used face recognition to unlock it. Notifications filled the home screen, but I was looking for one in particular and smiled when I read it. Athena hadn't mentioned the flowers, but after reading her text, I didn't give a damn about the flowers.

The best perk of running a travel agency was the travel. I made it a point to explore a new country every few months. Flying with different airlines was part of the adventure, but don't get it twisted—I had a soft spot for my Diamond Medallion status with Delta.

Some of my closest friends kept the travel industry humming—a cruise line ticket agent, an airline pilot, a luxury resort general manager. Davis Scott was an old friend wrestling with the launch of his new resort hotel. The Pearl on Black Diamond sat on a man-made island off the coast of Texas. He extended an invitation to stay at Elysium, one of the hotel's premier towers. It promised spacious rooms with ocean views, a health spa, a pool, and an entertainment complex. In exchange, I would offer insights on attracting travelers to the resort.

It was a perfect solution. I could get out of Houston, which I tried to do regularly…and meet Athena.

I grabbed a beer from the fridge and made my way through the glass doors to a stone-laid patio. A few steps away, a wrought-iron gate surrounded the best selling feature of the house—an in-ground pool. I snagged a chair from a round table and eased into it. With my phone in hand, I scrolled through my VIP list until her name was illuminated under my thumb. I set the phone down, leaning it against the sturdy pole that held the umbrella aloft.

A sunny day would usually find me under the shade of the wide multicolored umbrella. Since my youngest, Sedrick, had packed up and headed for UCLA, my life had settled into a predictable pattern. Wake up, clock into work, spend the whole day holed up in the office, clock out, then zone out in front of the TV until I passed out. I needed a reboot.

I had a passport and a job that could take me around the world. When I struck up a friendship with a kind, beautiful woman I met on Instagram, my plans for reinvigorating my life and someday having a beautiful travel partner blossomed. My mind wandered where it always wandered—how I'd fill the time if I could spend more than an hour with her. What I would do with her undivided attention for days.

"Hi, handsome." Athena beamed a tired smile as soon as her face popped up on the screen. Her voice was like honey even through the phone. "Out on the patio, I see. Was the day okay?"

When Athena got off work, she stripped out of her uniform and wrapped herself in a thick robe, then settled into a comfortable chair in front of the TV in her living room. We caught up while we made dinner, ate, or watched a show together.

I liked her natural, relaxed, unfiltered state. My need to see her, *all* of her, in 1080p resolution prompted our Zoom sessions, but a FaceTime call would do for now.

"The day was alright. I just logged out. I told you I had that sorority going on their anniversary cruise next week?" I shook my head and tried to suppress a chuckle. "A group of women that need to be somewhere on time? I hope they make it. The meetings have been...*interesting*."

I knew by her laughter that she recalled the stories about the meetings with the planning team before I decided that I only needed one point of contact. I didn't have three hours a week to devote to a group that bickered about every detail and tried to plan outrageous excursions with no break time between them.

"It'll go great," Athena said. "And if it doesn't, it won't be for lack of planning."

"Customers like to complain about everything that went wrong in their reviews, even if it wasn't my fault. You're right, though. They'll have a great time if they follow my instructions."

"That's a big *if*."

"Hence why I'm worried. Anyway, tell me about your day."

She brought a wineglass to her lips and sipped a mouthful, humming an appreciative tone. "It was pretty good. Nothing too urgent. There is a reason I moved to Obstetrics from Emergency. It's Nurses Week, so the administration is sucking up with catering and team building all week."

Her eyes rolled as she had another sip of wine. "There's food everywhere. I found too many pre-packaged snacks and some banana bread. Oh! I, uhm..."

She paused, then fought the smile that wanted to cross her

lips. "I got the flowers. I meant to text you, but the day got away from me. Nice touch, Vance."

I chuckled. "My mama ain't raised no fool. She said to keep the woman in your life happy, full, and surprised."

"My aunt used to say well-fed and well-fucked. Same sentiment. You're a great student. I was surprised."

"You're talking to me nice because you want me to fly you out somewhere."

She burst into laughter at how I broached the subject. "You're the one begging to fly me out."

"Are you sure? I want you to come, but I don't want you to feel like I talked you into it. I want you to be ready to get into some sunny weather."

Athena reached just out of camera view to set down her wineglass and pick up a notebook and pen. "I wasn't playing when I said I'd been thinking about it. Darius won't like it, so it *must* be the right thing to do." She shrugged, bringing her gaze back to the screen. "Why not? Let's go for it."

"Hell yeah! *Why not* indeed," I agreed. I'd never been much of a poker player, and I did not have a poker face. I was damn happy, and she was going to know it. "I'll call Davis and tell him we're coming. If there's anything you want to do down there, I'll hook it up."

Athena's gaze flicked up from the notebook to the screen, then she tipped her head and shot me a sly grin.

"Come on, now." I frowned. "Ima get up in that. If you want to—I'm not saying I expect—"

"Don't blow it up in my head and have to retract once we hit the island. I'm not trying to hear *I might have exaggerated my abilities.*"

"No exaggeration over here. I have every intention of turning you out."

Athena sighed, her eyes sliding closed, then reopening. "Alright now, Vance. My expectations are high as Snoop Dogg."

"When I tell you I can't wait to get you alone?" I ground out a grunt and pounded the table, making the phone bounce. "Might not see anything on the island on the first day."

"I don't know if I can take this wait. So, what's the plan?"

"Fly into Houston. I'll scoop you from the airport and drive down from here. It's a few hours south, then across a bridge. Davis will set us up with a nice room, great view, dinner reservations, and all access passes. I just need to let him know when we'll be hitting the beach."

We tossed around a few ideas and settled on a date based on Athena's work schedule. In three weeks, I would have this woman in my arms. I could hug her, hold her, kiss her...*fuck her*. Instead of dreaming about it, we would live those dreams out.

"I guess I have to break the news to Darius," she said, twisting her lips. He was about to turn thirty, hadn't ever left his childhood bedroom, and I didn't see him trying to, if Athena didn't put him out. "I don't want to tell him too early. I can't listen to his mouth for three weeks."

"Darius is too old to have an opinion about his mother's dating life." I saw her glare from miles away and didn't care. "Don't give me that look. I told you what I told my kids. You got to make your own way. You baby him, got him thinking his opinion matters on things."

"It matters on things. Just not these things."

"His grown ass got nothing better to worry about than what his mama is doing?"

"You know he doesn't. Unfortunately for him," she added, chuckling, "I've *been* grown. And you're on my ass like Kareema is going to jump for joy at the thought of her dad being with someone that isn't her mother."

Kareema was determined, strong-willed...*opinionated*. She assumed I could have done more to save the marriage, that I gave up and didn't fight. She wasn't wrong, but maybe I didn't see the use in fighting, in begging Alexis to fall back in love with me.

"I'm not looking forward to a conversation with Kareema. I'm the dad, though," I said, tapping my chest. "I don't need to ask my daughter's permission to move on from a marriage that had been dead for years."

"Her feelings still matter, Vance. You can't ignore them."

"I'm not ignoring them, but I'm not putting my life on hold because she doesn't want to see me move on. Does she want me to talk my ex-wife into leaving her marriage and coming back to a relationship she didn't want with a man she isn't in love with?"

I scoffed, shaking my head. "I'd like her to be okay with it, but I'll be alright if I don't get her blessing. Are you asking Darius for permission to take a vacation so you can meet your boyfriend?"

Athena moved into the corner of her chair and drawing her legs up under her. I straightened and got close to the camera, thinking I might see something. "You may refer to yourself as my gentleman caller. My beau. My paramour. I don't have a *boyfriend*. Out here sounding like a lovesick teenager."

"Well, shit, I'm a lovesick teenager, then. You're my girl-friend, all day, every day, baby."

Athena tossed her head back in laughter. "I'm not using that word. Darius will be okay. And Kareema will come around."

"And if they don't, we're still doing what we want to do." I shrugged, then pivoted on subjects. "I want to get on a call with Davis before he heads out for the day. Will you be up for a while, or are you turning in early?"

"Not you sending me to bed without my nightcap," she said, putting on that sexy tone she used because she knew it would grab me by the balls.

She tugged at the sash of her robe, loosening it, and slipping one shoulder from its warmth. Her bare breast hung heavy, the areola surrounded by a tight crown of skin with an erect nipple that begged to be sucked. She lifted the soft mound and brought it to her lips, circling the tip with her tongue before taking it into her mouth. Then she let out a throaty moan, eyes closed.

I heard a whimper, then I realized it came from me. Athena released the taut bud with a pop and let her breast fall. The entire scene was…breathtaking.

"I'll meet you in the room at the usual time, handsome."

I felt my body awaken at the thought of seeing Athena in real time in a finite number of days. I was already ready to hop on Zoom. "I'll be in the room."

I SWIPED TO MY CONTACT LIST AND SELECTED A FAMILIAR number, emptying the bottle of beer into my mouth while it rang.

"Now you know my number," said Davis.

I belched and set the bottle down on the table. "I've been texting when I can. It's tax return season. Business is booming up here."

"The only business I care about is the business you're sending my way. I hope you're calling to tell me you're coming down."

"The harassment worked," I replied, grinning. "I'll be down in a few weeks, and I'm bringing a…*friend*. I need to get an idea of what you want me to see so I can plan our trip, so—"

"Hold up! Wait. Back up!"

Davis had never been the type of guy who wanted to gossip over a new woman in my life, mostly because I almost never had a new woman. I had been with Alexis all through college and for more than twenty years after. The women I dated after my divorce weren't more than a passing interest.

"You can't just blow past that info you mumbled in my ear. Are we talking about the nurse? Have you met her yet?"

"Not yet."

"So you're bringing her to Black Diamond? For your first date?"

"Yes. To your hotel. So—"

"Hold. *Up!* Details! Are we chillin' or is this something more serious?"

"Athena's current assignment is in Minnesota, which is another reason I want to bring her with me. It's still snowing up there." I shivered. "I'm hoping this vacation will speed things up between us."

I heard the click of his tongue across the line. "Ugh. Are you about to *my lady* me to death?"

"Headed there, if I have my way," I admitted. I laughed, but I was serious.

"Alright, then. Rumble, young man. Does Alexis know yet?"

Though we remained cordial co-parents, our arrangement was based on the mutual respect and consideration we had worked hard to foster since the divorce. I didn't get intimate details of her life with Richard. She didn't get a play-by-play about my trysts with Athena.

"I can't say she's *happy* for me," I continued. "Lord knows she doesn't have a right to be upset. She and her husband should be too busy performing happy couple for all of Austin to be worried about what I've got going on. I just got the invite for their anniversary party at—"

"Bro." Davis interrupted. "Alexis invited you to her anniversary party? Like...to celebrate her marriage to the man she left you for?"

"Mmmhmmm," I hummed. The silence between us spoke

volumes. In the past, Davis and Alexis had been close. In recent years, the friendly feelings had waned.

"Interesting." I heard him tap the nearest surface with his fingertips. "Kareema is probably spitting nails."

"I haven't told Kareema yet because it will not go well. Athena is worth it. I was waiting for her to get the days off work, book it up, and then break the news to her before her mom tells her."

"I do not envy you, man. At least you get a little playtime to lick your wounds. So, when can we expect you lovebirds?"

I ran through the dates with Davis so he could alert his team to arrange our visit. "I want all the bells and whistles. Nice room, guest passes, meals, drinks—don't cheap out because it's me."

"Why are you talking to me like this isn't my whole damn job, Vance?"

"Because this is about more than me coming down to help you. I'm trying to impress this woman. Nothing but the best. Ramp it all the way up. Not for me—for her."

"We are about to show out."

"That's what I'm talking about."

I got up, carting the phone and the empty bottle with me back to the kitchen. I closed the sliding door and tossed the bottle into the recycling bin. As I headed to the living room, I tapped a panel on the wall to activate a pre-programmed set of lights, illuminating the darkening room now that the sun was setting.

"How's business out there? Is the hotel owner still on your ass?"

Crawford Calhoun, the owner of the Pearl Hotel & Resort on Black Diamond, owned several smaller hotel chains across major cities in Texas. Despite his previous successes, his tactics didn't work for a beachfront vacation destination. Unfortunately, he'd made it Davis' problem to solve.

"The island is great. Growing every day. Business is *okay*.

Which...isn't good for a hotel of this size," he explained. "Business needs to be screaming. My hair should be on fire. Calhoun calls every other day, threatening to bring his thousand-dollar custom cowboy boots down here if I don't increase occupancy. I do not want to see those boots in this hotel, Vance. And I haven't even told you the latest."

"Tell me."

"So, right after we completed the design on all four towers, he turned some of our VIP suites into condos. I have a person who tracks the number of rooms and suites we haven't booked across the property. Now a salesperson is in my office weekly to tell me how many condos we haven't sold."

"What, wait...condos?"

"Yeah," he confirmed. "The good news is that I got one of them as the GM, so I live on property now. They're nice, with views of the beach from every unit, plus amenities that come with the condo association fee. I just...I needed another thing to manage like I needed a hole in my head. I have to hire some help here or I'm going to walk out of this place one day and keep walking."

"To where? You live at work now."

"Right? Might regret that."

"Hang on until I get down there. We'll work something out." After a few moments, I asked, "Do you think you could hook me up with a tour? I might be interested in a move."

"I'll give you a tour myself if you're serious."

"I definitely want to leave Houston. I'm trying to decide where I want to go. The curse of being able to work anywhere is that I could work...*anywhere*." I sighed, slouching in the chair and propping my feet up. "I don't know. Maybe I just need a good option to slap me in the face."

"Consider yourself slapped. Maybe you need to stop and do nothing for a minute. Lay out on the beach for a day or two and enjoy yourself with Athena. While you're resting, put some time into thinking about where you really want to go. And maybe consider Black Diamond. It's a nice spot, and you're close to home if you need to get back."

He paused and then added, "And I'm here."

"That's a selling point?"

"The best selling point. Apartment 509, back together again!"

He and I shared a laugh, and a few memories from our old place tumbled around my brain. He had been my roommate in college dorms and our dingy off-campus apartment before I moved in with Alexis. He had become one of my best friends since then.

"So, listen," he said, bringing me back. "Speaking of condo sales, my weekly meeting is coming up in a few minutes. I'll get started on your stay, but I'm not planning four days of work. I want you to enjoy your guest and take everything in."

"Thanks, man. I'm looking forward to it."

I couldn't recall the last time I'd traveled where work was not the goal, where my focus was not on how to further the business, or which destination was next on my list. While I labeled work trips as relaxing, I never put my laptop away and my phone was plastered to my ear.

I scrolled to the calendar, marking the date three weeks from tonight when I would meet Athena, and vowed to make the time with her special. A true vacation—for at least a few days.

I wondered if I could lose twenty pounds before then.

"Man, whatever," I mumbled aloud to no one. "She's been staring at your middle-aged gut for six months. Don't trip."

It was too early to put pressure on myself, but I wanted everything to be perfect. If I had anything to say about it, this little work-play escape was going to be life-changing.

Athena

Vance-Wanderlust Travel: Don't let Darius get under your skin.

Thena W: I'll try. Easier said than done, though.

I SANK INTO IN MY CHAIR, WRAPPED IN A WARM ROBE FRESH FROM the dryer and cupping a thick stoneware bowl. It wasn't snowing every day anymore, but the temperatures were still frigid to this Southern girl. My blood was thin, and I would do anything for a bit of that sweltering Carolina heat my friends were already complaining about.

My day was stressful and seemingly never-ending, probably because it was technically two days. A few nurses were out at a conference and another two were on vacation, so we were short-staffed. I'd spent all but nine of the past thirty-six hours on my feet.

My shift was over. I was home. I was off for the next three days and my landlords left beef stew and a basket of fresh baked bread for me.

I hurried to undress and get comfortable so I could spoon

stew into a bowl and warm up a roll for dinner, pour a glass of wine to go with it, then climb into my chair to enjoy it. I wiggled my toes in excitement and reached for the remote. I planned to catch up on Real Housewives before I logged in for my nightcap with Vance. After some conversation, I had talked him into taking his daughter, Kareema, to dinner to tell her about our plans. She deserved a face-to-face, adult conversation.

In exchange, I had agreed to bite the bullet and talk to Darius. At least I wouldn't be facing him in person, so I had the better end of the bargain. I had texted him earlier to ask him to call me when he got home from work. I figured it would be a few hours before I heard from him, but the phone buzzed against the wood surface of the side table just as the TV popped on. I curled my lip and turned it back off. I wasn't full or inebriated enough for the conversation that I was about to have.

"Hey, Darius. You're off already?"

I wasn't met with the serene quiet of my suburban house, where the loudest noise I might hear would be the rumble of my neighbor's truck with the confederate flag sticker across the tailgate. I heard hammering and beeping and loud diesel engines in the background.

"Son, where are you?"

"Out," he replied. "What's up, Ma?"

I choked, then coughed to clear my throat. "What do you mean, *out*? And before you open that mouth again, take a minute to think about who I am and where you live rent-free. Let's try that again. Where are you?"

"Construction site, Ma. A guy called out; I picked up his shift for some overtime. I only have a couple of minutes to talk. Does that explanation do it for you?"

"You could have avoided the attitude if you talked to me like you had sense."

He sighed into the receiver. "I'm sorry, Ma. I'm exhausted.

My back hurts, it's been hot all day, and now I have to work until midnight. I'm kinda pissed I picked up a shift instead of going home to sleep."

"Do you have to be back on site at 7AM?"

"Yeah, I'm back in the morning, but overtime is good money. I can't pass it up. I can pay off my truck on the next paycheck. I need that more than a few hours of sleep."

"Okay. Congratulations on getting so close to paying off your truck. I told you that thing was too expensive. Now you're working extra hours to pay—"

"Ma, remember when I said I only have a few minutes? What's up?"

"Nothing," I replied, stalling. "I mean, nothing huge. I just needed you to know that I'll be gone for a few days."

"You okay, Ma? What's going on?"

I heard the concern in his voice. I pictured his face softening, his brow furrowed in that protective way it did when it came to me. Darius played the role of overprotective son well.

"I'm going on vacation. A little island getaway."

Coward, I chided myself.

"By yourself? With like…friends from work?" Darius paused for a micro second before adding, "You're not going with that guy from the internet, are you?"

I was so thankful he couldn't see the guilt flash across my face. "Actually—"

"Ma! Are you?"

"Vance invited me—"

"Please tell me you're joking, Ma."

"I'm not joking. Vance invited me to go on a trip he already had planned. I'm flying to Houston to meet him. We're going to drive together to a resort on Black Diamond. It's close to Texas. Just off the coast."

I braced for his response, plowing ahead when I was met with stony silence.

"He's paying for everything, including my flight and our stay at the resort and anything I want to do."

I paused again and was, again, met with silence. From him anyway. The noise behind him told me he was still on the line.

"Darius? Did you hear me?"

"I heard you, Ma."

"Okay. And...you have nothing to say?"

"I mean..." He clicked his tongue. I imagined his expression, his attempts to appear nonchalant masking anger and irritation. "Does it matter? You're going to do whatever you want to do, right? You're an adult, so you can have a ho phase, I guess."

Whew. This man was so lucky that I was states away and not across the room. "Darius, I didn't call you so you could—"

"You barely know this guy, Ma. He sees you on some random Instagram post and starts stalking you and you fall for it. Everybody knows those dudes are scammers. How much money have you sent him?"

"None!" I bit out. "I haven't sent him a thin dime. And thanks for letting me know you think I'm dumb enough to fall for that. I've spoken to him on the phone. I've talked with him on FaceTime—"

"Yeah, you do OnlyFans type shit so he can watch. He's a fucking creep."

My eyelids slammed shut as I was reminded of the time Darius had come home late from work and discovered me doing a lot more than talking to Vance. The lingerie set I wore was sheer and too sexy for my son to see me in it. I flipped my iPad over too late for him to not notice that Vance was naked.

Darius' lips twitched and his nostrils flared as he glared at me, then stormed from the room. He didn't speak to me for days.

"I know you have suspicions, and you should. But those suspicions are unfounded. Vance does not ask me for money and he's treating me to this vacation. I'll take your tone and commentary as high regard for my feelings and safety."

"Take them however you want to take them. Do whatever you're going to do; I don't need to know about it. But I'm not up there for you to cry on my shoulder when he turns out to be what I said he would be. I have to go. My shift is starting."

The line disconnected before I could get another word in.

I wanted to throw my phone across the damn room and would have, if I didn't still owe on the installment plan. Darius was more like his father than I cared to admit. He carried not only Kane's looks but his propensity toward jealousy, anger, and flying off the handle. Darius would hate to know how much he reminded me of Kane. When I finally ended our relationship, we were all relieved that it was over.

My anger flared, then evaporated, dissolving into sadness. It wasn't like I wanted him to do cartwheels that I'd found someone, but he didn't understand or wouldn't accept that I needed and wanted true love in my life.

I could have that with Vance. And it was too damn bad that Darius couldn't be happy for me, but I was going to go for it.

I put the phone down, grabbed my remote control, and turned the TV on again. Then I dug into my stew before it cooled off. I hoped Vance's conversation with his daughter would go much better than the one I'd had with my son.

A FEW DAYS LATER, I WAS DEEP INTO VACATION WARDROBE shopping. LaTasha, Valerie and I got a day off together, so we agreed to meet for a girl date. We drove to Grand Rapids, a city with an actual mall, to shop, have lunch and dish about work, our mutual friends, and my impending baecation.

I turned from one side to the other, examining the swim-suit I'd tried on over a pair of biker shorts and a tank top with a built-in bra. Bubble gum pop tunes rained down via the speakers above me in the changing room, but I wasn't paying attention. My focus was on the bold red, two-piece suit with a plunging neckline and high-cut bikini. It clung to virtually every inch of my figure perfectly.

And it was perfectly fanning the nervous flames I'd had about that figure being on display for a man I was about to meet in less than a week.

"You look *a-may-zing*," LaTasha sang. "Sprinkle, sprinkle, as the girlies say. You knockin' em out in that suit, Thena."

I scrunched my nose at LaTasha. "Is that…is that a kink thing? Should I ask about that?" She laughed and went back to flipping through the swimsuit options she'd brought me. "I'm serious. What the fuck does *sprinkle, sprinkle* mean?"

"It's a saying. Spreading joy, cheer, happiness. You're sprinkling all of that around in that suit. You need one of those in another color and a coverup. You know, something you can throw on to walk around the hotel lobby or something."

"I know what a cover up is. I'm not old or uncultured."

"You asked what *cringe* and *sprinkle, sprinkle* means, though. I'm just saying."

"If you could speak in English and not terms you learned from TikTok, I could understand you."

She ignored me and instead circled, nodding and murmuring appreciative noises.

"Am I vain, or does this look good on me? Minus the boy shorts and tank."

"Mmhmm. Vance won't know what hit him."

"I think I like this one," I replied, smoothing out the fabric across my hips, then testing the fortitude of the bust. It was sturdy. "Got the girls sitting nice, which he likes. And I do too."

Letting out a sigh, I rounded my shoulders, then added with a whine, "What if he doesn't like me in person? What if we don't have the same connection we have online? What if I get in the car and it's just silence for four hours because I'm not what he expected?"

"What if you hushed up that noise?" Valerie rounded the corner with an armful of evening wear, pulling out a purple sleeveless dress with an asymmetrical hem. "Try this on. We don't have much to choose from, but we don't have time to drive to Minneapolis. I did my best to pick up the nicest of the bunch."

"If he was going to run for the hills, he would've done that before he booked your flight," said LaTasha. "Men can smell fear and insecurity a mile away. You're going to need to deal with that before you get on the plane. If you don't, it will eat you alive and ruin your trip."

I grabbed the dress and pulled it off the hanger, then headed back into the dressing room to change. "I know you're right," I called out. "I have to stop overthinking. I just…I keep thinking about my conversation with Darius."

"We aren't considering the opinions of sons who only see their mother as a mother today," said Valerie. "Come on, now. I'm hungry and I want to see that dress on."

I slipped the sheer fabric over my head, pulled my arms through, and let it flutter over my hips. It was an attractive length, hitting me just above the knee, and the hem was high enough on one side to let a shapely thigh peek out.

I stepped out of the dressing room and twirled. "I feel pretty in this!"

"You *look* pretty in that," said LaTasha.

"I thought that would look nice on you," Valerie added, then dipped her head toward LaTasha, lowering her voice like she was sharing a secret. "Vance's favorite color is purple."

"With some cute sandals and silver earrings?" I suggested.

"With *sexy* shoes and *devastating* earrings. We're not going to church camp." Valerie shook her head and pushed me back into the dressing room, handing me an armful of clothing to try on. "Hurry, now. I'm so hungry, I'm about to chew my arm off. Try the rest of these on so we can get out of here."

After a full morning of shopping for swimsuits and loungewear, a brief break for lunch, and stops at DSW and Macy's for shoes, perfume and unmentionables, I was beat. Since we still had a drive back to Big Fork, we opted to cool our heels with drinks and dinner.

We chose a booth in a corner of a charming Italian restaurant near the Grand Rapids Mall. We placed drink orders with the server and while we waited, Valerie regaled us with plans for her wedding anniversary.

"Miller is building me a gazebo," she gushed, flipping through photos on her phone. "Well, I got the schematic, and all the materials are sitting in the garage. He'll start building as soon as the damn ground thaws."

"He's building it? With his surgeon's hands?"

"Miller is super handy," said LaTasha, butting in. "Last year, he redid her garden. He put in an underground sprinkler system and fountain, then planned out the flower bed. Miller Kennedy is out here making it hard for these new niggas."

I had arrived in Big Fork at the start of winter, so I'd never seen the garden in full bloom, but I had seen the expansive area set aside for it and the three-tiered fountain. I hoped I'd have time to see it before I left.

"I should be celebrating 30 years with somebody. I would be, if my silly ass hadn't hung around waiting for Darius' father to get his act together." The server arrived with our drinks. I sipped my wine and continued. "I should have known Kane wasn't gon' do shit but get on my nerves."

"You two were real young, weren't you?" Valerie asked.

"I was 16," I replied, nodding. "He was 18 and not ready to be a father, let alone a partner. Our folks pushed us hard to pretend, though. At least he kept a job so I could get child support."

"You are about to make up for all of those years with Kane," said LaTasha. "I can read men like the back of my hand, even the ones I haven't met yet. Vance is good people. Give him a chance to prove it."

"I can't wrap my head around a man that wants to handle everything. I haven't planned shit for this trip except what I'm wearing. All he asked for was my TSA number so he could book the flight. I just keep thinking he's going to pop up one day, like *just kidding*!"

"That's a trauma response," said LaTasha, nodding hard.

My eyes rolled so hard I almost gave myself a headache. "That is not what a trauma response is. That's me thinking men are trash. And expecting mine to be trash, just like Darius said he would."

"Thena, for real. Relax! Didn't you say he was a master… something-something?"

"Master Travel Coordinator," I corrected.

"Right," said LaTasha, pounding a fist on the table. "*Master* coordinator. Let that man handle business! When is the last time you let a man spoil you?"

I grimaced, staring down at the wood grain of the table. She and Valerie let out audible gasps.

"Never?" Valerie asked. "All those years with Kane and…never?"

I shook my head, frowning. "When I say he was a waste of my time? Never."

"That's why I want you to let that man work," said LaTasha. "If you think about all the good things you have done in your life, keeping your son clothed and fed all by your damn self, the lifesaving work you do? You deserve it, Thena. And don't let your brain tell you that you don't."

"I'm *trying*."

"Try *harder*."

I tapped her arm and crafted a sharp turn in the subject. "Not that I don't appreciate tales from the smug married, but tell us about who is spoiling you, LaTasha."

LaTasha was young, made great money, and wasn't in any hurry to settle down. She was a cute little thing, so slender that every pair of scrubs fit her like they were designed for her body. She kept her hair in a pixie cut and liked to spike it up whenever she wasn't wearing a cap. Her deep skin tone was gorgeous, crystal clear.

Every time I talked to her, she was heading out on a date or on her way back from one. She seemed to be enjoying herself, even if none of those dates turned into anything serious.

"I'm having as good a time as I can while I can," LaTasha said.

"And…where are you finding these men that you have a good time with?"

"I have three different dating sites going. The front-runner is a pleaser."

"A what, now?" asked Valerie. "Shouldn't they all be a pleaser?"

LaTasha laughed, laying a hand on Valerie's shoulder. "No, Val. *A pleaser*. He gets off on me getting off. And he doesn't require reciprocation. Unless…it would please me to reciprocate."

My jaw hit the table. I had never heard of such a thing. "Get the fuck out of here. That's a type?"

"Either that's a type, or this man is setting me up for a downfall. Either way, I am very…*very* pleased these days." LaTasha sucked down her cocktail while Valerie and I stared, mouths open.

"Where do you find the energy to manage all of that? I can't remember if I texted Vance or sent him a DM on Instagram or it was something we said on Zoom. And he's only one man."

"Oh, I'm very organized," she replied. "You almost have to manage it that way. Men are so suss; you're losing if you're not playing the numbers game. You know what I'm saying?"

"Not really," I said. "It depends on what *suss* means."

"Suspect! Funny acting! Like, you meet someone on a dating app, and y'all start talking, right? A little regular communication, and he's calling me *baby* and texting me *WYD* four times a day. And throwing a fit if he sees me making a comment to somebody on one of *my* accounts. Boy, please. Who the fuck are you?"

Valerie and I both laughed, bobbing our heads in agreement.

"I met a man on a social media app, and we became friends. And then more. And you two have been on my ass for months to take this man seriously. Shouldn't you take your own advice?"

"We're not talking about me, Athena."

"Actually, we are. I have transferred the conversation from me to you. So?" I stared, brows raised.

"You know what? I think I get it," Valerie offered. "I understand why Athena is so hesitant. I get why Darius is overly cautious. All I hear about in smug married land is how much of a scam dating is these days. The men aren't genuine, the women are gold diggers and the situation is rigged. How do you even have hope amid all of…"

She waved her hands around, gesturing in a flurry of movements. "This!"

"It's hard to know what's real," I said. "Are they interested in you? Are they looking for a hookup, but they won't say that because they know you'll curve them?"

"Or you end up with someone looking for a warm bed," LaTasha said.

"Been there, done that," I said. "That was Kane's thing—

ending up at my house for months at a time, threatening that if he didn't have a place to stay, he'd lose his job, and then I'd lose child support."

"How did you get that man out of your house?" LaTasha asked.

"I charged that negro rent," I said, snorting a laugh. "This man thought he could hold his little child support garnishment hostage. Please! Pay me or get out." I snapped my fingers in the air. "Like that, he met a woman that let him move in. I just transferred that hobo from my house to hers."

"Girl, stop!" Valerie cackled, doubled over until she almost lay on the table.

"And she loves the shit out of him! The only reason he acts right now is because of her."

"Well, there's a lid for every pot," said LaTasha. She raised her glass, prompting a toast. "And here's to Athena, finally meeting the perfect lid to her fine ass pot."

"Cheers to that." I tapped my wineglass to hers, then to Valerie's glass. Maybe it was the wine, but I was beginning to relax. At least until I got on the plane.

LaTasha waved her glass at the passing server, signaling for him to bring her another drink. "Thena, before you leave, come by my place. I can tighten up your edges for you. You want your hair looking fresh."

"Oh, God." I fingered my hairline, noting how much new growth peeked through my braids. I had them installed before I left Columbia and would be long overdue for a new set when my assignment was over. "Thank you. I was thinking about looking for a braider in Minnesota."

"I got you, honey. But..." She continued, leaning in. "How is the situation downstairs? Do you have a waxer? Do you need a Brazilian referral?"

"LaTasha..."

"What? Miss Kitty needs to make a good impression!"

I giggled. "Vance has already seen her."

LaTasha blinked, incredulous. "Not in 3D, life size, up close and personal, he hasn't!"

"You get on my nerves," I told her, laughing. "But...send me the referral. This man better be worth it."

"Remember, Athena—you are doing this for *you*."

"The hell I am!" I reared back in protest. "I don't care if she's bare."

"Not *bare*. We aren't shooting porn, just cleaning things up. Adding a lil' strip to wave him on down." She gestured, waving her hands toward her. "Welcome him in."

"Stop talking to me, LaTasha. Where is our server?"

VANCE

Thena W: Good luck tonight, handsome.
Debrief later?

Vance-Wanderlust Travel: Bet. Ima need you.

KAREEMA GLARED ACROSS A TABLE SET WITH CREAMY WHITE linens and gleaming silverware. Even at Amore, an upscale Italian restaurant that featured dark wood furniture and flickering candlelight, shadowed by merlot-painted walls and glass bowls of colorful flowers, the atmosphere between us was thick with tension.

The restaurant choice was hers. Though I wasn't a fan of what felt like an overblown Olive Garden menu, I'd decided that since I was meeting her to hurt her feelings, I could do it while she enjoyed Linguine alle Vongole, a dish of clams, white wine, pasta, and pancetta.

We agreed to meet at 7 PM. Kareema arrived at 7:35. I snapped at her because I felt she was late on purpose. Our conversation had been awkward and choppy ever since. Of all my children, Kareema and I were the closest until Alexis and I announced our divorce. We hadn't had a genuine conversation in some time, so we were well out of practice.

I shifted uncomfortably after an attentive server took our dinner orders. The weight of unspoken words hung between us amid the clamor of other diners.

"So," she bit out. She looked so much like Alexis in that moment—russet brown skin tone, her dark hair silk pressed to the gods, subtle but expensive skincare and makeup regimen on point. Her lithe physique looked good in everything, so she bought off the rack. Athena talked often about trying on clothes because she was never sure if something would fit her thighs but not her waist or vice versa. Kareema likely put little thought into whether the designer black suit she wore would fit her.

"So…" I parroted back to her.

She flipped a length of hair over her shoulder, then folded her arms. "So. It's been a while since we had dinner together, especially at Amore, so you're sucking up. You're not dying, are you?"

I cleared my throat, masking a chuckle. Humor was her defense mechanism, and Kareema could be extremely defensive.

"As far as I know, I'll be around for a good, long while. And you're right; we don't get together much. Which is a good reason to get together."

"Mmmhmm." She pressed her lips together. "We're going to chat like old friends after not really talking lately?"

I shrugged. "Why can't we—"

"Because you like to antagonize me by giving me all the reasons that you're no longer married to my mother." The brown orbs of her eyes glowed like fire. "And because we only have these dinners when you have shit you want to tell me. Like, say, you're divorcing my mother."

Here we go. This was about pain, anger, and the unresolved turmoil of the divorce. I couldn't combat it by meeting fire with fire, nor could I deflect it with therapy jargon. Kareema didn't believe in therapy; Kareema believed in burying her feelings in work. She worked a lot.

"I didn't *divorce your mother*. It was a mutual decision. You choose to view it from that lens so you can stay hurt behind it. Alexis and Richard are celebrating their anniversary next week."

She huffed. "Yeah, I got the invite. Do they plan to throw a big ass party every year?"

I did laugh that time. "Probably. You know how your mother is—any reason to have a party." We always joked that Alexis would celebrate the opening of an envelope.

She busied herself with the napkin, flapping it open and laying it across her lap. "I can't believe they're having it at some country club. Are you going?"

"No." I inhaled a strengthening, fortifying breath. "I won't be in town."

Kareema smirked. "Was that on purpose? You should be able to plan your trips better than that, Dad."

"Alexis is not my wife. I never had plans to attend a party celebrating four years with the man she left me for." I leaned back in my seat and let out a sigh. "Listen, I don't want to drag this out. You know I'm seeing someone."

Her expression did not change except for the rise in her eyebrows. "You're buying dinner so you can talk about that woman you met on Instagram?"

"I'm going on a work trip and I'm taking her with me. Mom knows. I wanted you to hear it from me."

She did not hide the irritated eye roll. "You're paying for her, though. Right?"

"It was my idea," I said with a nod. "I have to go anyway. It'll give us a good start—"

"How convenient. A free trip on you. And then what? Is she moving in? Is she going to live in the house you lived in with mom? Are your children supposed to be okay with another woman in that house?"

I paused, weighing each word carefully. It mattered, because I had no intention of repeating this speech.

"I want to give you time and space because I know the divorce hit you hard. But Kareema...you want a thing you cannot have. Alexis and I staying together would have ended in misery. We weren't happy. We hadn't been happy in a long time. She has moved on. I have moved on. I don't expect you to be okay with me dating someone new, but I do expect you to respect my decision."

She looked away, running her tongue over her teeth. Her eyelids, weighed down by false lashes, rapidly blinked. "You've never even met this woman."

"We haven't met in person, no. But I am more than familiar with Athena."

Her nostrils flared at the mention of Athena's name. "You're taking her on vacation for your first date?" She scoffed. "A little much, isn't it? She could be scamming you."

I chuckled. "Her son says the same thing about me. That I'm scamming her. Am I?"

She played with the napkin, folding it, then unfolding it and spreading it across her lap again. "I don't know," she snapped finally. "Probably not."

"Even if she was scamming me, it would be my business. If it was a *little much*, it's mine to do a *little much* with. Right?"

She sighed. "I guess, Dad."

"We think we owe it to each other to see if this thing has legs. I really like her, and I hope to introduce you to her soon."

"No, thanks," she shot back, probably as a reflex before she could think about it. I saw the regret in her eyes the moment the words landed on my ears and my expression changed. "I—I'm sorry. I meant that if you want to date, that's your thing. I don't need to be involved."

"Fair. Divorce is hard. I get it."

"Do you, Dad?" She shot back, eyes narrowed.

"All I remember about my parent's marriage before their divorce is that they argued about everything because they didn't like each other. When the conversation turned to divorce, your mom and I had already made peace with the idea. The decision wasn't a hard one to make, but we didn't loop in you, Sedrick, or Alex. In hindsight, we probably should have."

Kareema stared down at her lap, then up at me. "I'm sorry," she said softly. "I forgot about that. I know you were just trying to protect us from it all."

"We could have prepared you for the shock, and I'm sorry we didn't. I'm trying to do better. I hope one day you'll be able to see that this new person in my life brings me happiness."

Kareema sniffed, blinking away tears. "So you're happy with the way things are—divorced dad of three. You're cool with that?"

I paused, taken aback by her question, but the answer came quickly. "Nothing wrong with being a divorced dad of three. I'm cool with that."

"Are you the kind of happy you were when you and Mom were first married?"

I pondered her question. Alexis and I didn't have what I would consider a fairy tale relationship. We were a habit that just wouldn't quit.

"That was a different time," I told her. "I'm sure I thought I wouldn't ever be happier than I was back then. Today, I'm happy in a different way, a way that I don't think my younger self would have understood. I run a successful business. I have great friends. I'm excited about the future and whatever it might hold for me."

"And this woman? She's part of that?"

I nodded. "Athena is a part of that, yeah. I'd love for her to be a bigger part of that."

"Okay, so after your vacation, then what? Eventually, she'll come to Houston. Eventually, you'll want her to meet us. Eventually, she'll be a huge part of your new life and you won't even remember you had an old life before you knew her."

"I haven't even met her in person yet. There's no plan to move her here."

"Dad," she said, her tone seeming to scold me. "If you're talking about her being a big part of your life, eventually is going to come sooner than you think."

She wasn't wrong, though I cringed that I hadn't yet told Kareema that moving Athena to Houston wasn't on my mind because I did not plan to stay in Houston.

"I promise I won't try to shove her in where she doesn't fit, but I'd be lying if I didn't admit that I hope she fits into our family."

Kareema drew a shaky breath and wiped away the tear that had snaked down her cheek.

"I know this emotion is because you don't want to move into a new era, some unknown stage, because you don't know where you stand. But I promise I'm still your dad. I'm still here, like I always will be."

She sniffed. "Okay, let's not go overboard. I never said I didn't think you'd be here—"

"Mmmmm…" I hummed, shaking my head. "I don't know. I hear a lot of what amounts to '*don't take my dad from me.*'"

"Whatever." She rolled her eyes and sniffed. "You want happiness, so…I'll try to be happy for you."

"I'm not asking you to fake it. If happy is a bridge too far, then I ask for your respect that I'm doing what I need to do. I would want you to do the same." I cracked a smile. "You want to take a minute before dinner comes out? I know how you hate it when you don't look flawless."

She flinched, reaching for her bag, dug out a compact, and popped it open. "Oh, shit," she whispered at her reflection. She pushed her chair back from the table. "I'll be right back."

———

"HI, HANDSOME." ATHENA WAS IN HER BEDROOM WITH THE iPad propped so she could see me. She was in her robe, curled up on the bed, chugging a bottle of water. "You look like dinner was rough. Want to talk about it?"

"I'd rather talk about you modeling those swimsuits you said you found."

"Not before our vacation. They look good, though," she finished with a smile, putting some tease into her tone.

"Is that bad luck? Like the groom can't see the bride before a wedding?"

"That's me being neurotic." She tilted her head to the side, expectant. "Stop stalling. I went on and on about my conversation with Darius. I can listen to you talk about your adult child's inability to accept a parent moving on with their life."

"And that's exactly what it is, you know?" I sighed, rubbing a palm over my hair. "She is not the biggest fan of change. The conversation was rough, but it was mostly Kareema still feeling like that little girl whose world fell apart one day."

"How old was she when you divorced?"

"Twenty. Old enough to understand, and to witness the marriage falling apart in front of her."

"Interesting that she's mad at you and not her mother. Alexis moved on first, right?"

"I think Kareema assumed I'd caused that and didn't fix it. When I just…" I flopped a hand through the air. "Curled over, signed the papers, helped Alexis move out? I guess she thought I could have done something."

Athena mused. "Did she come around at all?"

"Some," I admitted. "I got her to understand that this is happening, and she can be okay with it or not, but either way, I'm moving on. She said she would try to be happy for me. That's really all I can expect right now."

"Okay…well," said Athena, perking a little. "That's a better outcome than I expected. You know it's about more than you dating someone."

"Yeah. It's a little tug of war for my love and attention. She and I need to rebuild that father-daughter connection. I don't know how to make that happen if I plan to leave Houston soon, but I'm always going to be her dad, wherever I am."

"Something to work on." She snapped her fingers. "Come on, Dad Goals."

I chuckled. "That sounds…*different* coming from your mouth."

"It *is* different coming from my mouth."

She began pulling her robe open to reveal a skimpy, sexy deep purple lingerie set. I'd bought it for her as a surprise and didn't know it had already arrived. The set fit her like a glove in all the right places, accentuating the roundness of her breasts, delicately outlining her body in the lace panty.

"Baby…that's fire on you. Hitting *all* the right notes."

Athena laughed, but I was serious. It looked amazing on her.

"I just wanted to make sure it fit." She skimmed a hand over each of my favorite curves. "What do you think?"

"It's perfect. So…*fucking* perfect. But, uh…" I licked my lips, leaning in like I could see more if I got closer to the tablet. "You were supposed to save that set for our trip, so you need to take it off. Nice and slow."

Athena smirked, running a hand through her braids, pulling them over one shoulder. Then she crawled to the edge of the bed and stood, letting the robe slide from her shoulders to the floor. I watched with rapt attention as she swayed to a beat only she could hear, her hands traveling the expanse of her body and teasing at the lacy edges.

"Got damn," I breathed out, feeling a tightness in my chest. "Hang on. I need to get comfortable."

I pulled at my clothing, cursing that I wore a shirt and slacks to dinner. I had never unbuttoned, unzipped, and tossed clothing so haphazardly in all my life.

Athena giggled as I hurriedly undressed. "I heard something rip over there. Take your time, baby. I'm just over here vibing."

Once I'd shed my clothes, I crawled back onto the bed and set the tablet in its usual spot, propped up just far enough away that she could see me. "Okay. Uh...continue."

She moved closer to the camera as she slowly lowered one strap of her bra. She did the same with the other strap, then reached behind her back to unclasp it, letting it fall away to reveal full, bouncy breasts.

She went back to her dance, swaying her hips and caressing her curves, cupping her breasts and flicking her thumbs over the nipples standing on end. I watched as she tucked a finger under the band of the panties and *slowly* dragged them down her thighs. She stepped out of them and threw her arms up, waving the garment like a flag. Her breasts bounced with the movement.

I pulsed, growing harder in my grip. "Shit," I groaned. "You are *killing* me."

Athena smiled. "Mission accomplished," she purred, crawling back onto the bed. She pressed a soft kiss to the tips of her fingers. "I can't wait to wear that for you."

"You don't even know how excited I am to see you."

Athena leaned onto her pillow, propped up on one elbow. "You know I can see you, right? With your hand wrapped around your dick standing at attention. I think I do, handsome."

She laid back, her mouth widening into a relaxed smile as she began to roll and tug at her nipples. She drew her legs up and spread her knees. "Tell me what you want me to do," she murmured, her tone deep and lusty.

I settled into the plush pillows, propped so I could lock eyes with her. "I want to see your fingers on your clit. Get warmed up for me."

A sexy smirk played on her lips as she traced around her nipples before heading further south. Her strokes were gentle at first, rhythmic movements that alternated between circular grinds and flicking her thumb over the hardening bud.

I fisted my dick, pumping in concert with her movements. "Watching you do that makes me so damn hard. That shit is so sexy, baby."

"Tell me what you're thinking about, handsome."

"*Mmmph,*" I grunted, falling into the mood. "The weight of your titties in my hands. How I can't wait to bury my face in your pussy. The way I want you to moan while I'm in your mouth. How I want those thick ass thighs locked around me."

"Mmmmm, yes. I want that, too."

"I want to watch you try not to come when I fuck you hard. Then soft and slow."

"Drag it out, baby. Make me work for it."

Athena whimpered, her voice shaking as she vigorously rubbed her clit, then brought an erect nipple into her mouth. I almost lost it watching her tongue circle and flick the tip. She moaned, not taking her eyes off the camera as she closed her mouth over the nipple again.

My breath caught in my throat as I uttered a strangled cry. "That pussy getting wetter when I'm slamming into you. Shit! I need you."

Athena's eyes glazed over. Her chest rose and fell with labored breathing.

"Help me out, baby. Let me see you slide that glass dick inside you. Like you're fucking me."

She spread her knees wider, lifting her legs so her feet were in the air as she dipped the head of a clear, penis-shaped toy into her opening. She moaned loudly, working it in and out until she could take it all.

"Fuck!" I roared, bucking my hips, fucking her in my mind. "Keep going. Just like that."

Thena's breathing grew heavier, more labored, her body trembling. I watched her approach her climax as she pumped the toy into her pussy with lightning speed. It wasn't long before she dropped her legs, using them as leverage to arch her body off of the bed.

"Shit! I'm coming!"

My muscles tightened as I reached my orgasm, flexing and releasing in waves. The sensation was delicious, only made better by the sounds of Athena at the height of her climax.

The room was hot, the air heavy with the musky scent of arousal. For just a moment, we were still, breaths slowing to their regular cadence. I picked up a remote from the night-stand and pressed a button. Above me, the ceiling fan turned. I sighed at the bands of cool air already beginning to dry the beads of sweat from my body.

My skin was raw and sensitive. Every nerve tingled, the hair on my arms and legs pricking to attention. There was something about this woman that made even jacking off an epic event.

"You still with me?" I asked. Athena groaned. "You should strip more often. That was impressive."

She sat up, pulling her braids back from her face into a ponytail and wrapping a hair tie around them. "I can't stop thinking about how fucking good you're going to feel in person. I can't wait to get on the plane."

The thought of seeing her in the flesh sent a wave of excitement through me. I was ready to bask in that energy, the spark that I knew we would have in person. I pushed myself up, then pulled open a drawer in my nightstand for a package of moistened towelettes. I snapped a few from the container to clean myself up.

"If this happens when we hang out on Zoom, we're not ready for how much better it's going to be in person."

"The days are crawling by so slowly."

"Yeah, well. You'll be back at work tomorrow. I have some travel plans I need to set before I leave so I don't have to work while down there." I tossed the towels into the wastebasket near the bed. "I just want a great time with you. That's all I'll let myself think about."

"Aw, baby…" Athena cooed, then she snickered. "You are simpin' *hard*, bro."

I laughed, settling in for after chat. "Guilty. So, tell me about your day in beautiful Grand Rapids, Minnesota."

ATHENA

Vance-Wanderlust Travel: No more sleeps.
Woke up thinking about the sheets we finna
fuck up tonight.

Vance-Wanderlust Travel: kinda excited,
kinda got bubble guts.

Thena W: Way to woo me, handsome.

I WAS TOO NERVOUS TO SLEEP, EVEN AFTER OUR NIGHTCAP. I WAS finally snoozing when the alarm went off and I didn't hear it. I woke up when Vance texted me.

Thankfully, I was more than ready and jumped into my travel clothes in time to meet my landlord, who was sweet to drive me to the airport. We left earlier than planned, and that was a good thing because he had my nerves on edge with his slow, meandering driving.

Just as he pulled up to the airport and I retrieved my suitcase and backpack from the backseat of his car, my phone rang out with the tone I'd assigned to Darius. I did not have time, patience, or energy for my son, but I would never hear the end of it if I ignored his call.

"Hey, I'm running late," I yelled as soon as I picked up, trying to move with the flow of airport foot traffic. "Is anything up, or can I call you when I land?"

"Land? You're still going on that trip, then."

I exhaled, squeezing my eyes shut for the briefest of seconds. I was lugging a suitcase through the Duluth, Minnesota airport, heart racing, phone pressed to my ear. How did I raise this man to not know how to read a damn room?

"Is anything up, or can I call you later?" I repeated.

"Okay. I see what you're on, Ma. Just think about what you're doing. You don't know this man, and you're about to fly to another state, then get into a car and drive somewhere with him."

Darius' voice had a desperate edge to it, and I understood why. I would react the same way if he suggested he was going to fly off to vacation with a woman he'd met online. I also knew that he wouldn't factor my displeasure into his decision. I was giving him the same consideration.

"You say that like I'm going to the middle of nowhere," I said, maneuvering around slow-moving passengers. "I'm not going to the Congo. Cell phones work on Black Diamond. You have the Find My Friends app so you can track me."

"You want me to track you and your sneaky link on your lil' fuck fest?"

"It's not like there's a camera," I replied, laughing.

"That's not funny, Ma. I'm not okay with this."

"You've made that clear. I wasn't asking for your permission. I was telling you where I'll be. I'm about to get in the TSA line, then get on a flight to meet a man I care about. Take however long you need to work that out. I'll call you when I land and when I am headed back. Love you, son."

"Ma, all I'm say—" I ended the call, mentally daring him to call me back, but he didn't. I pulled up my boarding pass and my ID and tried to forget that phone call. I refused to let my son's negativity spoil the adventure that lay ahead. In a few hours, I would be wrapped in arms I'd only dreamed about.

And in a few more hours, I hoped my feet in the air while I was getting my back blown out.

I settled into the first-class window seat Vance booked for me and puffed my cheeks, heaving a sigh of relief from my diaphragm. By the time the plane pushed back from the gate and was climbing into a cloudless blue sky, the conversation with Darius was forgotten and I was in a fugue state.

A flight attendant leaned in and smiled. "Miss, can I get you anything? Coffee, soft drink, juice?"

I requested coffee with cream and sugar and a fruit and cheese plate, and then, as if I could concentrate on a book, pulled out a tattered copy of Beverly Jenkins' *Indigo*. It was my favorite romance novel by my favorite romance author. I needed some romantic fortification and hoped it would seep from the pages and embed itself into my soul.

The hours passed by in a blur of dozing and foot-tapping nervousness, counting down to when I wouldn't have to daydream about Vance anymore. When the flight attendants announced they were gathering trash and to return our seats to the upright position, my heart hammered a steady, rapid beat in my chest. I pushed out a few Lamaze-like breaths, then dug through my backpack for the mints that I'd packed and a Fenty Gloss Bomb. The nude shade made my pillowy-soft lips shine bright like a diamond.

Then I decided I didn't want my lips to shine bright like a diamond. It would rub off on Vance's lips when he kissed me. I pulled a Kleenex from a travel pack and started over, applying a coat of Unveil, a chocolate brown nude. It would dry by the time I got off the plane and my lips would be kiss-ready.

Yes, Vance. Please kiss the shit out of this mouth.

VANCE

MAYBE IT WAS THE ESPRESSO I DOWNED WHILE I TOOK MY JEEP through the carwash, but my heartbeat thumped loud in my ears like a high school band. It had its own drum line.

I'd arrived at the airport early, mostly out of nervousness and because I never knew what traffic and parking was going to be like, and I could not be late to pick up Athena. I also didn't want to miss a second of seeing her in person.

I loitered at George Bush International, pacing and eyeing arrivals, pretending I hadn't been tracking her flight since its departure. My app showed her plane had touched down. I set an internal countdown, giving it roughly twenty minutes before I'd start searching the crowd. Passengers spilled out from the gate in a steady stream.

And then, I spotted her. I'd know those long blonde braids anywhere.

She wore light wash jeans with stylish rips across the thighs that offered a teasing glimpse of skin with each step. A black, short-sleeved crop top paired with the jeans, while a letterman-style jacket hung casually over her arm. Black and white converse sneakers, silver hoop earrings and designer shades completed the look. Even under those ugly airport lights, she was glowing.

"Thena! Athena!"

She looked around, then saw me waving like one of those inflatable things at a car dealership. When our eyes locked, she just...stopped walking. A few people came up short behind her, grumbled and moved around, but it was like she didn't see them.

Or didn't care. I was on the same wavelength.

She pulled her shades from her eyes and stared for what felt like forever but was probably mere seconds. After a few beats, her lips parted, and she beamed a smile that could have lit up the airport.

My heart did this weird little leap, and it was my turn to stand there. The moment that I'd been waiting for since I first sent her that Instagram DM was here. I didn't know how Athena thought about it, but it was momentous to me.

Her mouth formed the word, "Vance!" Then she took off, aiming right at me. I started moving in her direction. She laughed and broke into a run, her bag bouncing on her back and suitcase careening on one wheel behind her. When she was steps away, she dropped the handle, letting the suitcase fall and jumped into my arms, wrapping her limbs around my neck.

Her scent filled my nostrils—jasmine and vanilla and the coconut oil she used every day. She smelled good. She *felt* good up against me. It was as amazing as I imagined it would be.

I squeezed her until she laughed, protesting, "I can't breathe, baby!"

Knowing I had days ahead to hold her, I reluctantly let go. My hand glided down her arms, savoring the feel of the soft skin I'd watched her moisturize daily. Taking her hands in mine, our eyes met and held. I found myself lost in the deep espresso of her eyes, the laugh lines adding character, her emotions swirling beneath the surface.

"Hi, handsome," she said, her grin a mile wide. She reached out to grip one of my biceps, tracing an old tattoo with the tip of a finger. "And I mean *hello, handsome*. Damn, you fine!"

"Hello," I replied, fighting the flush crawling up my chest. "You are one million times more gorgeous in person."

I watched her brow wrinkle and a tiny V pop up in the middle of her forehead. She frowned; the edges of her thick lips turned down. My heart sank. *What'd I say?*

"Only one million? I thought you liked me, Vance."

I laughed in relief, the nervous thumps of my heart melting away. "I was trying to be sweet. You got jokes. You want to hand me that bag off your back?"

"You had me hyped up for a kiss. I need that first."

I pulled back to look into her eyes. "You want our first kiss ever to be at the airport?"

"It doesn't matter where it happens, just that it does. My mouth is ready."

I moved to stand in front of her, then cupped her face in my ands, my fingers buried in her hair. I gently pulled her to me, pressing my lips to hers. I wanted to keep it sweet, almost chaste, with a promise of what was to come.

Athena immediately went for more, stepping closer and sliding her arms around my body. She melted into me as she opened her mouth. I fell deeper into the kiss, our tongues mingling and getting better acquainted.

Every inch of distance, the fear of shyness, of awkward silence and nervous moments between us evaporated.

I pulled back first, not wanting to overwhelm her. Her hands found my face; her fingertips caressed my lips, traced my jawline, smoothed down my freshly trimmed beard. Her thumbs gliding along my skin brought goosebumps.

Our eyes locked. The pull between us was magnetic, the

air crackling with electricity. She smiled, then angled her mouth, leaning in for another kiss. A low, sultry moan rolled through her. I chuckled, breaking the kiss. She held onto the corner of my bottom lip with her teeth, then finally let go.

The minty taste of her mouth lingered on mine. She angled her head back, surveying me with heavily lidded eyes. "That was the best first kiss I've ever had."

"Same. But you can't be moaning like that, all pressed up against me in public."

"I can't?" she asked, eyes big and round, voice soft, feigning absolute innocence like she didn't have firsthand experience in what her noises did to me. "Why?"

I leaned in so I could speak into her ear. What I had to say to her was not for mixed company.

"Because it makes me want to throw you over my shoulder, run us out to my Jeep, and fuck you on the third floor of the parking deck at George Bush International. Have you ever been arrested for indecent exposure?"

"No." She laughed. "Sounds like a good time, though. I want to see some of that *pick me up and fuck me* action later."

"I'm only going to tell you once to stop playing with me, woman."

"You say that daily, Vance."

"You play with me daily, Athena." She winked, then slipped the straps of her backpack from her shoulders and handed it to me. The thing was heavy. "What is in here?"

"All the stuff I couldn't risk losing. A change of clothes, a few books, my makeup bag. My rose."

That last item made my head spin on my neck. Calmly, she picked up the handle of the suitcase, which was still on the ground. I slid the backpack over my shoulders, took it from her with one hand holding the other out to her. She slid her palm across mine and our fingers instinctively intertwined.

The airport was loud and bustling as we navigated

outside toward short-term parking, chatting along the way about weather and the flight and her conversation with Darius before she left.

Every few seconds, I wanted to pinch myself, hoping it wasn't my brain messing with me.

It wasn't. Athena was here.

ATHENA

Thena W: Hey, D! I landed in Houston safely. Vance is here and I'm good. Promise.

Thena W: Thank you for worrying. Keep an eye on the house and don't work too hard. Love you.

Darius: Be safe. Love u.

I LOCKED THE SCREEN, TUCKED MY PHONE INTO THE CROSSBODY bag that I'd dug out of my backpack and zipped it closed, then tried to relax while Vance stored my luggage in the trunk. The butterscotch leather seat was smooth, free of cracks, and cushioned my body like a hug. The wide screen in the center of the dashboard looked like command central, boasting an array of high-tech features. The car even carried his scent—a mix of masculine musk, wood, and an earthy spice.

Vance climbed into the driver's seat. The thunk of the door when he pulled it shut made me smile. We were all closed off. Alone. Together!

"You check in with the kid?"

"My almost thirty year old kid? Yeah."

"He good?"

"He has no choice but to be good," I answered.

He eyed me with the most sinful of grins. "He's probably worried about what I'm going to do to his mama."

I giggled. "Does he have anything to worry about?"

Vance pressed the ignition button and reached for the gearshift, but a local radio station popped on and blared hits from the '90s through the surround sound speakers. Vance turned it down before he leaned in, resting his elbow on the armrest. My eyes were drawn to the shifting muscle beneath his skin.

"Darius? Nah. You, on the other hand?"

I flicked my eyes up to his. They were smoky and full of want. "Tell me what I need to worry about, Vance."

"Bring those lips over here. I'll show you."

I felt the heat of his body as I turned in the seat. Our lips met again, but this time, Vance wasn't shy about letting his desire flow through him. The swirl of his tongue, the dance between his and mine was heady as it made each nerve ending sing and parts of my body thump.

He shifted, cupping my face in his hands. I gave in, moaning into his mouth. He returned the sound, then moved a hand from my face to my neck, gently massaging me before moving down my body.

I laid a hand over his, guiding him to a breast. I wanted him to experience the heft, the roundness, the fullness that he'd seen but hadn't yet been able to touch. He quickly found my nipple and stroked it until it stood at attention. A jolt of electricity shot through me, settling into a steadily building need. I squirmed, moaning again at the seam of my jeans riding my clit ever so slightly.

Vance must have heard me because he moved lower, then pulled my zipper and dipped inside my jeans. When he brushed across my clit, I gasped, opening my legs. I clung to his arm, not wanting him to stop.

"I can finally touch you," he mumbled against my lips, "And not just think about touching you. Your pussy feels good, baby."

He kissed me like he couldn't get enough. I attacked his mouth with matching fervor, delighting in the taste of him. If we weren't in short-term airport parking, I would have crawled over the center console, ripped down his zipper, and taken him until he was bucking his hips and driving his dick into my mouth.

But we *were* parked in short-term parking. I couldn't have him how I wanted him—his weight on top of me, his lips all over me, his arms around me, him deep inside me.

Breathless, I reluctantly broke the kiss and grasped his wrist. "I want this. I *really* want this, but if we don't stop now, we're going to have a problem."

"We already have a problem." I followed his eyes, noting the erection testing the strength of his zipper.

"There's time for all of this once we get where we're going."

"I guess, if you want to be a responsible adult about it." He sighed, dragging his hand back, then settled into his seat and pulled the seatbelt across his body, clicking it into the latch. I did the same. "I asked if you wanted to get arrested for indecent exposure."

"You asked if I had ever been arrested for indecent exposure."

"Same thing, Athena."

"It is not, Vance." He laughed, then leaned over with lips puckered. I kissed him, then kissed him again. When he leaned over further, aiming for another kiss, I pushed him back over. "Let's go before I drag you into the backseat. An arrest will fuck up my vacation."

Something hit me really quick, then. There was nothing in

the trunk when we had arrived at the vehicle. The backseat was also empty.

"Vance?" I straightened again and studied the side of his face as he drove. He'd slipped on a pair of shades since we had exited the parking deck into a sunny, cloudless Texas day.

"Yeah, babe?"

"Where is your stuff? Like…your suitcase and…you know? Your stuff."

"At the house," he answered. "I have a couple of things in the dryer. I thought we'd stop at the house, grab my bags, then hit the road. We don't have to be at the hotel until late."

His eyes left the road for a few seconds, then he asked, "Why?"

"Nothing." I settled into the seat and bobbed my head to the faint sounds of the radio. "I guess I wondered why we were playing grab-a-titty in the car when we could have been playing at your house."

"I had no intention of waiting to touch you, gorgeous."

Vance took my hand and brought it to his lap, tucking my fingers between his thighs. He pushed out a grunt, arching his hips up as I gripped him through his jeans.

"Don't move," he ordered, then pulled into traffic, headed south.

VANCE TURNED INTO A PAVED DRIVEWAY HALFWAY DOWN A QUIET suburban street. In the hour since we left the airport, I watched the landscape change from bustling city to busy suburb to quaint neighborhood. His brick rancher was charming from the outside, with plants that ran up a trellis flanking both sides of the front door and a wrought-iron bench on the porch.

He pushed a button on the dashboard and the wide garage door slowly rose, revealing a stuffed but neatly organized garage. Boxes were stacked in the space where another car would sit; tools were on hooks, and a ten-speed hung upside down from hooks screwed into wooden beams.

"Be it ever so humble," he said, pulling into the garage and pushing the ignition button.

I got out of the car, stretching my legs and arms while I checked out his neighborhood. It didn't look much different from a Columbia, South Carolina suburb. Both were stark contracts from Big Fork. I smiled to myself, so happy to be away or a few days. I had four weeks left in my assignment, and as much as I would miss Valerie, LaTasha, and my land-lords, I was ready to be in a state that was not still experiencing winter in May.

"Does the place meet with your approval?" I heard behind me. Vance had climbed a short set of stairs and was standing at the interior door to the house.

"So far," I chirped, rushing to catch up with him. He keyed in a code and the doors unlocked with a quiet whir. "You like fancy things," I commented. "Push button everything in the car, keypad entry for the house."

Vance let out a light patter of laughter. "You ain't seen nothin' yet, baby."

The inside of his home was just as bright and welcoming as the outside. The living room boasted a brick fireplace and a plush couch. A large bookshelf filled one wall, stuffed with books that spanned multiple genres from travel to personal finance to literary fiction and self-exploration.

"Make yourself at home," he said, gesturing to the couch. "Can I get you a drink? You're not driving, so you can have anything you like."

"What do you have that isn't water or booze?"

"Iced tea?"

"Is it sweet?"

"Why are you trying to hurt my feelings?" he asked,

turning to walk to the open kitchen. I followed. "I live in the South—of course, it's sweet."

"Thank God. I cannot get sweet tea in Minnesota. They hand me a glass of Lipton and a handful of sugar packets and wish me luck."

Vance opened one side of a stainless-steel refrigerator and pulled out a glass pitcher, the kind a Southern grandmother would use, with a spigot. He poured a glass of tea and handed it to me. I sipped the perfectly sweet brew while I scoped out his kitchen. It was immaculate, from the gleaming appliances to the spacious granite countertops.

"I didn't get good sweet tea unless I was at my grandparent's place in Georgia," he said, pouring himself a glass and putting the pitcher back in the refrigerator. He nodded with his head to lead me out of the kitchen and back to the living room.

We passed a panel on the wall, and he pressed a few buttons. Though the room didn't need it, lights illuminated the area over the fireplace, the TV, and the couch.

"Now you're just showing off," I teased.

"I heard a smart house was the wave of the future. After Alexis moved out, I redecorated, did some painting and renovation."

"It'll do a lot for resale value." I sucked down another gulp of delicious tea and made a mental note—a man that could make a perfect glass of sweet sun tea was a keeper. "You said your grandmother was from Georgia? Did she teach you how to make tea?"

He nodded, heading straight for a wall of photos in the hallway. He pointed at an old print so faded that it was sepia, lovingly framed and hung in the center of the photo wall. "Gloria and Vance Griffin. I'm named after my grandfather on my dad's side. Now, that there was a Southern woman. She got me hooked on it so bad that I had to ask her to show me how to make it so I can have it whenever I want it."

He turned to me and winked. "I made some just for you."

"It's delicious. You're so sweet, Vance. Thank you."

"I'm sucking up. Let me give you the tour. These are some places I've been to since I opened Wanderlust."

On the opposite wall, another collection of framed photographs hung, showcasing Vance's travels around the world. "Ooh, these are beautiful," I whispered, taking in each one. He took his time, narrating his adventures via myriad shots of him and others in exotic places. Some photos were in sunny beach locales. Others were of him in winter wear, standing in feet of snow.

"See, I would have been fine up in Big Fork."

"Mmmmm," I hummed. "I see. Wanderlust fits you to a tee." I made my way down the hall, studying the scenery in each photo. Every image was a different mood. "I don't see your...uhm...your ex or your family in any of these."

"The family is over on the wall around my grandmother," he said, pointing to a set of photos in frames. "Alexis is not a globe-trotter. She travels so much for work that it's not relaxing for her to get on a plane and go somewhere else. My kids love to travel. My youngest is backpacking through Brazil with a 9mm camera, filming first-person cultural interviews for some magazine."

He shrugged and walked on, shyly tucking away a proud dad smile.

"Okay, National Geographic."

"That's the goal." He stopped at a closed door and turned the knob, then ushered me inside. "This is where the magic happens, depending on what kind of magic you're looking for."

The little room had an enormous desk, a luxe executive chair, several filing cabinets, and a stack of labeled boxes amid another command center setup. Two monitors flanked the laptop computer on either side. Carved wooden letters that read *Wanderlust Travel* decorated the desk.

"I don't have to see this room for a few days, so we don't have to hang out in here long, but I wanted to show you my office."

"I love it. It's cozy." I pulled his chair from behind the desk and dropped into it, spinning a revolution before I stopped it from going around again.

"Is cozy code for sparse? I had my awards and appreciation plaques, some travel photos up on the bookcase, but they've been packed up for a few months."

"I like seeing where you run your empire. Now I can visualize it when we're talking."

Vance laughed softly. "It's a lot of juggling and putting out fires, trying to keep it all straight."

"I said what I said. I'm proud of you."

He pushed off of the entrance to the room where he'd been leaning against the doorjamb, then bent over the desk and kissed me. "Have I mentioned how nice it is to kiss these lips whenever I like?"

"Not nearly enough," I whispered. "I know the feeling, though."

"Are you ready to see where the *actual* magic happens?"

I perked, my face brightening. "The Black Man Cave? Your Black Man-tuary? Black Man-land?"

"More jokes. Come on here."

Vance led me to his bedroom. Dark curtains draped the windows. Two leather chairs with an ottoman between them sat across from the enormous bed and half-circle leather headboard centered above it.

"Wow," I marveled, feeling privileged to enter his personal space. "Your bed looks bigger than it does on Zoom."

"Everything's bigger in Texas."

"Lord," I replied, my tone dry, accompanied by an eye roll.

"I'm saving *'objects on Zoom may appear larger in person'* for…you know…later."

"You're still packing?" I angled my head toward an open suitcase laying across the ottoman.

"I've got it under control, baby. Maybe I had goals I wanted to accomplish before I threw some things into a suitcase and whisked you off to our romantic destination."

"Goals?" My brows rose. "Do these goals involve me? Or…*can* they involve me?"

He growled, drawing his bottom lip into his mouth and sending me a searing look. "Don't start shit you can't finish, woman."

"There ain't shit involving you I can't finish, man. Seems like we have a lot of that space and opportunity you're always talking about."

Vance had his hands on my hips in seconds, pulling my body to his. He pressed himself into my thigh as he took my lips again, skimming the sides of my breasts with his fingertips as he moved us in little steps until we stood at the foot of his bed.

My body went soft as my tongue swirled with his. Whatever this man wanted to do with me, for however long he wanted to do it to me, I was all in. When we came up for air, I was breathless, and my body strummed. I was ready to leap onto his bed and rip everything off. Or let it be ripped off.

Unfortunately, Vance pulled back, grabbed my chin, and tilted my face until we were eye to eye. "You know I want to fuck up these sheets right now. But we have plans, so…we need to make a decision."

"Okay. What…" I sighed. I did not have the brainpower for decisions. "What are the choices?"

He scowled playfully. "Fuck now or fuck later, obviously."

I laughed. "Why do we have to choose? We can do both."

"Don't you want to remember us making love for the first time with the sound of ocean waves in your ears?"

"Yes," I answered, nodding. "I also want to remember us *fucking* for the first time at your house. I want to remember you stripping me in your bedroom. Throwing me down on your big ass bed and ripping these drawls off of me, like you said you wanted to. I want to remember you giving me every inch…"

I reached for him, palming his length through his jeans. "…of what you're working with right here."

Vance's lips curved into a smile, his fingers tenderly tracing the contours of my face. "Say the word," he murmured, his voice sultry. "That can be arranged."

"Word, baby."

I grabbed the hem of his t-shirt, pulling it over his head. I understood his point—he had planned a special and memorable first time for us, but the past few months had been the longest, most intense edging session. Once the body I'd been staring at via Zoom screen was up close and personal, there was no turning back. I reached out to touch him, running my fingers through the layer of hair over his chest.

The muscle rippled as he pulled me to him. "Not yet," I chided, pushing him back, then deftly unfastening the button on his jeans and pulling down the zipper. The sound was sensual as it cut into the quiet of the room. I pushed the denim down his hips enough that he could step out of them.

His eyes never left mine as he stood before me in only a pair of boxer briefs, his arousal apparent. He pulled me into his arms again. This time, I let our bodies mesh from chest to thigh.

Vance tucked a hand between us and tugged at the zipper of my jeans, groaning appreciatively at the warmth that welcomed him when he slipped between my thighs.

I sucked a stream of air through my teeth, tearing my lips from his so I could toss my head back, throw an arm over his shoulder and hang on for dear life. I worked my hips, trapping his fingers between our bodies, seeking the sweet release that lingered just out of reach.

Vance's lips were wet, his breaths hot and heavy as they landed over and over, up and down my neck, dropping teasing little bites as he went. I used a free hand to push my jeans down my hips enough that they dropped to the floor.

"Have a seat, gorgeous," Vance said, dropping to his knees. I settled onto the edge of the bed in front of him. "I want to see these titties I've been worshipping from afar."

In a swift motion, he pulled my t-shirt up and tossed it somewhere behind me. I sat in front of him in the deep eggplant purple set, his favorite of the ones he'd sent me. The color against my skin was so decadent. Vance was gifted at picking colors and styles for my body, and it had become my favorite set as well.

I pulled my arms behind my back to unclasp the bra, but he stopped me, grabbing my hands and resting them on his shoulders. "I'll take care of that. You're going to need your hands for far more important things. Like holding on."

Vance was a simple, sweet, thoughtful man. He made me swoon with romantic gestures and smile at how he cared for me. But more than anything else, he made me laugh. He brought humor to a moment of vulnerability, not knowing if I was terrified for him to see me in my most private, intimate state. He wanted me to be comfortable and free to be myself.

I took his advice and latched onto his shoulders, watching him move from one breast to the other, kissing and licking the skin that I'd made sure was smooth and fragrant for him. He nibbled the rise of each breast, then nipped a raised nipple through the lace of the bra.

I gripped the back of his neck, gently tugging him closer. "Yes, baby," I muttered, then sighed. "That feels *so* good."

"Mmmmm," he hummed, moving to the other breast and doing the same, back and forth, biting, sucking, flicking. He used his other hand to nudge my knees further apart and slip a finger under the band of my panties.

"Tell me what you want me to do, gorgeous."

I smiled at the familiar question, an unofficial nod to begin our session. It was still so surreal to be in a room with Vance. I was tempted to shut my eyes, relying solely on his voice and gentle guidance, but that would be too much like retreating into my comfort zone.

"I want your lips on me. Suck my nipples, lick my clit. I've been dreaming about you touching me the way you said you wanted to touch me. I've played those words in my mind so much, I'm shaking. I need it."

He brought his lips to mine again, devouring my tongue with such passion I could have come right then and there, but I was holding back. He was not getting off easy this first go-round. I wanted him—or some part of him inside me when I came. While we kissed, he worked my bra clasp, releasing the hooks with an ease that should not have surprised me, given how long he was married.

My breasts fell with relief as Vance pulled the cups away. In seconds, Vance had taken so much of me into his mouth that I could barely see the areola. He sucked hard, sending sparks down my spine by flicking his tongue across the tips, moaning loud and long as he did.

When he got his fill from one breast, he moved to the other, giving it the same sensual treatment. His eyes rolled up to meet mine. They were smoky, the deep espresso pools smoldering with need.

"You are..." he whispered against my skin, punctuating each word with gentle kisses along my sensitive flesh. "So damn sexy, Athena. I love that you're here with me."

"I love that I'm here with you," I confessed. "I was afraid I'd be awkward, knowing I'd be seeing you and you'd be seeing...me."

"I see you." He laid a kiss on one breast, then the other,

then kissed my lips again. "How do you feel now?" he asked, his lips still near enough to graze mine. The sensation gave me shivers.

"Sexy. Wanted. *Wanton*."

"Wanton?" he repeated. "You tryna get a little wild?"

"I'm trying to get a lot wild. I have a lot of time to make up for. I'm ready to get into it."

I watched a glint appear in his eye. "These panties are beautiful on you. I like the way they look against your skin; how smooth and silky they are. But they have to go. They're keeping you from me."

"Ah, I was hoping you'd say that."

"Off with these!" Vance said, sliding two fingers under the fabric. I shifted my hips so he could pull them off, and he tossed them away. His eyes had not moved from my body, but now he had a new focus.

"Damn, woman. It's nice to see this pretty pussy up close."

Vance nudged my knees open a bit more, squeezing between them until his breath warmed my inner thighs. He teased me, swirling his tongue around the entrance to my body, then using the tip to explore the folds.

I whimpered, impatient. He rewarded my impatience by closing his mouth around my clit, bathing it with his tongue while the loudest, most pleasured moans roll from him.

My breath hitched in my throat, and I suddenly lost all sense of balance and core strength. I had to move a hand behind me to hold me up. The other had a vice grip on the back of his head. He wrapped both hands around my thighs and devoured my pussy like he was a starving man.

"Oh! Oh...shit!" I tossed my head back in so much bliss I was almost screaming.

Vance grunted in response. I rocked my hips, working my pussy into his face, riding his tongue, drunk in heady pre-orgasm. He sucked my clit between his lips and bathed it again with his tongue. I throbbed, the first inkling working its way through my core. My heart thundered in my chest, a rapid pounding. I don't know how Vance didn't hear the steady thump. All of my senses were turned up high, swirling together, clouding my mind, leaving me dizzy and light-headed and on the very edge.

"Oh, fuck yeah…" I heaved a long, loud gust, giving myself over. "Shit, baby…I'm coming!"

I exploded from the inside, my body led by thrusts and jerks as my climax rocked through me. Any other man would have been happy just to see me come, but Vance was on a mission. He held me tight, determined to lick and suck his way through my first orgasm with him. I held onto him, my back arching, his face buried in my pussy as I screamed his name.

When the pulsing and throbbing receded, he finally let up. I pushed myself up, cupping his face in my hands. I brought his lips to mine and kissed him, tasting the slick wetness on his mouth, loving that it was mine.

Softly, I ended the kiss and told him to stand. His erection, still constrained, was at eye-level. I pulled his briefs down, tracing my fingers up his length, then reaching the tip to tease the ridge. Holding his gaze, I watched his breathing grow ragged with anticipation. I licked my lips and leaned forward, dragging my tongue across the tip.

Vance let out a grunt of surprise. He shifted his weight from one foot to another, moving in closer. I took him into my hands and moved my palms along the shaft.

"You're about to tease the shit out of me, aren't you?" He didn't seem to dread the prospect since his lips were bent into a smile.

I shrugged, continuing my rhythmic strokes. Up and down, a twist, cup the balls, tease the tip, then start all over again. "After what you just did for me, that would probably be all kinds of wrong, wouldn't it?"

"And yet, my dick is not in your mouth."

"Is that what you want?"

"It's what I've been dreaming about. Getting off to."

"I like how you dream. I want you make you come for me."

"Do that shit, baby. I'm ready."

I looked up into his eyes and gave him a sexy grin before I took him into my mouth until I was full of him. Nothing compared to watching emotions roll across his features as I pleasured him for the first time.

Vance let out a low growl, beginning a slow, controlled thrust. His hands opened and closed, clenching and releasing, as if he had to fight himself to not reach out for me. I grabbed them and placed them on either side of my neck, then reached behind him and clutched his ass cheeks to bring him even closer to me.

"Damn, Athena! Your mouth! You know what you doin'!"

It was my turn to moan and mumble while my mouth was full. His breathing became labored as he thrust harder. We moved in unison, pushing, pulling, riding the oncoming wave until he tensed, his fingers tangled up in my braids as he pumped into my mouth.

"Ah! Fuck, I'm comin'!"

I sucked harder, swirling my tongue around him until I tasted his release.

Without waiting until I pulled back, Vance moved away. He fell from my mouth and bobbed in my face, still semi-erect. Gently, he pushed against my shoulders, encouraging me to lie back on the bed, then hovered over me as he stroked himself back to a full erection.

My fingers dug into his biceps, and my legs fell open. He held my gaze as he slowly pushed inside me.

"Thena…*shit*. You feel…" He hissed, shaking with the effort to maintain control. His features twisted as he pulled back, then pushed in again. "I...I didn't know you would be so—it's too good."

I arched my back and wrapped my legs around him, bucking my hips against his. "You don't have to go slow, baby."

Vance pushed out an animalistic growl and sped up his movements, his hips working like an oiled piston.

"Thena! Fuck!"

He slammed into me, hard and unrelenting, his chest pressed into mine, breaths hot against my skin. We were lost in heat and desire, our voices rising and blending together.

"I want to come. Not going without you—where you at?"

The desperation, the passion, the wild yearning but still wanting me with him step for step made my pussy convulse, and I was coming again.

"Yes, yes, yes, yes, yes!" I squealed, writhing. "I'm coming, baby!!"

He let out one last guttural moan, then shuddered and collapsed on top of me. His body was slick with sweat, our breathing heavy in tandem. I ran my fingers over his skin, riding his hard, panting breaths until they slowed. I loved being able to hold him while we came down together.

"Are you conscious?" I asked, after a few minutes of silence.

"Barely," he mumbled. He gently grazed my nipple with his teeth before he raised his head. "You?"

"I'm going to be saying this for days, but I'm so happy you got me to come down here."

A confident smile spread across his lips, then he pulled himself up onto his hands and knees. "You are not nearly as happy as I am. I'd better get my shit together so I can fulfill my end of the bargain. I promised I was gonna spoil your ass, and I'm about to get on my job."

I stretched up to kiss him, then I let him go. He rolled off me, then off the bed.

"You're a keeper, Vance Griffin."

"I'm glad someone thinks so. But give me a few days to really prove it to you."

He left the room, and after rummaging around in the kitchen, he returned with a fresh glass of sweet tea and a bag of chips. "Refresh yourself. I'm going to finish packing."

I sat up, grabbing the glass of tea and the bag of chips. "Can you bring in my backpack? That change of clothes I predicted I'd need would come in handy right about now."

VANCE

Davis Scott: Just wondering why I haven't seen your ugly mug yet. Your suite is ready, bro. GET HERE!

Vance-Wanderlust Travel: Remember when folks thought we were brothers because we looked so much alike? Watch who you're calling ugly.

Vance-Wanderlust Travel: Patience, brother. My lady and I had some business to attend to. Getting on the road now. See you shortly.

THE SUN BEAT DOWN ON THE JEEP AS WE LEFT THE CITY BEHIND us, headed south. It had been at least a half hour since we'd said a word to each other, and not that I minded the quiet, but Athena and I didn't ever sit in silence. We talked nonstop, either in texts or on FaceTime or on Zoom. We'd never run out of words. Even if we met up to have dinner and watch a show, there was constant conversation and chatter, especially during commercials.

Athena had pulled her braids into a high bun and

changed into an off the shoulder, fluttery sundress. It was a deep burgundy with a cheery yellow flower print.

"Have you ever been this far south before?" I asked.

"Hmmm?" She rolled her head toward me. Her peaceful expression made me regret the need to interrupt whatever solace she had found.

"Nothing, baby," I said, bringing our clasped hands to my mouth to kiss her fingers. "Go back to staring out the window."

"I'm sorry. I didn't even realize I wasn't talking. I'm just enjoying this ride and the music and the scenery. And the company..."

"Tell me anything."

She laughed. "Are you lonely? Are you getting sleepy? You need to talk?"

"Nah. I just...I guess I'm a talker by nature. I like to connect with people. Learn their story. Find out what makes them tick. Then, if we're talking about planning a trip, I try to match that for them."

"Okay." Athena turned her body so she faced me. "This trip you planned for us. I know I wasn't originally supposed to go with you—"

"Weren't you?" I interrupted. My eyes left the road for the brief second it took to glance over at her.

"No. You...said you had to go to Black Diamond anyway, so I should come with you."

"You didn't see through that?" I laughed. "I lied through all of my teeth."

"So you don't have to go?"

"Yeah, I do. But I don't have to spend three days down there. A site visit is a day, day and a half, tops. I don't need all the extras I asked for because I knew you'd be there."

She clicked her tongue, shaking her head. "You sneaky motherfucker. I should've known to not believe you."

"I can be pretty convincing. And you needed to get the

hell out of Big Fork, Minnesota. Any trick I can use to spend time with you is good."

Athena leaned back in her seat. "Well, Master Travel Coordinator, you've got me now. What's on tap for this vacation you tricked me into taking?"

"You'll find out. Don't worry. You're going to have a great time."

A few hours later, we arrived at the bridge that connected the Texas mainland to the islands. I rolled down the windows and set out along the four-lane highway across the Gulf of Mexico.

As we drove over the bridge, Athena leaned out the window, taking in the salty sea air. I stole glances at her, admiring how the light highlighted her smooth skin, her high cheekbones, the curve of her lips as she smiled.

A smooth five-mile ride later, we reached the outskirts of the beach town, the landscape on either side of the road dotted with beach-themed shops and restaurants.

"Welcome to Black Diamond," I announced, slowing as I drove through the rapidly growing town. It had been a few years since I'd been on the island and much about it was new to me. The place had grown from sparsely populated areas to a community that could support the thousands of residents and even more tourists that flocked to the sugar white sands and emerald green waters.

Athena looked around, her head moving right to left, taking it all in with wide eyes. "I understand why you use the word paradise to describe this island. It's unbelievable that this is drivable. Like four hours ago, we were at your house."

"I don't get down here near as often as I should, considering how close it is."

"I'm just as far from Myrtle Beach and I almost never go. Then again, I don't have a friend who works at a fancy resort begging me to come out there."

"Speaking of…" I pressed the call button on my steering

wheel. The music popped off, and the system beeped. "Call Davis Scott."

The sound of ringing filled the interior. After a few rings, the line picked up.

"Why aren't you here yet?"

"Why don't you ever answer the phone like a normal person?" I heard his laughter coming through the car speakers. "Just got over the bridge. Tell me where I'm going."

"The Pearl will be a big white monstrosity that you can't take your eyes off of. Just head in that general direction. The main road dead ends right in front of the hotel. Turn in at the front entrance. I'll head out now and meet you with a parking pass."

"Sounds like a plan."

I disconnected the call and kept driving. In the distance, just as Davis had said, a large resort loomed, and I understood why they called it The Pearl. The elegant white building gleamed against the ocean backdrop, with terra cotta tile roofs and arched porticos. As we came closer, I saw gorgeously landscaped grounds and immaculate pathways.

Davis was waiting, waving us over to a reserved parking space. I cut the ignition, and we stepped out of the Jeep. He was in a suit, his forehead shining in the heat of the late afternoon sun. He was stocky and athletic, with a warm chestnut tone and golden brown eyes.

It was no wonder people thought we were related; Davis was a good-looking man.

He embraced me, giving hard slaps on the back and loud gusts of laughter before turning to Athena, flashing a warm smile. "You must be Athena. I hope the next few days are just what you need."

Athena smiled in return, shaking his hand. "I've heard so much about you."

"I know it's all bad, and it's all true," he teased. "I'll show you to your suite. Leave your key with me and I'll get the concierge to grab your things and park your car. You'll be staying in the Elysium Tower. The view from your room is the best we offer."

Athena's hand slipped into mine as we followed Davis. As we entered the grand lobby, we smiled at each other. It was amazing to me that such a luxurious destination had a hard time attracting tourists. The hustle and bustle of the hotel, the guests coming in and out, the energy of the place—it was already intoxicating.

At a bank of elevators, Davis punched the call button. When it arrived, he ushered us inside and pressed the button for the fifteenth floor. "You'll get the grand tour of the place tomorrow, end to end. I made a reservation for you tonight at Breakers. It's our fine dining experience."

"Thanks, man. You went all out."

"You haven't seen the room yet."

As we stepped out of the elevator, Davis led us down a plush carpeted hallway lined with stunning artwork and elegant lighting. At the end of the hall, we stopped at a large wooden door with a brass plaque that read *Elysium Tower Suite 1505.*

"Here we are," Davis said, tapping a keycard to unlock the door and holding it open for us. "Your home for the next few days."

Athena and I stepped into another world. The suite was elegantly decorated and spacious, furnished with a plush couch and armchairs. The kitchen was fresh off the pages of an upscale lifestyle magazine. The bedroom had a king-sized bed and oversized, stately dark wood furniture, while the bathroom was double the size of my bathroom at home. Every window offered a breathtaking view of the ocean.

"Wow," Athena breathed as she moved around the suite. "I don't think I've ever been in a place this nice."

"Get used to it, gorgeous. First of many."

"I'm so glad you love it," Davis said, beaming. "Vance has

my mobile number if you need anything. You can also dial '0' from any phone to get the hotel operator. Everyone is here to ensure that you have a perfect vacation."

"Appreciate the hospitality, brother." I approached Davis with an outstretched hand. He took it, then pulled me into a bear hug. We laughed together and held the embrace for a few moments before he pulled back with a clap on my shoulder.

"Enjoy the suite. Tomorrow, have breakfast on us, hit the gym, whatever you like. Come down to the office whenever you're ready."

"It's on. I can't wait to talk about how to pack this place out."

ATHENA

Thena W: You should see this damn room!

Valerie Kennedy: Why are you looking at the room and not at the D?

Thena W: I already looked at that!

I WANDERED THROUGH THE SUITE IN A DAZE, ABSORBING THE tasteful decor, the lofty ceilings, and the roomy living space. I slid the doors open and stepped out onto the stone-tiled balcony that led to a stunning beach view. To one side of the balcony was a small bistro table, a pair of chairs nestled close together, and an umbrella offering a tempting oasis from the blistering sun.

I heard Vance before he buried his face in my neck, dropping a loud, wet kiss on my skin. "This is nice, isn't it?"

I turned, bracing my back against the iron rails that bordered the balcony. "Vance, this is all so…much. The view, this place. You."

Vance's shy smile was so endearing it brought a tear to my

eye. He'd worked hard to impress me. Impress me, he did. "It's our first trip. Had to go all out. Look at what I found."

He produced a bottle of wine, a deep red that looked expensive, and two stemless wine glasses. The label read *The Pearl Reserve*. I grinned, taking the bottle from him, and inspecting it. "They have their own damn wine?"

He poured two glasses and led me to the romantic seating area. As we settled into the chairs, a breeze whisked across my shoulders. I was very much looking forward to laying in that bed with Vance wrapped around me, a cool evening breeze wafting through the suite and the waves lulling me to sleep.

Vance raised his glass to toast. "To us. To this beautiful resort." I thought he was finished, so I tapped my glass against his and brought it to my lips for a sip. "And to women that fuck on the first date."

I almost spit my wine all over my dress. "Vance!" I gasped.

He took a sip, gave the glass an appreciative nod, and laughed while he rubbed my back until I stopped coughing. "It's true, isn't it?" he asked when I wasn't choking anymore.

I dabbed at my lips with the back of my hand. "It is true. And it was real good."

I moved closer, wanting his lips on mine. He tasted like the wine—ripe blackberries and chocolate with a hint of spice. We kissed deeply, tongues tangling. Vance's hands roamed my body, pulling me as close as he could get. I anchored a hand on his leg for balance and palmed his hardening length pressed against his thigh.

"Seems like we might fuck again soon."

"That's guaranteed, baby."

My brows hiked for a moment, then I stood and pulled my dress up enough to straddle Vance, settling onto his thighs.

"What you doin' up here, woman?" he asked, pecking my

lips. "Hm? You know what you doing? What you getting into?"

"I'm hoping you want to get into something."

My hands caressed his cheek before I brushed my thumb against his soft, thick, tempting lips. He lifted his face to mine and our mouths collided in a kiss that sent a shiver down my spine. I moaned into his mouth. Vance responded with a groan as he rocked his hips against me, pressing his heat into my core. I leaned in, grinding against him.

He opened up for me, giving me more room to slip my hand into his shorts. I traveled past the edge of his briefs until my fingertips brushed him.

"Pull me out."

I pulled the briefs down, exposing him to the air. I tightened my grip and worked my hand up and down his shaft. He shuddered, bucking up into my hand.

"That's good, baby. Shit, yeah. Keep going, just like that."

Without warning or hesitation, he pulled at the bodice of my sundress until he could see my bra. He worked the flesh until the nipple was exposed, then lowered his head and took it into his mouth, swirling his tongue around the hard bud. The sensation shot sparks through my core. One of his hands ran across the expanse of my thigh until he reached my warm center.

His eyes opened wide. He stopped pleasuring my breast long enough to ask, "You been bare ass this whole time?"

I produced a most sly and salacious grin and rolled my hips against his fingers. "This pussy is yours, Vance," I whispered. "Show her a good time."

Vance flashed a smile, sending tingles through me with each stroke of his thumb across my clit. I gasped, digging my nails into his skin. His expert fingers swirled, sending waves of sheer pleasure through my veins.

"Ooh, shit, Vance!" I panted.

"What do you want, baby? What can I do for you?"

I gave him a good, hard squeeze, and began a sinewy, sensuous wind of my hips. "Feel how wet you make me?"

"I'm feelin' you," he rumbled. "Pussy feels so damn good."

I used his shoulders as leverage and lifted myself enough to sink onto him. This was what I wanted—the ocean air on my skin and the sound of waves adding to the chorus of moans we had to keep quiet.

I gyrated on his lap, rolling and bucking my body, riding him while he reclaimed my breast and gently nipped my nipple. I shuddered, trying hard to keep my yelps to myself.

Vance wasn't doing much better, grunting out phrases in rhythm with my thrusts. "You...feel...so...damn...good...baby...fuck!"

I ground on him again, riding him so fast and hard, the chair thumped beneath us. I moaned and dropped my forehead to rest on his. My pussy clenched around him.

"I want to come," I whispered, catching his eyes. "Come with me."

He gave an imperceptible nod, but I saw the yes in the glint of his eyes. He grabbed my hips, his fingertips digging into my flesh as he worked his body under mine, thrusting hard and fast, sending a harsh *"fuck, fuck, fuck...yes,"* into my neck as he nuzzled my skin.

I squirmed and squealed, clenching and pulsing around him. We both came in hard gusts and whole-body shudders. Vance's head dropped to my shoulder, burying his face in my neck and hair.

"Well," Vance said after we had caught our breath, "the chairs are sturdy."

I giggled into his shoulder. "Able to withstand a good fucking."

"The balcony gets an A+." Vance dropped a kiss on my shoulder. I sat up and spread my arms in a wide stretch, freezing when three loud knocks sounded from inside the condo.

We burst into snorts of laughter as we rushed to tuck ourselves back into our clothing. "Not us about to get kicked out of this resort."

"I just poured the wine," Vance protested, gripping my waist to help me swing off of his lap. "That was all you."

"Don't pretend you had nothing to do with it."

"I'm not. I loved the fuck out of that." He stood, giving my behind a few taps as we entered the condo. "It's probably the valet with our luggage. Let's go for a walk around the resort. I'm anxious to see the place, and I want to know what you think."

VANCE

For the first time, I awoke with Athena in my arms.

Outside, Black Diamond Bay crashed against miles of sand. Morning sun peeked through the windows, illuminating the room and casting a golden light over Athena's sleeping form. Her soft curves molded against mine, her back and ass snug up against me, my arm flung across the rise of her hips. Her hair, twisted into two pigtails, was tucked into a silk bonnet. Otherwise, she was nude. Her skin was warm, and she smelled like vanilla body wash.

Although I wanted nothing more than to stay in bed with Athena all day, I had work to do. I could get started on a few details to share with Davis during our tour.

The evening before, Athena and I took a walk around the resort after a candlelit dinner at Breakers. The balmy air made it a perfect temperature to explore. The garden courtyards were calm and beautiful, with blooming flowers and swaying palm trees. Outdoor lanterns lined the pathways, creating a soft and romantic glow.

We strolled through two of the four towers that housed guest suites with balconies offering magnificent ocean views, creating a perfect spot for morning coffee or evening cocktails to watch the sunset slowly fade into nightfall. The lower floors housed an entertainment complex featuring a performance stage with room for an intimate crowd, a mini-golf course, an arcade lounge, and a bowling alley.

We meandered back to the Elysium tower where Athena noticed a pool and hot tub nestled in a corner of an oasis hidden by lush foliage. We decided to venture over there tonight after dinner.

Athena stirred next to me and rolled over, tucking herself back up against me and sliding her arm across my waist. I laughed lightly, then leaned down to drop a kiss on her forehead. "You trying to tell me not to move?"

"Mmmhmm," she murmured sleepily, snuggling deeper under the summer weight comforter and crisp sheets.

I kissed her again, then nibbled on her ear just enough to make her giggle. "The sooner I get this work done with Davis, the sooner I can play with you."

She grunted, curling her top lip. "I guess you can go."

Before she changed her mind, I slipped out of her grasp and crawled out of bed, heading straight for the bathroom. I washed up, brushed my teeth, and shaped and oiled my beard a little, trying not to pluck at the grays that seemed to multiply daily. Athena said she liked my grays. I gargled and rinsed, then coated my face and arms in moisturizer with SPF. I would be in the sun most of the day.

Athena must have gone back to sleep; she hadn't moved since I'd left her. I was quiet, pulling clothes from my suitcase and duffel bag, dressing in khaki shorts and a Wanderlust polo, then sliding on a pair of canvas shoes so I'd be able to walk through the sand. I grabbed my phone, sliding it into a messenger bag alongside my laptop, notebook, and a pen, and slung that over my shoulder. When I was sure I had what I needed, I tiptoed over to the bed and bent over Athena, placing a gentle kiss on her cheek.

She flipped to her back and smiled, her eyes fluttering

open. "Hey," she pushed out while bringing her arms up to stretch. "Heading out?

"Yeah." I pulled the sheets down, exposing her to the air of the room. Her full breasts rolled to each side of her body, and when she stretched both arms over her head, her nipples hardened. I really wanted to get back in bed and have her wake me up with her mouth. I could only sigh and lick my lips. "You need anything before I go? I can order breakfast for you—I'll walk right past Breakers."

"Mmmmm...nah. Maybe I'll grab a cabana and order something down there. I can read my book poolside."

"Rub it in, Thena." I dropped a kiss to her mouth, then one more to her nose and another on her forehead. "Bye, baby."

She caught my face in her hands and claimed my lips. I groaned and leaned into her. When she released me, I was panting.

"Reserve some energy for fun later," she called after me.

I strolled through the quiet resort, contemplating my plans with Davis for the day. Though it was a beautiful place to visit, The Pearl struggled to bring in guests. Compared to more prominent Caribbean destinations, the resort lacked visibility and allure for travelers. Davis would need a vigorous campaign to generate interest in the island, which would in turn boost tourism and natural word-of-mouth promotion.

Bringing people to the island was no problem. Sustaining increased occupancy was the challenge, and I feared that Davis needed more help than I could offer.

I entered the lobby, where large tinted windows offered views of the hotel's largest pool, swim-up bar, and the connected private beaches. Except for a few sunbathers, most were empty. Though it was still early, I'd expected the place to be hopping already.

A thin man with deeply tanned skin and shoulder-length

locs stood in a blazer, a white shirt and slacks at the concierge desk. His eyes lit up, and he beamed a wide, white smile. "You've gotta be Mr. Griffin. Mr. Scott said he was expecting you and that you and he favor a bit."

"He loves saying that. Yeah, I'm Vance." He introduced himself as Justin as we shook hands, then led me through the lobby to the hallway on the other side, pausing in front of a door with a nameplate that read *Davis Scott, General Manager*.

Justin knocked and swung the door open, ushering me into the office. The sunlit room provided a sweeping view of the sea through a wall of windows behind an expansive mahogany desk. Bookshelves displaying travel guides, management books, and nautical charts lined the back wall.

I paused for a moment, letting my pride overtake me. I'd never imagined that Davis and I would be where we are all those years ago at the University of Houston.

A curio cabinet to the right of Davis' desk housed a collection of miniature models of Harley-Davidson motorcycles. There were at least two dozen, ranging from vintage Knuckleheads to modern Softails and Touring bikes. Each was meticulously detailed down to the chrome trim and laced wheels.

Justin led me to a round meeting table surrounded by leather chairs at one end of the room. He left and returned shortly after with a rolling cart containing ceramic coffee mugs, a silver carafe of coffee and another of hot water, and assorted accompaniments of tea, cream and sugar.

"I hate to be that guy, but do you have green tea?"

Justin smiled, nodding. "I'll get a selection from hospitality for you."

"Thanks. Sorry to be a bother."

Justin stepped out and closed the door behind him. I moved to the glass cabinet and smiled at the collection that Davis had been maintaining since his teenage years. His Harley model bikes were among the things I could never, ever touch.

"You still have these, huh?"

Davis nodded, walking past me to the beverage cart. "It turns out that if you display them in a glass cabinet, people think you're less weird."

"You still ride?"

Davis snorted. "I barely drive. The bike cuts through traffic like a hot knife through butter. You should get one if you plan to move down here."

"We'll see about that."

Justin returned with a wooden box and a vast array of tea sachets. I picked one and thanked him.

"Since when do you drink green tea, man?" Davis poured a cup of aromatic brew while I prepared my tea.

"I heard it has health benefits. I'm about to hit fifty and real scared of it."

"Now you're singing my song." He took a seat across from me, pulling his jacket open. His button-down shirt was crisp and wrinkle-free. Davis might often be over dressed but he -was never sloppy.

After a few minutes of conversation and catch up, he got down to business. "Tell me you have some ideas for me. I'm drowning, and I don't know where to start to bail myself out."

"I've been thinking about it since we got in. This place is a dream—it should not be this quiet. Give me the rundown on marketing efforts. Do you even have a team?"

"Marketing isn't managed on-site. It's all centralized at Calhoun's corporate office in Dallas. They've only visited a few times since the hotel opened, and their strategy seems to be a one-size-fits-all approach across all of his properties. I've tried to convince him that his approach won't work for a hotel of this size and caliber. He's invested every possible dollar into this place, but he's under the illusion that it'll sell itself."

Davis shook his head and puffed his cheeks, blowing out a breath of frustration.

"I can help by putting together some packages to make the resort enticing to travelers. It's hiding in plain sight. But attracting a crowd solely based on the people I can bring here won't be enough to fill the hotel."

"It would be a start. If I could get a lift, maybe Calhoun would come up off of some funds for a person to manage events and do some marketing."

Once I'd finished my tea, I grabbed my notepad. "Let's take a walk. Point out the areas you'd like to highlight. I'll provide insights on what a traveler would value. We'll meet in the middle to offer a package including airfare, hotel, plus any added amenities and excursions to make the deal sweeter. What are your thoughts on a Wanderlust discount code?"

Davis and I walked the property from one end to the other. I snapped a few photos with my phone, but we agreed that he'd send me high-resolution images for my website and brochures. As we walked, I counted several pools and private cabanas around the resort that were underutilized.

"What's the rate for poolside cabanas?" I pulled my shades from my eyes and hooked them on my shirt.

"Cabanas go for $110 a day, and beachfront chairs are $150 a day, umbrellas included."

"How about bundling a poolside cabana into a package? Throw in a complimentary bottle of champagne, a two-hour spa slot. Add a dinner reservation, like the one you arranged for Athena and me. We could create an assortment of these. I know first hand that couples are suckers for a romantic getaway."

"I like that idea. I'd like to see the cabanas get more use. Right now, guests seem to prefer renting the beach chairs."

"That's because $100 is steep to only be poolside. Might as well splurge to be right on the beach. What about excursions? Have you partnered with any local tour companies?"

"A few, but there's room to expand. There are fun activities nearby that are popular with tourists, just none looped into a package. Snorkeling, exploring the local nature reserve, dolphin watching…"

"Those are nice and would be great to throw into a package. Delegate that to your concierge for now. He's charismatic, and could probably negotiate a good deal. It'll create a more seamless experience, and the more we include, the better the value for the cost."

We continued our walk, discussing variations on packages that we could offer. Reaching the beach, I observed a group of young adults immersed in a game of volleyball.

"How about concerts? Festivals? You've got that entertainment complex, but no events scheduled. You should already be promoting a 4th of July celebration. Think sunset bonfire, drinks, live music, fireworks."

"We have to contend with the fire marshal, get permits." Davis rolled his eyes and shoved out a grunt, sliding his hands in his pockets and widening his stance. "Look, I know we're behind the 8-ball. But it's another task that needs a dedicated person to handle."

"I'm not picking on you, but some of these ideas are no-brainers. Three things draw people to a location: price, experience, and convenience. With beachfront rooms going cheap these days, a deal needs to be tempting. You've got guest suites, event space, spas, miles of private beaches—all under-utilized. Ever heard the saying, 'it's easier to ask for forgiveness than permission'? Maybe you just invest the money and tell Calhoun '*I told you so*' when it pays off."

"And if it doesn't?"

I gave a casual shrug. "You can crash on my couch?"

By the time we'd finished touring the property and brainstorming ideas for me to develop, it was mid-afternoon. The heat caught up with me, and my shoes were full of sand. We rounded the corner to the Elysium tower. The pool and cabanas came into view.

"Let me put my ideas down on paper. I'll send you a preliminary project plan with target dates. If it's a go, let's try it out. I'll blast an email to my customer list and begin booking trips as soon as the inquiries start rolling in. I typically get great responses from..."

I caught sight of Athena lounging poolside in a cabana, wearing the most stunning swimsuit I'd ever seen on a woman. Its vibrant deep red color contrasted perfectly with her skin, the well-fitted cups cradling her breasts, the high waist emphasizing every curve. She sported a wide-brimmed straw hat and her Gucci shades, a tray of snacks and a frosty, berry-hued drink by her side. She was deeply engrossed in a book.

"Vance? You were saying?" Davis' voice broke through my thoughts.

"Yeah...I..." I shook my head, attempting to reboot my brain. "Sorry, I...I'm...I lost my train of thought."

"I see why," said Davis. "She is *wearing* that suit, ain't she?"

"Mmmhmmm." I leered like a creep, pushing out a manly, piggish grunt.

"So...what's going on there? You locking her down soon or what?"

Now Davis had my attention. "What?"

"You heard me. You're locking that down, right? The way you two were mooning over each other yesterday, I thought the suite might burst into flame."

"We...you know..."

"You're down bad, Vance. All that staring longingly into each other's eyes when you talk?" He chuckled. "Please. *Try* to argue with me right now, man."

"I can't say I haven't thought about it, but...." I sighed. "She's..."

"Beautiful? Funny? Stolen your heart and all your good sense?"

"Skittish, I was going to say. It took me weeks to convince her to meet me and I'm not trying to scare her away. I don't even know where I'll be living in the next six months. I don't think I'm ready to lock anything down yet, but wherever I am, I want her to be there, too."

"Speaking of where you'll be living, I've lined up a condo for you to tour tomorrow. I think you'll really like them. They're a step above the suite you're currently in."

"We'll take you up on that in the morning." I stuck out a hand and gave him a hearty shake. "I appreciate the hookup on this trip. I hope I can return the favor."

"Get people down here. How can I be more clear?" Davis laughed, then began moving away. "I've got a meeting coming up. Don't mess up that pretty lady's swimsuit. Catch up with you later."

I stood with my hand in the air, watching Davis move quickly back to the cool air of his office. Then I headed upstairs to our suite to change into something more vacation-conducive.

I was done working for the day; time to play.

ATHENA

Vance-Wanderlust Travel: You know when you're watching a cartoon and their eyes bug out? My eyes just did that.

Thena W: Why? What did you see?

Vance-Wanderlust Travel: You in that red swimsuit. Almost tripped on my tongue.

Thena W: You are so silly. How are you close enough to see me and didn't come gimme a kiss?

Vance-Wanderlust Travel: I'm on the way to kiss that mouth right now. Don't move.

I SET THE PHONE DOWN AND WENT BACK TO MY BOOK, MY DRINK, and the cabana shielding me from the sun. My friends back home would call me soft. It wasn't even that hot, but if there was shade available with drinks and snacks to order, that's where I would be.

Minutes later, I watched Vance turn out of the entrance to

the tower. My heart swelled watching his little blue swim shorts and *A Tribe Called Quest* slides saunter in my direction.

When Vance and I first started talking, we were more open with each other than if we'd been trying to date from the beginning. Standing just shy of six feet, he felt his stocky frame should be leaner. He maintained a close cut because his hairline had been receding since his early 30s. He didn't have molded pecs and a six-pack of abs. His dad bod was in full effect.

I hadn't ever been a slim, fit, taut woman. My ex spent years ingraining in me that no one else would ever want me and only he would put up with me. I'd spent the last few years undoing all of that. I worked hard to love all of my curves, lumps and bumps.

When we finally met in person, unfiltered by edited photos, we laughed at how we'd tried to set realistic expectations. However, we both found the other incredibly attractive. That attraction only intensified over the months we spent together. Not even a tall man with rock-hard abs and dancing pecs could lure me away from the man who stepped into my cabana, leaned over me, and graced my lips with a kiss.

"Hey, gorgeous."

"Hi, handsome. Slide that other lounger over here next to me." I pointed at the chair across the cabana.

"Remember when we watched *Titanic*, and you were screaming at Rose to move her ass over? Move yo' ass over!"

I snorted and scooted over, making room for Vance on the wide lounger. I snuggled up next to him, so close I could feel his body heat, then offered him a sip of my drink.

"What is it?"

I shrugged. "There's a little smoothie shack here called Tikis & Cream. This is their special of the day. Berry Sunshine or something."

Vance sucked down almost half of my drink. "What have you been doing all day?"

"A lot of this," I said, waving my hand round the cabana. "I put on my suit, ordered a snack tray and a drink, and I've been reading my book."

"Mmmhmm," he said, picking it up to read the cover. "*Indigo*. Beverly Jenkins. I've heard of her."

"You have not." I leaned back into the cushioned seat and opened the book again.

"I'm serious. I think my grandmother has a bunch of her books."

I pivoted to face him. "Ever read any?"

He wrinkled his nose. "Do I look like I read romance?"

"You act like you read romance."

"I do? Wait, is...that a bad thing?"

I laughed. "No. It means you're a natural at all the lovey stuff. I don't have to push and pull and beg for affection or attention."

"Sure don't," he murmured, his hand tracing over the top of my breasts. "I'm all about the lovey stuff."

I tipped my lips up to his and was rewarded with a deep, sensual, tongue-swirling kiss. He caressed my breast through the swim top as his tongue explored my mouth. My thighs clenched together at his touch. I tried hard to tamp down a moan but couldn't.

I sighed, tipping my head back. "I need you to keep your hands and your mouth to yourself, Vance."

"Where's the fun in that?" he asked, dipping his head for another kiss.

"Babe, for real. We cannot fuck in this cabana, and I'm not ready to go back upstairs yet."

"Fine, I'll settle down." He flipped to his side and propped himself up on his elbow. "Tell me about this book. You didn't buy it this tattered, so you've read it a lot."

"This one is my favorite. It tells the story of Hester and Galen. They meet when Galen is beaten for helping enslaved

DL White

people escape. Both are headstrong and they butt heads at first—"

"And then butt other things?"

"Vance! Romance is more than sex. *Indigo* is about the love that people found for each other against the backdrop of enslavement. Both are doing the work they feel called to do, and then boom...they meet the person meant for them."

"There is a lot of story here." He riffed a finger through the edges of worn pages. "Is there something in here you're wishing for?"

"I was nineteen when this book was published. I was in a bookstore consoling myself after Kane left me and Darius for the third time. I like to be reminded that there's hope, even in the darkest of times."

I sighed, trying not to get lost in my memories of days gone by. Kane was never a stable presence in our lives, but he also never completely disappeared, always returning when it suited him.

"I had a three-year-old," I continued. "My family was helpful, but the advice I got was mostly to 'pray about it.' The man who was barely a father to our child and wasn't a partner to me at all, wasn't present. When I read about how Hester's father sold himself into enslavement to be with the woman he loved?" I shook my head. "She was born from that union. It spoke to me. Still speaks to me. Imagine being loved that much."

"Mmmmm," he mused. "I should pick up some romance novels."

I clicked my tongue. "You're just going to flip through them looking for the sex." I went back to my book and the rest of my frozen fruity drink. "Although...the scenes are pretty good."

"So it wouldn't be a waste of time. You ever read before getting online with me?"

My mouth dropped in shock at his question. But then I

had to stop and think about it. I had read some steamy books as of late. But did I read them to get in the mood? Or *because* I was in the mood?

"You're talking way too long to answer for me to feel confident, Athena."

I burst into laughter, smacking him with the book. "You are disturbing my peace, sir. If you're going to sit in this lounger with me, pipe down. Close your eyes, enjoy the breeze."

He slid an arm across my body and pulled me up against him. "I'm going to take a nap, since you not gon' tell me you switch out the characters in your lil' sex books and put me and you in it."

I giggled. "They are not sex books. Go to sleep, Vance."

———

VANCE SNOOZED FOR ABOUT AN HOUR, THEN ORDERED A LIGHT lunch and took another nap. By the time he stirred again, the sun was beginning its descent across the sky. We packed up and headed back to our suite. We'd take our time getting ready for a nice dinner off the property. Davis had come in the clutch again with a reservation at one of the island's nicest lounges. We had plans to have an intimate meal and enjoy the entertainment the island offered.

The dress Valerie had picked out for me was perfect for the atmosphere at Clinks. The lavender hue complimented my skin tone, and the flirty hem added a hint of feminine allure and let a hint of thigh peek through. Vance, looking dapper in dark trousers and a button-down shirt, helped me clasp strappy silver sandals onto my feet, taking every opportunity to run his hands over my legs.

I put on a pair of sparkly earrings, twisted my braids into an elegant chignon, and threw a few things into a clutch before tucking my hand into Vance's elbow. A car waited to give us a scenic tour of Black Diamond and drop us at Clink's Restaurant and Lounge.

Earlier in the day, LaTasha and Valerie had each texted to ask how things were going. I looked forward to filling them in later about how proud I was that I could sit back and let myself be treated like a lady. Vance was hell-bent on spoiling me and having a great time doing it.

Clinks was an elegantly appointed restaurant with a patio on the edge of a marina and an outdoor stage where local musicians played live music. Sailboats sat in the harbor, dotting the bay while the runners clacked together in the breeze. Whimsical strings of lights wrapped around trees and lanterns hung on posts, casting dancing shadows over the tables.

Vance pulled my chair for me as we sat at a table for two. The food was amazing, the music was shoulder bump inducing, and the company was handsome and charming. Vance was attentive and sweet and funny. I was trying my hardest to not think about going back to virtual sex via an impersonal Zoom connection. We were only on day two, but I was ready to make plans to see Vance in person again. The trip was a dream, and I wasn't ready to wake up.

We danced and ate, then had dessert and danced more. Sabrina Forrest, a jazz vocalist, and her accompanying band were fun and so talented, transforming popular hits into new tunes. After more than an hour of entertaining the crowd, the band announced they were going to take a break.

Vance and I took our seats and waited for our server to approach to refill our wine glasses. I heard something that sounded like a scream—more like a yelp, followed by an uproar just offstage. I glanced at Vance. He glanced at me. We seemed to ask each other, without saying the words, if we should see what was happening.

The hostess ran out to the patio and broke into the small crowd that had gathered. The hairs on the back of my neck were on end. I stood and folded my napkin, leaving it on the table.

"I'm just going to go check. I feel like something's up."

Vance stood as well, following me over to the group. I broke into an opening in the crowd and gasped. Sabrina Forrest was laid out on the ground, her black cocktail dress askew, her caramel skin covered in a sheen of sweat. Someone had rolled up a jacket and placed it under her head.

I kneeled next to her and introduced myself to the musician who appeared to be helping her. "I'm a nurse. Can you tell me what happened?"

"She just dropped," he said, his deep tenor voice shaking. "Just…she was standing there. She said she wasn't feeling well, so she wanted to take a break and…she just collapsed. She would have face-planted if she hadn't fallen into me."

"Sabrina?" I tapped her arm, and she stirred. "How do you feel, honey?"

"Lightheaded," she muttered. "Like my head isn't attached to my neck. Hot. Nauseous."

"Did anyone call an ambulance?" I asked the crowd.

I was told an ambulance was en route but that it would come from the other end of the island, so it would be a few minutes. "An ambulance is on the way. I'm going to take your pulse," I informed her, placing two fingers along her wrist. Her heart rate was elevated, her skin clammy. "Has this ever happened before?"

She nodded slowly. "I get lightheaded and sweaty a lot. But…it always goes away. I've never passed out before."

"Have you had anything to eat today?" I asked.

She shook her head, guilt spreading across her features. "I don't like to perform on a full stomach. I was on my way to the bar to order a burger when I just…" She shook her head, then retched.

"It's okay. Just relax," I assured her, swinging around to

locate the hostess. "Can we get some juice over here? Orange juice, apple juice...anything sweet. Quickly."

The hostess rushed off, returning shortly with a glass of orange juice and a straw. I lifted Sabrina's head gently and positioned the straw against her lips. She managed a few sips, coughing a little as she swallowed.

"Sabrina, have you spoken with your doctor about diabetes? Hypoglycemia? Any problems maintaining blood glucose levels?"

Wearily, she wagged her head from side to side. "I don't know what any of that means."

"Hypoglycemia is low blood sugar," I explained, outlining the potential symptoms and how it could lead to episodes of dizziness, disorientation, and even fainting. "Your symptoms seem to be getting more intense, especially if they're happening more often and you've never fainted before. I recommend having your doctor look into it."

"I...I don't have a doctor here yet. I moved here for this gig," she admitted.

The wail of approaching emergency sirens intensified. Within minutes, two medics donned in BLACK DIAMOND EMS uniforms rushed onto the patio, a gurney trailing behind them.

"I'm Athena. I'm an RN," I told the first medic to arrive.

He kneeled next to Sabrina and asked, "What do we have here?"

I provided a quick report. "Patient's name is Sabrina. Suspected hypoglycemic episode. Tachycardia, disorientation, nausea, and a brief loss of consciousness. She hasn't eaten today. Episodes have become increasingly severe, especially over the last few months. I gave her a few ounces of orange juice for fast-acting sugar."

The medic nodded, beginning his usual assessment. Vance helped me to my feet and stood with me while the medic checked Sabrina's vitals and examined her pupils. After the assessment, he gently helped her onto the gurney and secured her with straps.

"I want her to come with me!" Sabrina wailed from the gurney. She stuck out her hand, reaching for me as it rolled. "Please! Please come with me!"

The medic looked at me skeptically. "Are you family?" he asked.

"No," I answered. "But I can help."

He paused for a moment before nodding and motioning for me to follow him into the ambulance. I glanced at Vance. He gave my shoulders a reassuring squeeze. "Go. I'll follow in the car."

I chased after the gurney, grabbing Sabrina's hand which was still outstretched for mine and held it tight. Her eyes met mine. I saw panic and fear in them.

"You're going to be okay," I soothed. "You're already looking better. I'm here with you."

In the back of the ambulance, the medic started an IV. In minutes, we arrived at the small island clinic, where they rolled her to an exam room. Once inside, I helped her onto the table, held her hand, and mopped her brow while we waited for a doctor.

The doctor on call was young. A mask and scrub cap obscured sandy brown skin and dark hair, but eyes were visible and kind. He introduced himself as Dr. Patel and began his assessment, asking Sabrina a litany of questions and details about her symptoms. I stood by, chiming in with my own observations and suggestions when needed.

Dr. Patel slipped his stethoscope back around his neck. "I'm going to have a nurse get a glucometer reading. It'll tell me where your levels are. But I think your nurse friend is right—your symptoms point to hypoglycemia. I'll get you some glucose gel to help stabilize your blood sugar."

He nodded and quietly stepped away.

Sabrina sent me a weak smile. "I watched you and your

man dancing. I'm so sorry to pull you away. It's still early; you can go back to your date."

I pulled over a chair, wanting to cringe because it looked uncomfortable, but I was determined to stick it out. "Honey, right now you're my date. I need you awake, so talk to me. Tell me about yourself. You said you moved here last month? To sing at a restaurant?"

Sabrina nodded. "I was up in New York trying to make it in the club scene, but..." She sucked her teeth with a roll of her eyes. "I got a tip that a restaurant on an island off the coast of Texas was looking for live entertainment. I came down, begged the coordinator for an audition. Knocked it out."

She smiled. Her pallor was looking much better, and she was perking up.

I motioned for her to continue. "Do you have a genre you're fond of? Or do you do a little of everything?"

"A little of everything. We get better gigs as a cover band than if we perform original material. Jazz, blues, and throwback pop are fun, though. I love to mix it up. Keep it fresh, do something different, something challenging."

"It takes a lot of nerve to move across the country on a whim. So, what about when you're not performing? What do you like to do for fun?"

Sabrina laughed. "Seriously...what's your name again?"

"Athena," I reminded her.

"Athena. I know I begged you to come, but you don't have to stay here with me. They're just going to confirm what you told them and send me home."

"If I know patients, and I know patients, you'll slip out of here before you get the official word. You made the mistake of falling out in front of me. Now you're stuck with me until you're discharged."

"Lawd, this nurse you sent me is mean!" Sabrina cackled, then motioned that she wanted to sit up. I found the button to raise the bed to a sitting position and grabbed a gown from a cabinet in the room to cover her thighs. "Make yourself at home, Nurse Athena."

"Don't mind if I do. Now, out with it. Hobbies and shit. Talk to me, or tonight's gonna be real boring."

Sabrina and I chatted away like old friends while a nurse came in with a kit to prick her finger and collect the blood on a strip. The device she used beeped after a few seconds.

"Hmph," she said. "I want to see your levels a little higher, given how long it's been since you had juice and IV. I'll be right back with some glucose gel."

"Glucose gel sounds gross," Sabrina whined, her youthful face screwed up in disgust.

"Well, it's not candy. But you'll be alive."

Sabrina pouted but didn't argue. She took the gel when the nurse brought her a few packets, grimacing at the texture and flavor. As she swallowed it down, Dr. Patel returned with her lab results.

"You'll need to make an appointment with an endocrinologist for monitoring and treatment. I hear you're a singer; that's rough on the body. Singing and dancing, even walking around in heels—all that exertion without fueling your body isn't a great habit to get into."

Sabrina nodded, looking as if she had been appropriately chided.

"We'll do another test in a few minutes. If your levels are normal, we can let you go, but please take care of yourself." Dr. Patel turned to me. "There's a gentleman in the waiting room looking for you."

"I'll be right back, Sabrina. Enjoy me not asking you annoying ass questions to keep you awake."

I rushed out of the exam room, the door swinging shut behind me. I turned a few corners until I found the waiting room. Vance was sitting in a chair, his ankle resting on one knee, scrolling through his phone. He had my clutch on his lap.

"Vance." At the sound of my voice, his head popped up. He leaped to his feet and came to me. "I'm so sorry. I had to—"

"Don't," he said, pulling me to him. He dropped the lightest, sweetest kiss on my lips. "Don't apologize. Is she okay?"

"Yes, she's fine. She—" I paused, remembering that I was not at work and could not disclose her medical information. "She's okay."

Relief seemed to flood his features. "I knew my favorite nurse had her all squared away."

I chuckled. "She called me mean when I was trying to keep her alert. The nerve of these kids today."

Vance laughed, then kissed my forehead.

"I feel bad that our night got cut short."

"We have plenty of night left. I took a long nap and I'm ready to un-pause whenever you are."

I closed my eyes and let my head tip forward into his chest. "I wanna say some cheesy shit like I don't deserve you. But for real, I—"

"Shhh," he soothed, bringing both arms around me. "Do you know if you're off shift yet, Nurse Wilcox?"

"I just need to make sure she has a way home."

"I'll take care of her," I heard from behind Vance. The band member that had assisted us at the restaurant stood and joined us, still in his white shirt and black pants but looking considerably disheveled. He introduced himself as Nathan. "Thanks for your help. We're just some guys with instruments without her. She's the entire show."

I flashed a smile at him. "I'll let her know I'm leaving. Make sure she takes care of herself, alright?"

When I returned to the exam room, Sabrina was back on her feet, attentively absorbing the nurse's detailed instructions. "Get yourself a glucose meter from a drugstore and monitor your levels regularly. Once you have your appoint-ment with your endocrinologist, ask about a CGM—that's a continuous glucose monitor you wear all the time. Pair that with an insulin pump to manage high readings, and always carry some sugar for the lows, and you'll be all set."

The nurse's gaze found mine as I hovered in the doorway. "Quick action may have saved her life. Are you looking for a job out here?"

I laughed, draping an arm across Sabrina's shoulders. We walked together to the lobby. She saw Nathan and rushed into his arms. When they kissed, I glanced over at Vance. He shrugged, his brows hiked in curiosity.

I got Sabrina's mobile number and promised to check up on her, then we said goodbye to the young lovers walking hand-in-hand out of the clinic.

The car Davis had arranged for our evening – the one intended to chaperone us on our romantic outing – sat idly in a corner of the parking lot. "Our driver's probably real tired of our shit," I said to Vance.

He clasped my hand and walked with me to the car. "He's getting paid by the hour, and by now, it's overtime. I don't think he's too upset, but I'm sure he's ready to go home. And I am ready to get my gorgeous lady back to her vacation."

Vance tucked me into the car and slid in beside me, then scooted close and held me in his arms. We settled in to watch the lights of Black Diamond twinkle as they rolled past.

VANCE

Vance-Wanderlust Travel: hey man, FYI—
your bill from the hired car is going to be
high. Let me know how much extra we owe
you. I'm good for it.

Davis Scott: Ain't no thing, brother. Tell me
you and Athena spent the extra time and
money doing something fun.

Vance-Wanderlust Travel: Nah. There was a
medical emergency at the restaurant. Athena
had to roll in the ambulance to the hospital. I
had the car follow and wait for her.

Davis Scott: Shit! Everybody okay?

Vance-Wanderlust Travel: All good. I got to
watch my girl do her thing.

WE RODE THROUGH BLACK DIAMOND IN SILENCE, THE
adrenaline from Athena holding a life in her hands beginning
to wear off. The car weaved through the resort and around
each of the towers before dropping us at Elysium. I swiped us
into our suite, then flipped on the entry lights.

Athena stopped short when she saw the surprise I had arranged. An assortment of chocolate and raspberry ganache mini cupcakes, plump strawberries, and a spicy and sweet artisanal liqueur awaited us.

"Look, handsome!" She clasped her hands to her chest and squealed, turning to reveal a wide smile. Then her eyes playfully narrowed, and she planted her fists on her hips. "Is this your doing?"

"It is," I confirmed.

"So you're going to be a sneaky motherfucker the entire trip?"

"Wow," I replied with a laugh louder than it should have been at damn near midnight. I walked around her to inspect the spread myself. "The way that term describes me so literally is amusing. I hope you're not too tired to spend some time with me, but this can wait until—"

"I'm not tired at all," she quietly interrupted, her sweet, impressed smile returning. "It's the perfect lead-in to our nightcap." She reached to pick up the tray. "Should we—you want to take it out to the balcony?"

"Actually..." I grabbed her hands, then pulled her to me. "I was thinking we would head down to the hot tub. It's late, it's probably empty. Let's unwind. De-stress. You game?"

"I am so game." She began pulling me by the hand to the bedroom. "But don't think you're slick, Vance. You're just trying to see these swimsuits I brought."

"And you're trying to show them to me. You're not slick either."

We changed into swimwear and rode the elevator down to the lower level of the tower. We were pleased to find the heated indoor pool, jacuzzi, and hot tub complex deserted. We picked up a few towels, then set down our tray of sweets, drinks, and a few shot glasses I grabbed from the bar service in our room. Bubbles broke the surface and powerful jets soothed tired muscles as we sank into the water.

Athena wore a black and tropical print swimsuit that made my mouth water. The halter bodice tied around her neck, which let her breasts hang like teardrops. The bottoms were cut high to show off as much hip and thigh as possible. As soon as I settled onto the built-in seat around the perimeter of the hot tub, I pulled her onto my lap, wrapping both arms around her. She reclined with her head on my shoulder, her back flush against my chest, her hands gripping my biceps.

Her chest expanded with a deep inhale. Then she pushed it out in a lung-clearing sigh.

"Word," I replied.

I plucked a mini cupcake from the lined tray next to us and fed it to her, then poured her a shot of liqueur.

"You know what, Vance?" Athena tossed back the shot and handed the glass to me.

"What, babe?"

"This whole resort vibe we've got going? The beachfront room, the cabana, the valet to bring me whatever kind of fruity, frozen drink I want? The spa, the hot tub, the sunrises and sunsets and constant sounds of the ocean in my ears while we fuck?"

"Sounds familiar. What about it?"

"I'm with it. Any time you're traveling to one of these high-end ass places for work, I need you to slide me an invite."

"Okay." I laughed, mostly to myself, and set about pouring her another shot. "But stop pretending this is an original idea you came up with, Athena. I been saying that shit for months."

"I know. But before, it seemed like some silliness. Like… just talking. We hadn't even met in person."

"I was never just talking, gorgeous."

"But since we have met and we are here, I'm just saying that I now agree it's a good idea."

"Uh-huh. You convince yourself that you thought of it, and it's suddenly a good idea. Here."

She took the drink and finished it, then picked up a plump strawberry and fed it to me. I took a bite, moaning as the flavors rolled across my tongue. She finished the strawberry, then poured us both a shot. We knocked them back and set the glasses aside.

I leaned down to capture her lips, mixing the taste of the liqueur with the sweetness of the cupcake and strawberry. That kiss was delicious.

"So, just checking in," I lobbed softly, feeling guilty that I was more concerned about getting all of my time with her than making sure she was okay. "How are you? About Sabrina and having to jump into nurse mode on vacation."

"I'm fine," she said quietly. But it sounded like a robotic, automatic answer. Something someone said when they really wanted to answer *terrible, thanks for asking*.

It reminded me of the night I had called Athena after she'd had a terrible shift. She seemed fine at first, just tired. She asked me about my day, and I jumped into a rambling story about a trip I had planned to send a group to Egypt— except everything that could go wrong did.

Too late, I realized she was not okay.

She was driving and sobbing, the sounds of her tears like a dagger to my heart. I stayed on the line with her until she made it home, and even then, I didn't hang up. I gently prodded her to talk, to release the tumult of emotions she was holding inside. She wasn't used to having someone to talk to that cared about her day and how she felt about her work as a nurse, the impact she made, what it was like to lose a patient.

It was the beginning of a different era for us. I learned to decipher her moods from the words she chose in a text or the inflection in her voice. If she needed space to unwind after a grueling shift, I caught on quickly. I sensed that Athena was putting on a brave face, attempting to sound more upbeat than she truly felt.

"Just fine?" I prodded.

"I mean…I'm glad I was there. I just wonder how long she has been sick and ignoring it. Young folks think youth is like having a bulletproof vest. They think they're invincible, that bad things can't touch them. Remember when I said there's a reason I switched to Obstetrics from Emergency? They're *wrong*. I've seen it. I tell Darius that shit all the time, but don't ask me when was the last time that boy saw his doctor—"

"You're right," I interrupted, soothing her. "It's good you were there. You could have saved her life."

"That's what scares me. Tonight could have ended so much worse, Vance. Can you imagine if…" Her voice drifted off, but I knew where she was going.

"That would be a nightmare. But baby, that nightmare didn't happen." I stroked her skin, which I hoped was helping. "It didn't happen because you were there."

"Yeah." She shrugged a shoulder, nonchalant. "I don't mean to downplay what I do, but…it *is* what I do. I acted because my instinct was to jump in. I can't stand to feel helpless."

I let out a short snicker. "Like me? I was just standing there watching like you were Angela Bassett on an episode of 9-1-1."

"You know her name is Athena on that show, right?" She chuckled, tapping my arm, soothing me back. "No, you were the best support, handsome. I appreciate you were there to come get me and bring me back. Otherwise, I feel like I would have tried to take care of her. Followed her home. Put her to bed, maybe baked her a cake."

I laughed, recognizing her attempt to brighten the mood and inject some levity. "You know, I've been thinking about our conversation. The one about the book you're reading. So, the young sister…"

"Hester?" she offered.

"Yeah, her. She met…um…ol' boy…"

"Ol' boy?" Athena chuckled. "You mean Galen?"

"You're gonna make me forget my point."

"Okay, sorry." She tapped my hand and giggled again. I loved the way her laughter felt against me. I locked that sensation away in a vault for when I wouldn't have her with me. "Continue your lecture on a romance novel you haven't read featuring character names you can't remember."

"Thank you. So Hester was doing what she does and then boom—she meets Galen. He gets on her nerves until she likes him. And then they bump stuff."

"Vance! Griffin!" Athena cackled in laughter, kicking her feet.

"I was watching you do what you do while we're on a trip I planned." I laid my hand on my chest, puffing it out proudly. "Because I had to come down here and do what I do. So, we're kind of living in a romance novel. Wouldn't you say?"

"I would say that." I heard the smile in her voice. "It's super dreamy and romantic. And…sexy. Actually, the way your dick is pressed into my ass, we're living an erotic romance novel."

"We could act out one of those scenes."

"We should. Right here. Right now."

"Don't play with me, Athena. This resort will hear you screaming my name."

Athena laughed and wiggled her ass in my lap, grinding against my growing erection. "What if I'm not playing?" She tipped her head back and kissed me, her tongue sliding into my mouth. "These people will never see us again, Vance."

I slid a hand along the side of her body and up her bare midriff, then under the low-cut swimsuit top. "You really want to play? Right here, right now?"

She grabbed my hand and placed it atop her breast, then

squeezed our fingers together. I found the erect bud of her nipple through the fabric and gently rolled it between my thumb and forefinger.

The sound of her whimper went straight from my eardrums to my dick. Shifting her on my lap, I turned her so her legs were draped over mine. I kissed across her jaw, down her neck, smoothing my hands down her body, across her belly to the junction of her thighs. She smiled, making room for me to slip a finger under the material of her swimsuit and explored her smooth lips.

Athena rolled against my fingers; her moans were most welcome in my ears. Our lips reconnected as I fingered her, teasing her clit, using soft strokes that kept her on edge. She broke the kiss, starting a quiet, pleading whine.

"Vance..." She sighed, her chest heaving. "Baby, you're *killing* me."

"Already? I thought you wanted to play?" I mumbled against her mouth. "Tell me what you want me to do for you."

"Remember..." She laid a hand on my chest, then slowly circled my nipple with a fingertip. "When we were at the airport, and you said I can't be making all that noise when we kiss in public?"

I laughed, recalling our conversation after our first kiss. "Because it makes me want to pick you up and cart you off someplace I can fuck you? Probably where we could get arrested for indecent exposure."

"Mmhmm. And I said..."

"And you said you wanted to see some of that *pick me up and fuck me* action later."

She tipped her head back, making a show of looking right to left. The area was still as empty as it had been when we came in, and greenery and a waterfall effect obscured us. She brought her gaze back to mine, brows hiked.

"Like I said…right here, right now."

"Seriously?" A slow smile crept across my lips. "Did I know you like public sex?"

She stood, sliding off my lap and bringing me up with her. I leaned in to kiss her again, our tongues intertwining as I tugged her bikini bottoms down her hips and pushed my swim trunks down, then backed us up to the edge of the hot tub.

I placed my hands on her hips and, buoyed by the water, lifted her. Instinctively, her thighs closed around me, her breasts smashed against my chest. I wedged us up against the wall of the tub, tucking her up against me.

"You said you wanted to know more about the things I've never done, Vance. Sex in a hot tub is one of those things."

Athena's thighs wrapped around me had been a fevered dream for nearly a year. I almost blacked out, realizing this was an actual moment and not a daydream I was jacking off to. Eager to live out my fantasy, I guided myself to her, reveling in the warm, slick wetness of her.

"*Fuck…yesss.*" Her body tensed around me, then she relaxed with a low moan. "You feel so fucking good to me, baby," I hissed into her neck, pushing deeper.

Athena's teeth dug into my shoulder as I felt her clench around me. The sensation made me lightheaded. Feeling her pleasure in kind made me harder. "I need you to fuck me," she whispered, tugging at my ear with her teeth. "Fuck. Me. Hard."

Obliging, I slammed into her, gripping her thighs as she matched my thrusts. Every moan from her pushed me closer to the edge, electrifying my nerve endings. She reached behind me to grab two handfuls of my ass and pull me to her. I held her tighter, thrusting deeper, moving faster until we were rocking together, making waves, hearing our sex sounds echo through the cavernous, empty room.

I was lost in her. Lost in the way her body responded to mine, in the sensation of her pussy milking me, in the muted grunts of pleasure coming from the both of us.

"It's so good, it's so good, it's so good," she chanted. "You're gonna make me come!"

"Go for it. Come for me, gorgeous."

I took her mouth again, but Athena couldn't maintain a kiss so close to orgasm. She tore her lips from mine and flung her head back. I pulled the strings just barely holding the bodice of her swimsuit up. Her breast fell from the cups; I wasted no time in picking up the luscious flesh and closing my mouth around the taut nipple, flicking my tongue across the surface as light as a hummingbird wing.

I throbbed inside her as her walls clenched in waves. She shuddered, head still thrown back, her body trembling. "Vance! Vance! Vance! Shit, I'm coming!"

The sight, the sound, the sensation of Athena coming undone was all I needed. I pulled her to me and pumped into her, letting my orgasm take me.

"Thena! Thena! Thena!" I grunted her name into the arch of her neck, over and over until I was empty.

My head dropped to her shoulder. I was limp and wilted, both of us fighting for a few moments to get in a full breath.

Her lips on my temple brought me back, reminded me of where we were and what we were doing. I glanced around, happy to see that we were still alone and appeared to not have drawn attention to ourselves. I caught the glint in her eye and smirked.

"Okay, now," she began, joining me in laughter. "We're *officially* guilty of indecent exposure."

I pressed my mouth to her chapped, kiss-swollen lips. "My gorgeous exhibitionist, I think we covered that yesterday when we almost got caught fucking on the balcony."

The jets turned off on the hot tub and the bubbles died to a slow boil before dissipating. The lights above us dimmed.

"I guess The Pearl said to take our asses to bed," Athena said.

"We were gonna get there eventually."

Athena didn't bother to put her swimsuit top back on again. She shrugged out of it, giggling as she watched me collect our clothing from the bottom of the hot tub. She reached for the large towels that the hotel handed out and gave me one.

I wrapped myself in a towel, then helped her put hers on, tucking the corner up under her arm, then grabbed our tray of drinks and snacks, and followed her back up to our suite.

"I was thinking," she said, leading me to our bedroom. "Maybe we could try out the hot tub at every hotel we visit."

"I'm trying to get invited back to these places. We can't fuck in every hot tub we see."

"Damn. You're right."

"We'll pick a select few."

I tugged at the corner of the towel wrapped around her body, delighting in watching it fall and revealing her. I pulled her to me, making sure she felt me coming alive again.

"I can't lie," I said, taking in her nude form. "I like seeing the towel drop in person much better than online."

"I like showing it to you in person much better, too." She rose onto her toes so our lips connected in a kiss. "Let's grab a shower, wash the chemicals off of us. I'll even let you rub me down with oil after."

My brows danced as I moved us toward the spacious, elegantly tiled bathroom with a dual head shower. "I can't wait to put my hands on you. Let's get in and out, though. We have a long day tomorrow."

Athena turned in my arms and led us to the bathroom, heading right for the shower to turn on both heads. "What's tomorrow?"

"Aht! You can't put that bomb pussy on me and think you can get details. I said I was going to spoil you and I'm not done yet." I tapped the high, round rise of her right ass cheek and nodded toward the steamy glass cube. "Let's go, baby. I want you well-rested for our day."

ATHENA

LaTasha Nixon: Not to fuck up the vacation vibes, but have y'all come up for air?

LaTasha Nixon: I haven't seen a text, a photo, a carrier pigeon since you went running out of the building after your shift.

Valerie Kennedy: LaTasha, get out this woman's text messages! She is BUSY.

Thena W: I just texted you thirsty bitches yesterday! Don't nobody wanna talk to people at WORK. I am on vacation with my man, my man, my man. 😉

"AHH! GOD, YES, VANCE!"

Rays of golden sunbeams crisscrossed the room, brightening the dark corners and finding us waking up in our favorite way—my sleep shirt pushed up over my hips and Vance's skin slapping against mine as he thrust into me from me behind.

One arm was wedged under my body so he could grip a breast in his hand. The other hooked under my knee, holding my legs open and giving him access to stroke my clit while he drove into me with such force, I felt the sting on my skin each time our bodies connected.

I rocked my hips, riding him, grinding against him. My mouth gaped open in erotic bliss as the live wire of climax wound through me. Vance's cheek was pressed against mine, his hard, staccato breaths beginning to stutter.

"I wanna come. Where you at, baby?"

"About to come with you! Don't stop!"

I felt Vance pulse inside me, a forced "Shit!" slipping through clenched teeth. A low moan rolled from him, building to a crescendo until we were both spasming, gyrating, crying out in orgasm.

His energy faded almost immediately. He released my leg, allowing my knees to draw close together, but he didn't pull out. He fucked me slow, his hands caressing my body until we came to a second, sweeter climax and finally went limp.

"Jesus. You got that magic stick."

"I believe those expectations you said were high as Snoop Dogg have been met."

I laughed as Vance kissed my shoulder, then left a trail up my neck to my cheek. He slipped out of me, then pulled me back against him. I couldn't remember the last time I'd laid in bed with a man's arms around me. Kane was a hit it, quit it, then roll over and turn on the TV kind of lover. The few men I'd slept with between Kane and Vance gave nothing but a desire for something battery operated to finish the job and a need to change the sheets.

Vance's arms were made to hold me. His physique was made for my body to fit up against him. I wanted to savor it, but he had hinted at plans for the day, and though I would be content to lie in bed with him, I was also eager to see what he had in store for us.

"I guess we have to shower again," he mumbled.

"Oh *noooo*," I moaned, fake dread coating my tone. "Together?"

"It'll save time."

"Dammit, you're right."

Vance laughed, then tweaked a nipple before pushing himself up. "Alright, smart ass. Let's go. We have one errand before we need to head out."

My joints popped as I pushed myself up. I couldn't decide if it was because I was forty-six years old or because I'd sat on his face until I cramped and we moved to a different position. I'd had more sex in contorted arrangements in the last two days than I'd had in all of my life.

"How do we have errands on vacation?"

"Did I tell you that one of the towers at The Pearl is all condos? Davis set up a tour for me."

"What?" I twisted around to face him, almost falling off of the bed. "You're touring a condo?"

Vance stared at me, his eyes seeming to search mine for a few moments. "Yeah. I thought you might come along. Let me know what you think."

"Okay, but why—" I shook my head, deleting all of my arguments and questions. "Alright, let's get in the shower, then."

"Whoa." He tapped my arm. "What's that? If you have something to say, Athena, say it."

I didn't intend to start an argument. Vance's ex-wife had found it hard to express displeasure in their relationship, so they never squashed minor irritations until the irritations were major. By then, resentment had built into a hurtful, explosive revelation of emotion. He was hypersensitive to my moods and, as he mentioned, we'd agreed we wouldn't hold things back from each other.

When words were all we had, we couldn't afford to weaponize them, or their absence, against one another.

"I'm...surprised," I explained. "You didn't say you were looking to move down here. You might have mentioned that before we fucked on the balcony. Or before we had a sweaty sex session in the hot tub last night."

One corner of Vance's mouth tipped up, probably at the thoughts of our hot tub escapades. "I haven't decided if I am moving down here. Davis mentioned the condos. I said I'd tour one. You knew I was planning to sell the house and go somewhere. I just hadn't decided where."

"Yeah, we talked about that. So..." I worked a pillow out of the crevice between the mattress and the headboard where Vance had shoved it during an earlier session and stuffed it behind me. "Is Black Diamond a contender? You'd live on this island for the foreseeable future?"

Vance shrugged his shoulders. "It's an option. Davis could use the help to make the hotel a big player. I could work from here to bring tourists to the area and still run Wanderlust. Last night, you talked about the resort vibe and how much you like it. I do, too. When you come to see me—"

He reached for me, tucking a finger under my chin and pulling me toward him. He kissed me, low and slow, a sultry meeting of lips and tongues before he released me.

"And you *will* come to see me," he continued, "you'd come here. It would be like a vacation every time we get together. Unless you're traveling with me and we're really on vacation."

"And you've said since I met you that you want to move on with your life. Alexis is remarried. The kids are living their own lives. You deserve to improve your life, too."

"I have," he said, leaning over to drop a soft kiss on my lips.

"You know what I mean, Vance."

"Yeah. We'll see. If it looks anything like the suite we're in, I might not want to go back to Houston. And I'm not even playing."

My head swirled with all of those words. Vance was making moves, clearing a pathway to the life he wanted to live. And…where did that leave me?

Was I really going to keep flying back and forth to see Vance, spend a few days of vacation-like bliss with him, then return to real life where I toiled for twelve hours a day at a sometimes far-flung location for three to six months at a time?

Was I going to keep arguing with my son about my relationship with a man I cared deeply about?

I threw the covers back and rolled out of bed, lecturing myself that I wasn't upset that Vance hadn't told me about his possible move to Black Diamond.

I was jealous that he could do so.

He'd built a life that afforded him that opportunity. If I wanted to continue the career I'd been building, I would have to work in some inhospitable locations. If I made the choice to leave South Carolina, my son would likely stay near family. Making a major change at this point in my life meant striking out on my own.

An hour later, I was at the mirror, laying down flyaway hairs with a brush and gel. "What does that look mean?" Vance asked after watching me arrange my braids to keep them out of my face. "What's going on in that head of yours?"

"Life," I admitted with a derisive chuckle. I worked the fine brush around the perimeter of my forehead, then checked out my work. "I'm fine, handsome. I'm just thinking about stuff."

"Okay. Anything you want to—"

"No," I said, cutting him off. Cupping his face in the palm of my hand, I used my thumb to smooth down the hairs of his beard. "I'm on a dreamy island vacation. I don't want to talk about real life right now. Are you ready to go?"

I stepped back, modeling a sexy two-piece boho shorts set in a summery yellow. My bare midriff and legs looked golden and luscious if I had to say so myself. Underneath, I wore a swimsuit, per Vance's instruction. Also per his instruction, I skipped jewelry, put my things into a crossbody bag, and wore sneakers.

He took my hand and kissed the palm. "I'm not imaginary, Athena. I'm not make-believe. This isn't fantasy—I'm real and I am in your life. That makes me and our relationship real life."

He dropped my hand and stepped back to leave the bathroom. But before he turned away, he added, "Let me know when you're ready to talk about real life stuff."

"THE RESORT OFFERS A UNIQUE CONCEPT," DAVIS BEGAN, swiping his card to enter a condo in The Pearl's Paradise tower. "Units in this tower are privately owned condominiums. Elysium, Nirvana, and Eden Towers offer guest rooms and VIP suites."

We entered a light-filled space, our steps echoing on sturdy bamboo flooring up to high ceilings lit by pendant lamps every few feet through the open-concept living area. A plush sectional sofa sat near a stone fireplace, an extravagant wet bar was on the right wall, and a fully equipped kitchen with sleek, modern appliances beckoned us.

My pulse quickened at the thought of Sunday afternoon meal preparation. The nature of our relationship meant that we didn't have those everyday casual moments. Not in real time, anyway. We'd had plenty of Zoom sessions where we talked while I cooked or Vance grilled. Here, I could be at the stove, a glass of wine in hand, the scent of something delicious wafting up from the skillet, and Vance on a stool on the other side of the island.

We toured the primary bedroom, our mouths dropping open at each revealed feature. Vaulted ceilings, a sparkling chandelier, a large sitting area with built-in shelves, a spa-like bathroom complete with a Jacuzzi tub and separate shower stall, and enormous windows that overlooked the beach.

"This is some fancy shit," I whispered to myself as I imagined afternoons lounging on the beach or exploring local attractions, then coming back for dinner, drinks, and conversation before being tempted to the bedroom for loud, sweaty vacation sex, which was much different from run-of-the-mill Tuesday night sex.

I wanted run-of-the-mill Tuesday night sex, too. The prospect was appealing and made me smile.

"Check it out," said Vance, nodding to the plush loveseat facing the rows of built-in shelves. "That's where we'll keep our romance books."

Davis' raised brows and surprised expression made me laugh aloud. "Vance drinks green tea and reads romance? You're not the same guy I lived with for five years."

"That's not nearly enough room for my collection. And Vance doesn't actually read them."

"Yet. I have insightful thoughts about them though. Also, someone said I'm like a modern-day romance hero."

"Someone named Vance Griffin."

"You didn't argue when I said it. I have evolved, Davis. Look into it."

"I don't think I can compete with you on that. You...you got that." Davis laughed, eyeing me. "Let me show you the other features of this condo."

"Wait, now. Before we get into the gold-plated closets or whatever...how much are we talking? What's the bottom line?"

"Well, this is a model unit, right? And it's decked out— three bedrooms, two bathrooms, around 1800 square feet of living space," said Davis. "It's eco-friendly, it's got automated window treatments, pre-wired surround sound, Wi-Fi thermostats, security controls, home automation, and so on. Given all of that…it's a bargain at just over $945,000."

"*Sheeeeeit*!" Vance flinched, hissing at the number. I understood the reaction; I had to turn away to avoid coughing.

Davis nodded, his jaw firmly set. "Between us, it would be wise to view a regular unit and of course offer less than asking, especially after reviewing my sales report. Not that the unit isn't worth the price, but Calhoun would love to get another sale under his belt."

"I'm scared to ask. What's the annual fee look like?"

Davis consulted the tablet he'd brought with him, scrolling through a page or two. "The Condo Association fees come in around $10,000 a year—just under, actually. They cover exterior maintenance, premium amenities, and contribute to the sustainability fund for community initiatives."

He paused, scrolled more, then added, "You also get membership to the Owners Club with access to all pools, cabanas, beach service, discounts on green fees at the golf club, spa treatments, plus…you know, entry to various events and preferred seating at the resort restaurants. There's also housekeeping and concierge garbage services available to you."

In my bag, my phone buzzed. I zipped it open, my eyes popping wide at the name on the screen—Sabrina Forrest. I was supposed to check on her.

I pulled open the doors to the wrap around balcony and propped my arms against the railing. The sun was a bright ball in the sky, but a breeze wafted through, bringing with it the scent of salt and seaweed. And in the distance, palm trees swayed in the wind. Paradise was a perfect word for this place.

I swiped my finger across the screen to answer the call. "Sabrina! Hi. How are you?"

"Hey, Athena," she replied, sounding brighter and much more alert than the evening before. "I'm feeling much better. Nathan won't let me do anything, even though I'm feeling fine."

I smiled, though she couldn't see me. "He promised he would take care of you, and he's doing just that. You don't want a visit from mean Nurse Athena."

"I actually wouldn't mind. I got an appointment at Corpus Christi Medical Center tomorrow. You wouldn't happen to be free to come with me, would you?"

"Oh…" I turned to watch Vance and Davis chatting in the living room of the condo, both with arms crossed and feet planted wide. "Tomorrow is our last day on the island. We're checking out and riding back to Houston. I don't think I'll have time, but you have my number. Text me any questions you have, and I'll do my best to help."

"I understand," she replied. She sounded so disappointed, it almost broke my heart.

"Can Nathan go with you?" She assured me he would accompany her to the appointment. I confirmed we would speak again as soon as we arrived at Vance's house. "Don't forget to ask about a wearable glucose monitor. There's a process to get approved for that, and some training you have to go through, so get yourself one of those testing devices from the drugstore. The finger prick thing we saw the nurse using."

"Yeah, Nathan got me one today. I keep pricking my fingers just to see what the number says."

I laughed. "That'll wear off. And testing strips are expensive."

"I know." Her sigh traveled over the phone line and lodged in my heart. "Thanks for helping, Athena. I keep thinking about what could have happened if you weren't there."

"We don't have to even think about it. You're going to be fine. When do you think you'll hit the stage again?"

"Well, we have rehearsal tonight for shows this weekend."

Sabrina and I chatted for a few minutes before she had to hang up to meet her band for rehearsal. I tucked the phone back into my bag just as Vance stepped out onto the deck.

He joined me at the railing and smiled at the breathtaking view.

"Just got off the phone with Sabrina. She has an appointment tomorrow. It's probably just an intake and paperwork deal, but it's good she got in to see someone so quickly."

"That's great. She'll have someone watching over her and making sure she is okay."

"So…" I tipped my head toward the condo. "What do you think?"

"I think…" Vance inhaled deeply, then blew the breath out, puffing his cheeks. "I think on my way back to my little shack in Houston, Ima rob a bank."

I snorted. Vance laughed aloud, bumping my arm repeatedly until I burst into laughter with him. "Davis stepped out to take a call. While he's gone, let's be real and honest. What do *you* think?"

"Honest? Real?" I glanced at him. He gave me a solitary nod. "I love it. I think you love it, too. It's…a lot, though."

"Yeah. This is a big place with a lot of extras. Maybe if they have something not so…" Vance turned, leaning back on the railing, crossing thick arms over his chest.

"Appointed?" I suggested. "Highbrow? Sadditty?"

He laughed. "Yeah. That. I like the bennies, though. Even if a grand a month is a lot to pay for people to tell me not to paint my front door. Waking up here every morning sounds good to me." Vance gestured, arm outstretched. "And not for nothing, but it's not completely out of the realm of possibility. My house appraises well. I've taken good care of it, and I've done some upgrades. Alexis and I agreed I wouldn't ask for alimony if I got out of the marriage debt-free except for the house and tuition. Our youngest graduates next year."

"So you could actually make this work? What about travel?"

He shrugged a shoulder. "That's the one thing I don't have to worry about. I know how to get us where we want to go."

Us. Without making a big deal about it, he was already wrapping me into his plans. The intensity of his feelings, the confidence in his tone, was both thrilling and...unsettling.

Here I was, being careful and considerate to not assume he would be a part of my life a year, five years, ten years from now. Based on a hunch, nine months of conversation and a lot of great sex, Vance had already laid claim to a future that included me.

"Makes you feel better about spending a cool million on a box to live in."

"It's a beautiful box," said Vance, turning around again. "I'm dreaming about coming out here every morning, drinking green tea while we watch the sunrise."

That twinge of envy when I thought of Vance spending his life doing what he wanted to do, where he wanted to live, twisted my insides. In a little more than a day, I would be back in Big Fork, Minnesota, hoping the temperature would stay above freezing and no one went into premature labor.

Vance and I had known each other less than a year, had only been talking to each other for a few months, had been closely intertwined for mere days—how could I already be despondent about getting on a plane and returning to a life I worked hard to build?

We would still spend more time apart than together, between my work assignments and his frequent trips for Wanderlust, but since meeting Vance, I found myself restless in a way I'd never experienced or thought I'd be. My feelings for him made me question if the solitary life I'd led for so long would ever be as satisfying.

"I'll be honest," he said, leaning in to whisper since Davis had come back to the condo and was walking through the kitchen with a handkerchief, rubbing out fingerprints. "It's tempting."

I nodded, still staring out at the ocean. "It puts your plan to revamp your life into overdrive. No more half-packed rooms. Selling your house, moving hours away, starting a new life."

I turned to him. "Telling Kareema that you're leaving Houston. You ready for that?"

"I am not ready to tell Kareema anything." Vance met my gaze, a determined look to his eyes. "There's one thing I am ready for, though. I want to wake up next to you in the morning. I want to fall asleep next to you at night. I want to explore the world with you. However I can make that happen, I'll do it. I want us to make this decision together."

My heart surged, swelling with emotion. I reached out to him, squeezing his arm. "Vance, you are so...*so* sweet, but this is something you should think about outside of our relationship. I get you want to open your door to me—"

"I'm not just talking about opening my door to you." The quiet ferocity in his tone brought my argument to a halt. "You'd have a key. You'd have input on decorating and half the closet and most of the drawers and all of those bookshelves."

"Van—"

"And your own parking spot, and a standing appointment at the spa, and a favorite cabana."

My heart raced. His words were a siren song, luring me in with promises of a life that felt too good to be true.

"How would we even make that work?"

He grinned. "That would be the fun part. We weren't splitting up after this trip, were we?"

"Of course not. But I don't want to rush into something that we'll regret."

"I'm never going to regret knowing you, Athena. Getting you to come down here and spend some time with me. Letting me fall hard for you."

He ran his fingers through my braids, gently massaging my shoulder with his thumb. "This is a lot to think about, but I need you to understand what I was saying this morning. This is real life, Athena. Whenever you're ready to accept that you aren't dreaming, I'll be right here."

Movement inside the condo caught his eye. "Let's let Davis get back to his day. And then you and I have lunch plans."

He winked and stepped back into the condo. I heard the two friends ribbing each other, laughing, and chatting, and then the condo door closing. Vance's footsteps sounded faint, then louder as he walked back to the balcony, his phone in hand.

"Ready for lunch?"

I followed Vance back inside the condo, my mind racing, and my heart flip-flopping in my chest. I wasn't paying much attention until I realized we had exited the hotel at the parking deck level. Just off the elevator, we hopped into a golf cart, which wound through the vast underground of the hotel and came out at the dock at the southernmost tip of the island.

Moored there was a cute little white yacht, gleaming in the sun. As we stepped closer, I saw the intricate details of the sleek design, from the polished metal railings to the gleaming anchor at the bow.

Vance and I were greeted by a seasoned sailor with a salt-and-pepper beard, dark brown hair, and a friendly smile. He introduced himself as Liam, then waved over his first mate, a young man with a cheerful disposition named Carlos.

Vance grinned at me, his hand on the small of my back as

he helped me onto the boat. He jumped on board behind me and let our captain secure the ropes. Once we were both on the deck, he took my hand and led me to the stern as the captain moved the vessel away from the dock and expertly navigated the yacht through the open waters.

"How's lunch at sea for romantic? Are you spoiled yet?"

VANCE

ATHENA'S EYES SPARKLED AS SHE STOOD AT THE RAILING OF THE yacht I reserved for an afternoon excursion. The sun reflected off the waves in a dazzling display as it cut through the waters of Black Diamond Bay.

"For the record," she said when I joined her at the railing after checking in with Captain Liam, "I don't need to be spoiled. Just being here with you is more than enough."

"I know," I replied. "But it don't sit right to have you here and not show you the finer things. Think about all the places we can go together. I'm planning a trip to Cartagena in a few months. I might go check out the Canary Islands in the spring, and I'm planning my annual trip to Ghana in December. We had just met last year when I went."

I'd tried to get her to come with us, but traveling to a different continent with a man she had never met seemed a step too far.

"Last year, we took a corporate group to Qatar for FIFA. No way am I doing the most and not bringing you with me."

"If you're casually throwing out plans to go to Cartagena, I'm in. I just wanted to let the record show that I don't *need* it." She turned back to the view, then leaned in so I could hear her over the motor of the boat and the surf against the hull. "I sure like it, though. This is *amazing*, Vance."

"There's a cove with a private beach not far from the island," I explained, my chest puffing with pride. "I thought we'd have a picnic lunch."

Athena glanced over at me, her mouth in an impressed downturn. "Well, now. A picnic lunch, a yacht ride to a private beach, scenic views, and the most handsome company a girl could ask for is—"

"Over the top? Trying too hard?"

She laughed. "Romantic as hell, I was going to say."

"Sure you were." I leaned forward, bending to rest my forearms on the railing. "That's what Kareema told me, by the way. Taking you on vacation was doing too much and you could be scamming me to get a free trip."

"Am I scamming you?"

"If you are, you took me for everything I got. Hook, line, sinker. Heart."

"Heart, too? I made out like a bandit."

"You're ducking again," I lobbed softly. "Do you not want to discuss anything past this trip? Should we wait until we get back to real life, as you call it, for you to decide if I'm too good to be true?"

"We should at least wait until we're not on a fairy tale magical vacation. I'm liable to agree to anything if you ask me on a yacht."

"Then let me ask you everything I need to ask before we get off of this boat."

"Vance…" She huffed, twisting to face me. "I get it. You like me and I like you, and we are *very* sexually compatible, and we are both almost fifty, and why waste time? That is leaps and bounds away from helping you decide if you're going to buy a condo because you want to give me a key and a parking spot. We haven't talked about what that even means."

"You can't tell how I feel about you? If I say I want us to make a decision together, what do you think it means? Why does everything have to be black and white and under contract to get you to believe that I feel something real for you?"

"Because it feels like we met fifteen minutes ago, Vance. How do you know that's what you want already?"

I tried not to laugh, but the thought made a chuckle bubble up. "It don't take a man but fifteen minutes to know if a woman is someone he wants to build with. I've known what I want for the last eight months. You know it, too, and it scares the shit out of you. I'm not alone over here on Love Island, am I?"

"Vance…" I waited with bated breath for the rest of that sentence to drop. "No. You're not alone. I just…"

She turned away again, her skin flushing pink beneath her deep skin tone.

Maybe I picked the wrong time to get clarification. Maybe, like with my marriage, I had a tendency to put my foot in my mouth, push too hard, say too much, or say the wrong thing at the right time.

Or the right thing at the wrong time because admitting my feelings for Athena would never be the wrong thing to say. Either way, I wasn't trying to push her back to the place we'd been before she landed in Houston. We were miles ahead of that place now.

"Okay. I'll back off." I straightened, then dropped an arm across her shoulders and pulled her body close to mine.

"Vance, I don't mean to be—"

"I know, gorgeous." I dropped a kiss on her lips and tipped her chin up in what I hoped was a reassuring gesture. "Let's enjoy lunch and our day. We can talk when you're ready. But I want to talk, Athena. Soon."

As we rounded the tip of the island, the cove came into view. It was a stunning sight, nestled between two rocky cliffs. Clear turquoise waters lapped at the shore of a white sand beach. Our captain expertly navigated the yacht, and soon we were anchored just offshore.

"We'll get lunch set up," he said, passing us on his way to the lower deck. "I'm sure you two can amuse yourselves in the meantime." He winked and disappeared around a bend, then reappeared with Carlos. Both had their arms full of baskets and boxes.

While they worked to set up lunch, Athena and I stripped down to swimwear and dove into the ocean. The water was warm and inviting, so clear that we saw a school of speckled trout swimming by us as we floated near the shoreline. I swam a few feet away, taking in the view of the island and the yacht from the water. When I glanced back, Athena was paddling toward me, her emerald swimsuit accentuating every curve of her figure as she cut through the sea.

I couldn't help admiring how the sunlight played off her skin.

"You're staring," she said, laughing as she reached me.

"I am." I pulled her into my arms, groaning in pleasure when she locked her thighs around mine, pressing every contour of her body against me.

"I've never been on a yacht before."

"It's *barely* a yacht, baby. But I'm glad I could be the one to take you on your first ride." I trailed my fingers up and down her back, over the roundness of her backside, then back up.

"You want to hear something funny? It's related to the book we've been talking about."

"Sure. Tell me something funny."

"So, Galen is a Vashon, right? After *Indigo*, the author wrote other books with men down the Vashon family line. Each of them claimed to have this...genetic tendency called the *spoil your woman to death* trait. They all say they inherited it from Galen."

"Mmmhmmm." I nodded, deep in thought. "So, you're saying I need to check if I'm a Vashon."

She laughed. "I mean...you flew me to an island for our first date. You have fucked me senseless and treated me like a queen. We took a yacht to lunch in a secluded cove. I'm pretty damn spoiled. And I'm..."

She blushed, her lashes sweeping her cheek as she dropped her gaze. "I admit I'm having a hard time with a Vashon type. I'm used to having to work for the smallest amount of affection. And I know you're not him. It's–"

"A hard habit to break," I broke in. "It's a lot of work to rewire your brain to know that you deserve a Vashon. To know that love and affection isn't a reward for good behavior. To know that you don't have to earn love."

"I'm not trying to deny what's happening between us, Vance. I want this. And I don't want to lose it because I was impatient and greedy. Or because you're the first man that's nothing like my ex. I'm scared to do too much, too soon or that it'll burn bright and flash out. The way I feel about you is how I have always wanted to feel about someone."

I held her tight against me and kissed her forehead. "I understand. And I respect how you're feeling right now. Take your time."

Athena rolled her eyes up to mine, her gaze full of long-ing. "Thank you," she said softly before pressing a kiss to my lips.

I deepened the kiss, enjoying the taste of saltwater on her skin. It was slow, sensual, a perfect complement to the gentle waves lapping against us.

I fought an urge to drop my trunks, slide the panty of her swimsuit over, and take her right there in the bay. Our picnic lunch was waiting, and as much as Athena seemed to enjoy public sex, she was probably not interested in performing for an audience.

We swam together for a while, eventually making it back

to the cove where a portable table and chairs shaded by a colorful umbrella awaited us. Carlos and Liam had laid out a smorgasbord of fruits, cheeses, and sweet treats to finish the meal, paired with a tart fizzy punch. The aroma of grilled steak and seafood, combined with the salty briny air, made my taste buds tingle.

As we ate, we talked and laughed easily, just as we had when we were having dinner over Zoom. It was as if time had stopped, and we were in a world all our own.

After we had eaten our fill, we went back into the water, this time with snorkeling gear. We explored the world near the cove, pointing out the coral and the variety of sea life that surrounded us. The colors and textures were so starkly contrasted with the deeper blues and greens of the ocean below us.

We headed back to shore again and lay back on loungers with umbrellas that Liam and Carlos had set out for us. I heard the strains of an early 2000s station adding to the atmosphere. Athena tapped a bright blue toenail to Usher, K-Ci & JoJo, Beyoncé and Keyshia Cole as we sipped frosty, fruity beverages and watched the clouds drift by.

After a long bout of comfortable silence between us, I felt Athena's hand slip into mine. I rolled my head to see her.

"Thanks for today. Not just all of this," she said, gesturing. "You're right to call me out when I duck the hard conversations."

"Well, sometimes you're not ready to verbalize things. I'm not very patient, but I'm trying. What did Quincy say? *I been lovin' you since I was eleven...*"

"*...and the shit won't go away*," she said, laughing as she finished the quote from *Love & Basketball*.

"Yeah. That's where I'm at. If you're heading there too, give me a sign. I'm not going anywhere."

"I'm counting on that. I'm not walking away either."

The sun had moved, so the umbrella's coverage was off. I

adjusted my body, slouching down in the lounger, which tipped Carlos to hop off of the yacht. He adjusted our umbrellas and took drink refill orders.

"I'm thinking about ol' boy from the romance novel," I said, tucking a hand behind my head.

"Lord…" Athena groaned, turning away so I couldn't hear her laugh, but I saw the way her chest bounced with the giggles she tried to hold in.

"So…it's not all about the sex. Two people that are meant for each other, who show up where they're supposed to be, will eventually find each other. And I could be genetically predisposed to spoil the shit out of you."

Athena cackled. "I want you to actually read the books, baby. But yeah. You get it. And when it's very much a fairy tale, they get to bump stuff, and it is life-changing."

I gave myself a round of applause. "See, I knew I was a romance novel hero."

"I can tell it's about to go to your head."

"Well, so…" I flipped to my side. "And I'm not pressing, I promise. But tell me you're thinking about that bathroom. What about the bedroom? Or the kitchen. I liked the kitchen, too."

"I loved everything. It was beautiful. And honestly?" she said, pulling her shades from her eyes with a contented sigh. "I'm trying not to pick out paint colors. If you decided to buy, when would you move out here?"

"As soon as I can. There's nothing holding me in Houston, really. The kids, but two of them don't even live there, and Kareema is back and forth between the Houston and Austin offices."

"They'd probably love to come visit Dad at his beach condo."

"I'm actually nervous about making a big, sudden change."

Athena squeezed my hand. "Remember what you tell me

about Darius. You do what's best for you, and the kids—who aren't kids—will adjust. You deserve to be happy."

"As do you," I reminded her. "Easier said than done, though. Which is what you tell *me* about Darius. Because real life sometimes works differently than we wish it did. But what about you? Set aside all of your arguments…if you wanted to say yes, if you wanted to move with me, could you?"

She reared back. "Are you asking how much I'm putting in the pot?"

"Athena…" I shook my head. "Wherever I am, I want you there. I want to take care of you and that means providing cover and making sure this move works for you. If you wanted to say yes, is your hesitation a heart thing, a head thing, or a wallet thing?"

She pondered my question for a few beats. I appreciated her giving it a good amount of consideration.

"It's some heart," she answered finally. "But it's coming around. The wallet is okay—travel nursing is lucrative and I'm in a good position. So, it's mostly head. This is fast and it shouldn't make sense, but…I'm excited, the more I think about it. So…"

She shifted, moving to one side to face me. "Let's talk specifics about how we could make this work."

Some time later, Carlos suggested we head back, luring us with cocktails as we sailed. With a reluctant sigh, we gathered our things and climbed back onto the yacht.

On deck, the interior was aglow with the soft flicker of candles on a table set for two. A flight of cocktails and a few plates of fresh fruit surrounded a bowl of cut flowers. The drinks were expertly crafted, with just the right amount of alcohol to bring on that warm, giddy feeling.

Dusk blanketed Black Diamond as we approached the island. Captain Liam moored the vessel at the dock and cut the engine. The sky was awash with all shades of pink, purple, and orange. It was one of the most beautiful sunsets I had ever seen, and I had seen my share of exotic island sunsets.

But I'd never seen them with Athena.

We stepped off the yacht and climbed back into the golf cart. Athena scooted in close to me and settled under the arm I laid across her shoulders.

"So, what's next on the list of new experiences?"

I chuckled. "Are we talking about tonight? Or our next trip together? Or more than that?"

Her smile was soft, a little shy. "Any and all. What if…"

She glanced away, watching the cars parked in the lower deck of the hotel whiz by. "What if I just let go? If I stopped being careful and expecting to be hurt? What if I stopped thinking you're wasting my time? Stopped thinking like Darius that this is going to end up a tragic, embarrassing mess on Instagram?"

"What if?" I asked her, my lips grazing her temple. "What would that mean for you?"

Her voice was barely above a whisper. "If I let myself love you, I could have everything I never knew I wanted. I could start over. And have someone to start over with."

"And I would do everything in my power to make sure that you never regret it."

Athena's eyes returned to mine, full of emotion. "I think I'm ready for that, Vance."

The golf cart stopped at the elevator. Athena and I stepped into the cube and climbed to the ground floor, then crossed the lobby to the paths that wound throughout the property. This would be our last night at the resort, and we wanted to take it all in one last time.

We ended our walk on a grassy stretch facing the endless sea as the sun sank below the horizon. My mind was murky with all the things I wanted to say to Athena.

She squeezed my hand, moving to stand in front of me.

My view of wayward braids falling from the bun she'd twisted her hair into, her clothing haphazardly thrown on over her swimsuit, freckles standing out from a bare face that glowed with her tan, and the surf and sand behind her was one I wanted to tuck away in my memories.

"This trip has been more than I could have dreamed. I can't believe I have to go back to Minnesota and that tiny little house and Big Valley Hospital in two days."

"Yeah. I'm dreading the return to the grind and the routine. But we don't have to go back yet. And, for real, we don't have to go back forever. We could decide, right now, that it doesn't have to stay that way."

"We could," Athena agreed. "We could make this thing official."

"I mean…" I spread a hand across my chest. "It's *been* official for me. I told you that weeks ago. *You* are the one that needs to make things official."

"Wow, the hits keep coming." Athena laughed, dipping her head low in faux embarrassment. "So that makes you my…." She cringed, scrunching her nose, then continued. "*Boyfriend.*"

"It's that hard to push that word out?" I cackled, tossing my head back to indulge in not only the laughter but the moment.

"Fuck you, Vance Griffin."

"Yes, please. Often." I tucked a finger under her chin, tipping her head up so her lips met mine. "I am honored to be whatever you want to call me as long as it means you're with me."

I tugged at her bottom lip with my teeth, then traced its contours with my tongue. Athena sighed into my mouth, melting into the kiss, her arms snaking around my neck as I pulled her close. Our bodies molded into one another, the heat between us intensifying.

I nuzzled my nose into her neck, inhaling her jasmine

scent. I pulled back again, leaving butterfly kisses along the curve of her neck.

"I think you know this," I whispered, close to her ear. "But I have to say the words. I need you to hear it and know it. You are so easy to love. And I do. I love everything about you. The way you laugh, the way you smile, the way you make me smile. I love that we can talk about anything and everything, how we lean on each other and keep each other lifted. I love how I feel around you. I love that we've found each other and what we're building. I'm serious about you, Athena. It's not for play anymore, and it's not online anymore. It's real life. I am in love with you."

Those words never held the weight they did now, with my heart in my throat and the shine of tears in her eyes and joy in her expression. I realized I had never loved someone so much in my life.

Athena's voice was soft and shaky with emotion. "I…" She blew out a steadying breath. "I…love you too, Vance. I know I don't need to thank you for loving me, but…thank you. For loving me."

My mouth curled into a wide smile. I pulled her into my arms, then squeezed her tight. "You're shaking."

Athena clung to me like I was about to float away. "A man has never said those words to me before. Not like that."

"I think it's about time to hear it regularly, then." I tucked a stray braid behind her ear and traced the line of her jaw. "There's no pressure, no rush. I'm not proposing tomorrow or anything. But I meant everything I said today. I want us to plan a future together. We can talk about what that looks like for however long you want to talk about it, but you're stuck with me. I need to know you're okay with that."

"Stuck with you?" she repeated, then laughed. "That's not how I'd put it, but I am more than okay with that."

"One more thing."

"You're pushing me hard today."

"It's an easy one," I said. "Can I hear it one more time? I like the sound of my name on your lips."

"I love you, Vance." She rolled the word over her tongue, letting it fall easily. She tilted her head back to look me in the eye. "We should go up to our room so you can hear your name on my lips over and over again."

"Over and over," I repeated, turning us toward the front doors of the Elysium Tower. "Sounds like the lady has plans."

"Baby, you have no idea."

ATHENA

Thena W: okay, not too much on the "told
you so" but...

Thena W: The L word landed last night. Both
ways.

Valerie Kennedy: See! I told you! Didn't I
tell you?

LaTasha W: I think you told her! I told her too!

Thena W: Y'all don't follow directions for shit!

"Mr. and Mrs. Griffin, we're ready for you."

Two spa attendants stood at the ready in white sleeveless
tank tops with the *Haven Spa at The Pearl Resort* logo across
the chest and black shorts. Each held a towel, a robe, and slip-
pers while patiently waiting for us to complete our
paperwork.

I rolled my head to playfully glare at Vance. He was trying
hard to maintain a nonchalant, unbothered expression, but it
wasn't working.

He shrugged. "I booked a couple's massage and gave my name. They assumed we were married."

"You didn't try to correct them, either."

"Oops." He handed me his clipboard with a wink and a smile.

I snorted a laugh, then handed both clipboards to the receptionist. "We are ready," I told our attendants, and followed them to the changing room.

Once we changed into robes and piled our clothing, jewelry, shoes, and other belongings into an assigned basket, we followed our attendants to a private massage room. It was dark, moody, romantic, with calming mint and jasmine candles lit in each corner, and lo-Fi music wafting from over-head. Vance and I slipped out of our robes and laid side by side on massage tables.

Two massage therapists covered our bodies in warm, fragrant oil and began working their magic on our tired muscles. The past few days had flown by so fast, but my bones and muscles still remembered sex in a chair, in the hot tub, not to mention morning, noon, and night in our suite. I breathed a soft sigh of relief, sinking further into the table. Vance let out a content groan beside me, then reached out, his hand finding mine and lacing our fingers together.

The massage was blissful, our therapists working out every kink and knot. I felt myself slipping into a dreamlike fugue, the combination of the music, scent, and skilled hands lulling me into a state of pure relaxation. And yet, I was acutely aware of Vance's presence beside me. Our conversa-tion the day before had been playing like a record on skip in my mind.

And then I consciously fast-forwarded past every argu-ment and impossibility that I came up with to distract me from what I wanted. Real love. True love, with a person who loved me out loud.

I sighed again in deep bliss and contentment. Whatever I had to do to keep this man in my life, it was on.

The hour-long massage came to an end and I slowly sat up, the world coming back into focus. Vance did the same, his eyelids at half-mast. We headed to a joint manicure and pedicure. Vance had never had a paraffin wax treatment before, so it was fun guiding him through it.

When our hours of relaxation at Haven ended, we poured ourselves back into our clothing.

"I am starving," Vance noted, zipping his shorts and slipping his feet into a pair of deck shoes.

"Oh my God, I'm ravenous. Is a massage supposed to make you hungry?"

I pulled a peachy-pink jumpsuit with spaghetti straps up and over my body, ensuring that the strapless bra was tucked inside. The topknot I crafted was still perfect and no wisps were out of place around my forehead. I took a moment to admire the golden tan I had acquired over our vacation.

When I was back in Minnesota, it would remind me of these blissful few days.

"The massage? No, I'm pretty sure it was all the…activity."

Vance winked at me, then waited for me to leave the changing room first. He followed, sliding a palm across my behind as we left the spa and headed to Breakers. I planned to eat all the crusty, fresh baked bread with handmade honey butter while Vance and Davis met to discuss their mutual ideas for promoting the resort.

Davis was already seated at a table with a view of the pool and the beach in the distance. I was delighted to see we had already been served a basket of bread and butter.

I was only half-listening, ignoring the shop talk, distracted by the feel of Vance's hand squeezing my knee under the table. I pulled out my phone and exchanged a few texts with Valerie, LaTasha, and Sabrina.

My head popped up at the sound of my name. "Huh? What'd I miss?"

"I said that by the time our anniversary rolls around, we'd probably be residents of Black Diamond. We should plan out some things to do that week."

My eyes widened with surprise. "Our anniversary?"

Vance nodded. "September, right? That's when we started talking."

"Yeah, but we didn't—" I stopped short, remembering Davis was at the table. "We weren't really dating until, like…January."

"December-ish," he said, bobbing his head side to side. "But close enough. I told Davis about putting the house on the market and making the move. It sounds better every second I think about it."

"Wanderlust could set up shop in an office near mine," said Davis. "I like the ideas you came up with, and it would be easier to collaborate if you were on property."

"An in-house travel agency is not a bad idea," Vance said. "It would be nice to spread out into an office. Plus, we don't want to take up bedroom space we could use for guests. I know my kids will be down a lot. And hopefully Darius will want to see his mom."

"Okay, so…" Davis grinned. "Y'all are getting serious. I hear co-habitation plans and kid visits."

The batting around of ideas and talk about relocating would have scared the shit out of me weeks ago. Or maybe three days ago. Today, my heart pitter-pattered with excitement, although I didn't see Darius coming around for a while. And I wasn't planning to wait for him. Vance and I would be right here living our best lives, watching his sourpuss turn upside down.

Vance flexed his fingers around my knee. "We've had some healthy conversations. We're excited about the future."

"Either that, or we're out of our minds," I added. "But we'll be together.

"That's beautiful. Really...congratulations."

"Thanks." Vance I gave each other wide, silly grins. "We're excited. So, Wanderlust would have an office on the property?"

"That's the idea," said Davis.

"That would give me space for my coordinators to work when they inevitably make their way down here. I could actually have in-person team meetings that aren't built around trips we've planned."

The excitement in his voice, the lift in his shoulders was contagious. I saw his vision clearly; it made my heart swell with pride for Vance. He had worked hard to build his business, and now he was expanding into office space and partnership opportunities. Watching him do his thing, live out his passion for his work, was sexy.

I longed to join him in that. I just had to figure out how to make that work.

"WHY IS YOUR PHONE SO BUSY?" VANCE ASKED.

The device had been in my face most of the morning, throughout lunch, and while we walked through the suite to make sure we hadn't missed anything. Davis had arranged to have Vance's Jeep brought to the area just outside the elevator landing, and it would arrive in a few minutes. Vance had stacked our baggage near the door and was waiting for me to come in from the balcony, where I was taking in the last few minutes of our beach vacation.

I would sure miss this suite, this strip of land, the scent of salt in the air, the resort vibes.

"It's Sabrina," I told him. "She's nervous about her appointment. She has a lot of questions."

"I'm sure she's scared. But she can't fall out again like she did the other night. Is Nurse Athena on the job?"

I laughed, my fingers moving across the keyboard to respond to her latest text. "Kind of. She wanted me to come to her appointment with her, but I said we were leaving the island today."

"Do you want to? She seems like she could use the support."

"I—" I wilted, resting the phone in my lap. I stared up at Vance through the tint of my shades. "I don't want to throw our plan off track. And her boyfriend is there. She'll be okay."

"You don't sound confident. And he's not you. We can ride up there. It's on the way home, and it'll be far better than your thumbs cramping from all that typing."

I pushed out a sigh, feeling the worry lines on my forehead already receding. "It would actually mean a lot to me if we could. And...while we drive, I'm thinking through some things about my job. Maybe making some changes."

"Ch-ch-changes!" Vance crooned, singing the word as he held out a hand to help me stand. He pulled me up and dragged me inside, ignoring my laughter at his inability to sing.

"Nobody asked for a solo, Vance."

"Please, you love my voice. Ask her where we can meet them so my lady can do her thing."

We slowly made our way to the front door of our suite. Vance handed me my backpack. I slung it over my shoulder and let him handle the suitcases.

"I love your voice saying things like, '*come for me, Athena. Let me spoil you, Athena.*' I do not love your voice defiling David Bowie."

"Lemme fix it, then." Vance turned, taking my cheeks into his hands and pulling my face to his. He dropped a tender kiss on my lips before pulling back to utter beautiful words. "I love you, Athena."

"I love you, too. But you can't sing."

He laughed, released me, then pushed me out the door. We loaded up the car in time to get Sabrina's text. She was overjoyed that I could meet her at Corpus Christi General and attend her appointment with her.

We drove toward the hospital, a breeze blowing through the cab of the Jeep and Vance's hand resting between my thighs. When we arrived, Sabrina and Nathan were waiting in the lobby, looking nervous and exhausted. Sabrina's eyes lit up when she saw us. I pulled her in for a tight hug while Vance shook hands with Nathan.

"Thank you so much for coming," she said, her voice tight with emotion. "I don't think I could have done this without you."

"Of course, you could have," I whispered, patting her back. "But this makes it easier. How are you feeling?"

"Tired. We rehearsed until late last night. And I'm starving. I had to fast for this appointment."

We rode up to Endocrinology together and checked in. Sabrina was called back almost immediately, and I stayed with her while the nurse took her vitals and asked her a few questions. Vance and Nathan hung back, already engaged in chatter about music and sports.

Sabrina's appointment was routine, Labs, including a urine and blood sample, full medical history, and an array of questions between Sabrina and I. By the time we left the room, armed with printouts, pamphlets, and a prescription for a wearable glucose monitor, the nurse practitioner had earned her hourly rate and then some.

"I'm so grateful you could make it. You asked some questions that I hadn't thought of." Sabrina's long, thin arms wrapped around me as she held me in an extended hug. "I really wish you lived close. I don't want to bother you all the time with medical questions, but I'd just like to have someone who knows what's going on is nearby."

"Well, you have Nathan." I nodded to her boyfriend and Vance, standing by. "And now you have a doctor you can call. And...Vance and I are talking about moving to the area. Nothing is set in stone, yet, but..."

I glanced up at Vance. He flashed a smile in my direction. "I'll keep you posted about our plans. In the meantime, reach out to your doctor if you have any issues and check in with me. You have no excuse for not taking care of your health."

"See what I have to deal with?" Sabrina turned to take Nathan by the hand, ambling toward the elevators. "Mean."

"I get it, too," said Vance. "She told me today that I can't sing."

"He can't, and please don't ask him to prove it." We laughed, spilling out of the elevator on the ground floor. "Take her to get some food immediately. And you might want to keep a few snacks handy just in case she has an episode."

Nathan nodded. "We're going to a pool party. They're grilling her a burger as we speak." Both waved as they headed toward their car, and Vance and I walked to his Jeep.

I pushed out a happy sigh. "That was a productive appointment. It went exactly as I thought it would."

"You were great with her. Are you thinking about doing more of that?"

We climbed into the Jeep, pulling down our sun visors. Vance pressed the start button; a chill filled the cabin as the air kicked on.

"I'm actually thinking really hard about it. There's a business concept called a Concierge Nurse. I can do consultations, home health care, even some maternity care. Maybe the hotel needs an on-call nurse? And I can do contract work for the Black Diamond clinic and the hospital in Corpus Christi."

"What you do now, but you don't have to go to like...Big Fork, Minnesota."

"Exactly. I'd get to stay here. In Black Diamond." I paused, staring at the side of his face. "With you."

"And...just being clear. You want that, right?"

"Once I start making moves, that's the point of no return. So, let's be clear. *You* want that, right? Me around all the time, slowing you down, distracting you—"

"Athena."

He interrupted, trying to level a glare at me. Since he had his shades on, I couldn't see his eyes, so it wasn't working. I stared back, awaiting his response.

"That's not a concern," he finally said. "Do you know how pissed I am to go back to being with you on Zoom after tomorrow? That shit is what's distracting. Thinking about how I want to be with you and I can't? That shit slows me down. You being with me all the time is all I want."

"Okay," I said. "Just making sure. Because I'm thinking of not renewing my contract with my agency and starting the process to validate my nursing license in Texas."

"Alright, Nurse Wilcox."

Vance leaned over the console, lips puckered. I met him halfway and savored the kiss. As we parted, Vance's eyes held a mischievous glint. "There is a patient that needs your attention."

I grinned, knowing where he was going. "And...what is his problem?"

"Severe case of *needs to put his mouth on you*."

I felt a familiar heat building. I'd nearly forgotten that we had one last night together before my return to reality. I intended to make the most of it.

"Well, I'm not a doctor..." I slid my shades over my eyes and snapped my seatbelt on. "But as a treatment, I might suggest that he take me home and eat my pussy until symptoms subside."

His brows furrowed in faux serious concern. "I concur, Nurse Wilcox. You're damn good."

"Better than you know. Let's go. We have an appointment."

Vance put the Jeep in gear and pulled out of the lot, headed north. I sank into the seat, nodding my head to the hits of the 2000s pouring from the speakers and dreams about what my life could be flashing through my mind.

VANCE

Vance-Wanderlust Travel: Hey, hey. Good to be back in the land of WhatsApp.

Vance-Wanderlust Travel: Dropping my girl off at the airport tomorrow. Then we can check in.

Whitney: Vance! How was the vacation?

Vance-Wanderlust Travel: I'm sure you're not surprised, but I'm heavily considering moving there. Working out the details over the next few weeks.

I WANTED MY LAST MORNING WITH ATHENA TO CRAWL BY SO I would have more time to explore her body, to feel her softness and warmth, to hear my name on her lips. We hadn't stopped touching each other, kissing each other, indulging in each other since I pulled into the garage. After dinner and a few glasses of wine, Athena dragged me to my Texas-sized bed and wore my ass out.

Still, knowing I had to say goodbye to her in a few hours, I could not resist one last rumble between the sheets.

The first rays of sunrise crept across my bedroom, highlighting the silky smoothness of Athena's bare skin as she lay beneath me. Her hands were bound to the headboard above her head, her thighs spread wide and breasts undulating with every thrust as I drove into her. She was tight, hot, wet around me.

I pulled out, then paused to balance my weight on one elbow to hold the silicone rose against her clit. Athena gasped, arching her pelvis to increase the pressure against the stiff, vibrating bud. I moved the toy from her clit to her folds, teasing the sensitive area.

Athena writhed, growling low. "Hmmm, shit! Put it back!"

I pinched her nipple, then dipped to take it into my mouth. Athena inhaled sharply, shuddering at the sensation. I pressed the toy against her clit again and she moaned, biting her lower lip. I teased her, pulling it away and applying it again. Her moans grew more intense until she was near a scream, bucking her body furiously. I pushed the toy harder against her and moments later watched an orgasm rip through her.

I pulled the toy away and drove into her again, riding her orgasm and galloping toward mine. I wanted to make it last, but the sensation of her spasming around me was too much. On the edge of blacking out, I felt the first waves ripple through me, traveling up and erupting in a volcano. I hissed and groaned, grasping her hips as I ground against her, riding out the last throes of climax.

"Shit, shit, shit! Untie me! Hurry!"

I pulled the loose knot and removed the scarf that bound her hands together. Once free, she pulled me to her and kissed me, our tongues dancing, expressing what words could not.

Athena pushed against my shoulders, urging me to roll us

over and lie back. I complied, savoring the weight of her on top of me, the feel of her flesh against my flesh.

"Hey, gorgeous," I whispered, watching her balance herself. "What you thinking about doing to me?"

Athena rolled her hips, pressing into my groin, smiling as she worked her hands down my body. She stroked and licked me, goading my erection back, then balanced herself over me.

"Damn, baby," I moaned. "You got another one in you?"

Her eyes flicked up at mine before returning her attention down below. "Fuck, yes. So do you."

She sank onto me, her jaw dropping open with her loud, pleasured groan as she took me. I watched her pussy swallow me, her thick thighs straining with the effort, her round ass bobbing as she rocked back and forth. My hands cupped her breasts, my thumbs grazing the hard peaks of her nipples. She anchored her palms on my chest and rode me hard, switching between quick and shallow, then deep, slow movements.

Athena's eyes were wide, her mouth open with ragged breaths. She moaned aloud, frantically maneuvering her hips in circles and grinding against me. I felt her shudder.

"Ooh, shit, I'm about to come. Where are you, Vance?"

"Come for me, gorgeous. I'm right behind you."

I held her hips, bucking hard and fast to meet her. She tensed, her muscles contracting, milking me. We exploded into orgasm together like dynamite detonating on a mountainside. I closed my eyes, threw my head back, and let out a bellowing growl as I emptied into her.

Athena collapsed onto my chest. I slowed to a stop, heaving hard breaths to match hers. I pulled off her silk bonnet since the band was soaked in sweat anyway and kissed her forehead.

"You, uh…you think you're all stocked up for a bit?"

"Not hardly," she answered, the sound muffled by my chest. She rolled her head to drop a kiss there, then worked her way up my body until her mouth claimed mine in a slow, heady tangle of tongues.

When we parted, she pulled back, her eyes boring into mine. "I get it now."

"What do you get now?"

"Why Valerie yelled at me for not meeting you sooner."

I rolled us until we laid on our sides, facing each other. "See?" I said, settling us into a new position. "You should listen to your elders."

"Well, my elders didn't tell me it could be like this."

"Some of us have to learn our lessons the hard, slow way."

"Like you're God's favorite over there," Athena said, her eyes only open halfway. "This has been the best vacation. I like Texas hospitality."

Her hands caressed my skin, coming to rest on my chest. I smiled, draping my arm over her waist. "I do like to make my vacations memorable."

"If knew that, I'd have booked with you a long time ago."

"You did know that," I argued.

She laughed. "Have you ever met a woman as stubborn as me?"

"No," I answered. "But you came around. Any time you want a repeat, I'm game."

Athena wiggled closer to me, her face buried in the space between my neck and shoulder. "You should book yourself to beautiful Big Fork, Minnesota."

"You're actually inviting me up to Big Fork? You must be serious about me."

"Valerie and LaTasha will want to meet you," she muttered, her voice already thick with sleep. "I'm warning you, though. There's nothing in Big Fork."

"*You* are in Big Fork. I am not flying to Minnesota to look at the scenery."

"I tried to warn you." She sighed, then said, "I only have four weeks before I'm done there."

"And then what? You're not renewing, you said. You're not going back out?"

She inhaled deeply, then slowly released it. "No, I'm not going out again. I am going to see my son and check on my house. I want to work out an arrangement with him. He can get a roommate and pay rent, or leave so I can rent the house out. Then I am going to box up some things to ship here because—"

I felt her cheeks round with her smile. "I'm moving with my man to the beach."

"I love the sound of that every time you say it. So, if you're not going back out, you have time to help your man pack up his house."

"Hey." Her palm made a flat, slapping sound against my chest. "We did not discuss manual labor."

"I thought *move to the beach with me* covered all of that."

She grunted in answer, burrowing deeper under the covers. I pulled them up around her bare shoulders. "We have a couple of hours before we have to get ready to head to the airport. I don't want to be stuck in traffic."

I heard a groan from under the covers. I let my eyes slide closed, joining her in a post-sex nap. Soon, but not nearly soon enough, we would be like this every day. No more separations or goodbyes, just us together.

I fell asleep to the sound of her rhythmic breathing and the warmth of her body tucked close to mine.

ATHENA

Vance-Wanderlust Travel: No more sleeps, gorgeous.

Vance-Wanderlust Travel: Get that mouth ready.

Thena W: Mouth is ready for the foreseeable future.

Vance-Wanderlust Travel: I told you to let me take you somewhere so I could spoil your ass.

Thena W: Still on the job. Fly safe, baby. I love you.

I PACKED A FEW ITEMS FROM MY TEMPORARY WORKSTATION AT Valley Hospital into a cardboard box, fitting the lid snugly on top. The final weeks of my assignment were grueling. The hours were long, the work was demanding and often thankless, and to make matters worse, my schedule didn't align with Vance's travel plans.

With the mounting tasks we both had to tackle before our

impending move, I wouldn't get to see him until he showed up in Big Fork to drive me down to South Carolina.

It had taken unbearably long to arrive, but my last day at Valley pounced on me like it was hiding around the corner. Though I was not as ready to leave as I thought I'd be, I completed my exit paperwork and moped to Valerie's cubicle.

"That's it, I guess," I said, handing her my badge.

"I guess." She took it, the edges of her mouth turned down as she wrapped the branded lanyard around the card and clip.

"Don't pout. You'll make me cry. You knew I was only going to be here for six months."

"Yeah," she muttered, tucking the badge into a drawer. "I was hoping you might extend. Stay a little longer."

I didn't mean to laugh in her face, but I did. "In Big Fork, Minnesota? You thought I would stay longer in a place where it still snows in May?"

"Minnesota is beautiful in summer!"

"You know what's beautiful in summer? My house. My boyfriend's house. Our future home on Black Diamond."

"See, there she goes," said LaTasha, turning into Valerie's cubicle, both hands propped on slim hips. "Ol' bragging ass."

"I know you're not talking, Miss *Let That Man Work*. He worked, okay? I took all of your advice and he worked his ass off. You're supposed to be happy for me."

"I didn't say come back here with plans to move to the beach with him. I'm salty because he's taking you away from us."

"I know you know this, but I'm a contract nurse. I was leaving anyway, Tash."

I set the box down on Valerie's desk and extended my arms, folding them both into a hug. "I really want y'all to stop performing. I told you both to come down to the island as soon as we're settled."

"You say that now," said Valerie, "but you two will get

your place all cozy and romantic and decide you don't want to be looking in anyone else's face."

"Please." I huffed an impatient breath. "If I do not look into these faces before the end of the year, there will be problems. I'm not playing. Vance already said he'd hook you up with a package."

"Yeah, yeah, Miss *My Boyfriend is a Master Travel Coordinator*. Keep bragging."

I laughed, my head cocked back. "Y'all need to stop, or I'm going to start second-guessing myself."

"No, you are not!" LaTasha pulled back from the hug and poked me with one of her nails. "You're going to ignore our whining and tell us the story again."

"I'm not telling that story again. I have things to do at the house and then I'm picking up Vance in Duluth. I'll see you both tomorrow. Can we bring anything?"

Valerie frowned and playfully pushed me away. "I already told you not to bring a damn thing but that smile and your man so we can get a good look at him before you two ride off into the sunset."

I hiked my full work bag over my shoulder and picked up the box. "Kiss, kiss," I said, tapping their cheeks with mine before I shuffled toward the exit. "Don't call me tonight."

"Hadn't even planned on it!" LaTasha called after me. "We know you're about to be busy with your man, your man, your man."

MY HEART LEAPED INTO MY THROAT AS I WATCHED VANCE approaching from the arrivals terminal at the Duluth airport. I'd been casing baggage claim since I saw that his flight from Houston had landed. Weeks apart had felt like an eternity, and I craved being in his arms again.

I tried to play it cool as I watched him walk toward me,

but my ridiculous grin and impatient twitching from foot to foot gave me away. He broke into a smile when he saw me and doubled his pace, rolling a black Samsonite suitcase behind him.

"Hello, gorgeous."

He dropped the handle of his suitcase and pulled me into the tightest embrace possible, and I still wasn't close enough. The warmth of his touch was all I needed to forget the teary goodbye at the Houston airport a month earlier and the weeks following where we hungrily soaked up time by text, FaceTime, or our nightly sessions on Zoom.

I clung to him, breathing in the familiar strains of jojoba from his beard oil. I welcomed his mouth on mine. After a few bumps from passengers in a rush, we slowly came back to reality.

"Hi, handsome," I mumbled against his lips. "I missed the shit out of you."

He laughed, his chest and belly bouncing against mine, dragging out the embrace until we had to part. I finally released him, allowing him to slide his palms down my arms until he held my hands in his. He looked tired since he'd taken an afternoon flight out of Houston after working on the house all day, but he was a sight for sore eyes in a dark blue Wanderlust Travel t-shirt and jeans.

"I missed the shit out of you, too. Zoom is just not the same."

I almost squeaked, knowing that Zoom would not be a regular part of our relationship anymore.

The past month had been a whirlwind of activity for Vance and me. Vance had his home appraised, and after a few repairs and some paint, it would be ready to list for sale. He also made an offer on a smaller, less appointed three-bedroom condo at The Pearl. The offer was quickly accepted and Vance anticipated sailing through closing in a few weeks. Our to-do list was pages long.

I passed the remaining time in Big Fork researching requirements to set up my business as a Concierge Nurse. To be licensed in the state of Texas, I had to pass an exam. I spent my spare time studying so I could take the exam as soon as we moved. Vance and I had robust travel plans for the holidays, so the goal was to launch my business after the new year.

"Come on, handsome." I slipped my hand into his and led him out of the airport toward short-term parking. "The sooner we get on the road, the sooner I get you home. How much did the painters get done today?"

"They made pretty good progress. They think they'll be done in a few days. It's a good time to leave, so I don't have to breathe in paint fumes."

Vance and I carried on a lively conversation about the projects he'd begun on the house to prepare it for sale, from painting the interior to brick work on the fireplace in the living room. He even hired a landscaper to trim the hedges and give shape to the bushes that flanked the front door.

The drive to Big Fork from Duluth went so quickly, before I realized it, we were turning into the driveway of the home I'd been renting for the past few months. I pulled into my space in the garage for nearly the last time, fighting a misty, melancholy feeling about leaving Big Fork.

My landlords beamed with happiness when I told them about moving to the beach. They had already requested information from Vance to book a winter trip to Black Diamond. I would miss their kindness, but in a few weeks, they would have a new tenant to spoil.

"Home, sweet home." I ushered Vance inside and pushed the front door closed and tossed my keys into a decorative bowl nearby. "Don't blink. You'll miss it."

As soon as I turned to give him the nickel tour, Vance's hands were around my waist, pulling me up against him. I had no plans to fight him. After weeks of separation and a long drive, I finally had him to myself.

Vance's groans were loud and appreciative. His hands roamed my body as if they needed to memorize me again. The tour ended by giving my full, round cheeks a firm squeeze.

"It's all still back there."

"Good. I missed this ass. I've missed every part of you."

"*Every* part?"

Vance smiled, his hands exploring as his lips landed on mine. When the kiss ended, he spoke in a soft whisper. "Every part. You want me to call them out? The lips. The nipples. The dip in your neck I like to lick. Your belly. Your thighs…really missed your thighs around me."

He stared, his eyes narrowing, growing smoky. "Should I keep going?"

I shrugged. "I haven't heard my favorite part yet…"

He leaned in for another long kiss. His hands roved my body again, coming to rest at the juncture of my thighs. His fingertips brushed across my mound, sending my heart rate sky-high.

"Your clit," he added in a husky tone.

"Getting there," I replied, breathless and almost panting.

His fingertips caressed me with a gentle, rhythmic touch. As the sensation intensified, I fought a full-body shudder.

"Your pussy," he pushed out, pressing his lips to mine while pressing a finger to my clit. My breath caught at the answer that I knew was coming, but the way he said it, in a barely controlled growl, set me aflame. I had waited for what felt like an eternity for him to explore every inch of me until I unraveled.

"There are parts of you I've missed, too."

"My text message inbox says there is at least one part that you've missed a lot. So, you know what it's time for, don't you?"

I ran the date through my head. It wasn't a particularly special day—just the day I'd marked on my calendar that I would see Vance again.

"Remind me."

Vance took my arms, threading them around his neck, tracing each curve of my body with his hands until he reached my thighs.

"Some of that *pick me up and fuck me* action. You ready?"

"Oh, my God! Vance!" I screamed in laughter as he gripped my thighs and lifted me off the ground.

"Already screaming my name. I like it," he said, laughing with me. "Wrap those legs around me like I know you know how."

I complied, cackling hysterically as he fought to maintain balance and move us from the living room to the bedroom.

"Cute place," he said, huffing while he spoke. "It's like a Barbie house."

"It's just enough," I protested. "Look at this bed."

He angled his head around me and laughed aloud at the bed shoved into the bedroom. With the addition of my packed crates and boxes, we barely had room to move.

"Shit," he said, then dropped me at the edge of the bed.

"I told you."

"It's a good thing we don't need much room for what I'm planning to do with you," he said, his eyes dark and hungry as they roamed my body.

I kicked off my shoes and scooted back on the bed, giddy with anticipation. "What do you plan to do with me, handsome?"

"It's been a month. I have a list."

Vance began pulling at his clothing. His t-shirt and jeans were quickly discarded at the foot of the bed, and his briefs joined the pile. He was already erect, more than ready for this moment.

"You too? We should compare lists."

Vance kneeled on the bed beside me and gripped my left ankle, pushing the loose yoga pants I'd worn to the airport up and over my knee and revealing a leg that had lost its island tan. I watched as he ran his lips along my skin. It tickled, but I was already thumping too hard to laugh.

I pulled my pants off, yanking them down so fast I heard the fabric tear. I kicked out of them, then pulled my t-shirt off and laid back, quietly waiting for Vance to notice the bra and panty set I was wearing.

Eventually, a grin spread across his lips, and he gave an approving nod. "The purple Fenty. You thought of me."

"I don't think about much besides you."

"Somebody is about to get very…" He resumed his exploration of my body, nudging my legs open so he could nibble at my inner thigh before slowly inching up. My head fell back. I writhed and whimpered, anticipating his next move.

"…very lucky," he finished, just as he arrived at my core. He toyed with me, lightly biting me through the delicate fabric.

"Oh, shit. Vance…" I moaned, angling my hips up toward his mouth, my voice raspy with need. "Don't tease me, baby. I need you."

A deep, throaty hum escaped him as he used his teeth and fingers to pull my panties off and give him full access. I palmed his head, pulling him back to me as my hips began a sensuous roll. I'd been thinking about this moment since the last time his mouth was on me. I wanted to scream, I was so on edge.

"Fuck yes, Vance. Lick it, suck it hard."

As if he was waiting for the invitation, he swirled his tongue across my clit, then sucked me before diving into my pussy. He thrust in and out in a rhythmic pattern that radiated sparks to the tips of my toes. His hot breath ghosted over me as he lapped with long strokes of his tongue, teasing and tormenting until I was begging for release.

My thighs clenched around him, my hips bucking against him. He braced himself, gripping my thighs, not missing a stroke.

I propped myself up, using one arm to stay balanced, my ankles locked firmly behind his back for leverage to grind against him. I flung my head back, indulging in loud, pleasured moans as I rode his mouth.

"Vance! Oh....*fuck*! I'm coming! I'm coming! I'm coming!" I screamed out to him as the peak of climax rippled through me. My muscles tensed, slowly releasing as I fell back on the bed, limp and overcome.

Vance smiled up at me before planting a soft kiss on my mound, his lips lightly grazing my body as he made his way up. He stopped to give a lick at the flap of belly near my pubic bone, kissed my navel, and gave a little nibble to both nipples before hovering over me.

"I love the landing strip, by the way. I kept getting distracted. Forgot to mention it."

My fingertips traced the lines of his jaw. I pulled him closer until our lips met. "We don't have to be anywhere until tomorrow, so I hope you have more rounds in you."

"You're always clockin' me," he teased. "I wasn't done with my list."

"You're moving like it hasn't been a month since I've been fucked with anything but a glass dick. I'm ready."

I pulled him on top of me, then guided him, sighing as he pressed into me. His long strokes sent waves of pleasure through me as he filled me.

"Tell me to take my time." My jaw clenched as he dragged his hips back. I felt every vein in his dick as it passed my entrance. "Tell me to fuck you slow."

"I don't want it slow," I whined.

"You don't want it slow?"

I hummed, vigorously shaking my head and rocking my

hips up and into him. "I need you to fuck me hard. Fast. *Please.*"

"Fuck, I missed this," he grunted, his breath hot on my neck. "Touching you, tasting you. You smashed up against me when we fuck. I missed those sounds you make when you're about to come." He took my earlobe into his mouth and nipped it with his teeth, then sucked it before releasing it. "I missed feeling you pulse around me."

My fingers dug into his skin as I worked my hips under him, my body meeting his thrust for thrust. "I missed you so much. I need...*shit.* I need you."

It was a slow climb, and with each stroke, his thrusts became more aggressive. He covered my mouth with his, swallowing my gasps of pleasure as he drove into me.

For the rest of my life, I wanted nothing more than to always be wrapped around him, joined with him, our sweat-coated skin sticking together as our bodies rocked toward climax.

I felt his quickening, stuttered breath on my skin. "Where you at, baby?"

"So close, Vance. Harder. Fuck me harder."

He gripped my thighs, pumping harder, pushing deeper, our bodies sending a satisfying slap into the air. "Let it go, baby. I got you."

My moans became yelps as he pounded into me. His muscles tightened beneath my fingertips. I clung to him, wanting more until it was more than I could take.

A cry ripped from my throat. My body tensed, my pussy spasmed, drawing him deeper. "Now! Come with me! Come with me, Vance!"

My orgasm sent a rush of heat and lightning through my body, from the bottom of my feet, up my calves, pulsing in my core. Vance pumped with wild abandon until his body stiffened and he roared through his release.

He panted as his muscles reached exhaustion and softened. His limbs gave out, and he settled on top of me. I savored the feel of his weight on me, his heart pounding into my chest. When he seemed to return to consciousness, he slid his hands until his fingers intertwined with mine, then anchored our hands together above my head.

He dipped to the right, his mouth capturing a dark erect nipple before moving on to the other. Then he moved to my mouth, fluttering his lips over mine.

"I love you, Athena," he whispered into the quiet of the room. "I want to love you, just like this, for the rest of my life."

My eyes watered as I met his gaze. "I love you so much, Vance. I'm never letting you go."

The sun had long since set, and the room had grown dark. We lay tangled in each other, listening to the sounds of a Midwestern evening until my stomach rumbled in protest of a long day with not enough sustenance. Valerie had ordered in lunch, but I'd been too nervous about seeing Vance again to do more than gossip with the nurses and doctors that I would truly miss. They'd made me promise to put Big Fork on the list if I ever returned to contract nursing.

"I didn't even ask if you were hungry," I mumbled, rolling my head in his direction. "Just got right to the fucking."

"No complaints here." His palm slapped against his belly. "I don't miss many meals. I missed my girl, though. I got my fill of her."

"Well, you have to eat more than pussy. I guess I can get up and make us something."

"What are you going to make for us in your Barbie kitchen?"

I tossed a dry patter of laughter over my shoulder as I forced myself to sit up. I reached for the lamp at the bedside table and pulled the string, bathing the room in a warm glow.

I glanced over at Vance lounging next to me. "My landlords brought over a few things so I don't have to cook."

Vance pushed himself up as well, then noticed the camera and tripod set up on the dresser across from the bed. "About time to pack that thing up for good, huh?"

I grinned at him before kicking my feet over the side of the bed. "Hell, yes."

VANCE

Vance-Wanderlust Travel: Got your feedback on the packages. They'll be ready to go live on the Wanderlust site as soon as I can get them to my designer.

Vance-Wanderlust Travel: I'll be out of pocket for a day or so. Picking up my lady to bring her home.

Davis Scott: Just like I said. You 'bout to 'my lady' me to death.

BIG FORK, MINNESOTA, POPULATION 446, WAS BEAUTIFUL...LUSH, green, peaceful. Athena practically vibrated, she was so excited to show me around her temporary home.

Our first stop was Moose Tracks, a quaint local coffeeshop where I managed to find a surprisingly good cup of green tea. Then we took the scenic route, driving along the edge of the Wilderness National Scenic Byway, boasting miles of unspoiled forests and shimmering lakes, offering a level of quiet that was hard to find in the city.

I'd spent my whole life in major cities and suburbs,

always in the thick of the action. But in this small town, life moved at a slower, quieter, more relaxed pace. It was a change, but a welcome one. Since we were planning a move to a beach town, I was learning to slow down.

We headed back to the house so we could take our time closing down Athena's existence in Minnesota before a blast of a going away dinner at her former supervisor's rustic country home. We got back late, then we were up early to load up the car.

"That's the last box," I announced, coming down the steps. "I don't understand how you've collected so much stuff on a temporary assignment in a place called Big Fork."

Athena made room, shoving over a suitcase and a stack of bedding and pillows. After I added the box to the trunk, I closed it. Athena did a last-minute walk through the house and came back outside, shut and locked the door, and dropped the keys in the mailbox.

"If there's anything left, it's not going with us." Athena propped her hands on her hips as she surveyed the car that was stuffed from end to end. There was just enough space to see out of the rearview mirror.

"We ready?"

"As ready as we'll ever be."

Athena glanced over at the rambling home across the driveway. Her landlords had come by early that morning to bring us breakfast. There was a long, tear-filled goodbye, followed by an hour where she was quiet and sullen. It took a conversation about our to-do list before we made the move to Black Diamond to pull her out of her funk.

"Don't go back over there. We'll never leave."

"I know," she mumbled. She tapped my ass as she passed me on the way to the passenger side of the car. "Let's go before Marian comes out here. She'll beg me to stay."

"I will drag your ass out of here."

I slid into the driver's seat of Athena's car, a metallic blue BMW that fit her personality. Classy, bougie…a little ratchet. Like Athena and her platinum goddess braids and shapely figure, the car stood out. Athena snapped her seatbelt on; I did the same, then pressed the ignition button and put the car in reverse.

"Last call," I told her.

She leaned over the armrest to press her lips against mine, then sat back and slipped on her shades. "Let's go, handsome."

The drive from Minnesota to South Carolina would take two days. We hit an early summer storm during the last few hours of our first day. I was tense and stiff from gripping the steering wheel, ready to maneuver around cars and trucks on the slick roads. We finally made it to the Chicago area, where we had planned to get a good meal and solid rest.

The next morning, Athena was chipper and in a great mood as she slid into the driver's seat for her shift. I was groggy, still exhausted from the long drive and a late dinner before passing out, but I felt guilty about letting her drive.

"I can take over later after I get a few more hours of—" A FaceTime notification ringing through the car's Bluetooth system rudely interrupted me. "Who is FaceTiming you at 6 AM?"

Athena grinned and pressed accept on the phone. On the screen, two women in hospital scrubs were smashed together, and a high-pitched squeal-fest was not doing anything for my headache.

"Hey, you two," said Valerie, who I'd met a few evenings before. We had a great time sharing one last meal with the people that Athena had grown close to over the past few months, but Valerie and LaTasha were the two I connected with the most. According to Athena, they were the reason she was with me, so I'd made sure to thank them.

"The morning shift ain't the same without you, Thena!"

LaTasha leaned in to say her piece, then blew air kisses before moving off screen. "I gotta go get reports!"

"I'm just checking in to see how the road dawgs are getting along. I see you're up and at 'em."

"We have a long drive today. If I put my lead foot into it, I can be home before sunset."

"I know you're looking forward to seeing your house. And your son."

Athena nodded, flashing a smile. "We had a great time at dinner. Didn't we, baby?"

I leaned in and tried to smile.

"What did you do to that poor man? He's looking rough."

"I am rough," I said. "Hi, Valerie."

"We hit a storm on the way to Chicago. Vance needs a few more hours of sleep and some caffeine, so we're going to hit the road. I'll let you know when I'm home."

"Alright, honey. Don't let that lead foot get you in trouble."

Athena and Valerie signed off. She pulled out of the hotel parking lot and followed the GPS directions back to the highway.

"Are you nervous about me coming to your house?" I asked.

"Nervous?" I could just make out her eyes through the dark lenses of her shades as she glanced at me, then back to the road. "Not especially. Are *you* nervous about coming to the house?"

"Just thinking about meeting Darius and how that's going to go. You're not nervous about meeting Kareema?"

"Yeah, I am," she acknowledged with a nod. "I just figured I would do my best to respect her feelings and your relationship with her. I thought you were coming with me specifically to meet Darius?"

"I'm coming specifically to get you home. But he'll be there, and I won't be able to avoid meeting him. And I don't want to avoid him. He's a part of your life, and I plan to respect that. I'm just…"

I bumped my shoulders in a shrug.

"He clearly doesn't like me and doesn't approve of us. I don't want to be a point of contention between you and your son."

"Nor do I, with your kids. But I promise, if it wasn't my relationship with you, it would be something else. He barely talked to me during my first travel assignment. He didn't know any different than me being at home every night to make him dinner and pack him a lunch and wash his clothes. He's much different from Kareema."

"I can tell he doesn't want to make the leaps he needs to make right now. And I'm the reason he has to—"

"No, you're not," Athena argued. "This has been a long time coming. We've sped up the timeline. Just remember—it's not about you, it's about me. I've coddled him. Our family, including his father, has spoiled him. I'm making him grow the hell up, and he's not interested."

A part of me still felt like I had a point—Darius didn't like the idea of sharing his mother any more than my daughter would be welcome to sharing her father.

"Darius and I have had to move past huge transitions over the past few years. He is slow to change, and a lot has changed quickly. We just need to give him some time."

She glanced at me again, this time with a smile. "And we're about to."

"So he's not going to swing on me or anything, right?"

"Darius?" She snorted. "He'd better not, if he plans to stay in my house. He doesn't have to love the idea of us, but he will respect it."

"I've never met a woman's children before. I don't know the right way, or the right time or the right approach. I guess I just needed some reassurance."

Athena kept her eyes on the road, but reached across the

seat to land a hand on my thigh. I rested my hand on hers. "I love that you're concerned about meeting my son and doing it right. Darius will be fine. Kareema will be fine, too. You should get some sleep."

I yawned, very tempted to close my eyes. "You stayed up with me yesterday."

"So? You look exhausted."

As if my body needed permission to rest, I suddenly couldn't keep my eyes open. I tipped my head back against the headrest and, lulled by the gentle rock and hum of wheels on pavement, drifted off into a deep sleep.

I woke up a few hours later, still groggy but feeling more rested. My eyes opened to the view of passing scenery. I-65 southbound stretched out in front of us, creating a monotonous landscape. It had been cloudy earlier in the day, but the sun eventually burned away the gray and replaced it with a stunning blue sky.

Athena hummed along with the radio, her eyes fixed on the road. I watched her for a moment, taking in the way her braids, swept into a pony tail, swayed gently with the move-ment of the car, the sweet pucker of her lips as she quietly hummed so she wouldn't wake me up, the slight furrow of her brow as she concentrated on driving.

"Morning," I growled, my voice still rough with sleep. "Wait, is it still morning?"

She glanced over at me, her lips bending into a warm smile. "Hey, handsome. I didn't realize you were awake. It's almost ten. Feeling better?"

"Yeah, actually. What's...uh.." I sat up, rearranging myself. I'd turned to my side and was slumped in the seat. "How's the drive?"

"Smooth. We can stop in Indianapolis for gas and lunch."

"You're making good time."

"I did this drive in December, remember? We talked the whole way."

"Ohhh....yeah." I leaned my head against the headrest and laughed a little. "Man, that was a lifetime ago."

"Mmm," she hummed, nodding. "You were still some guy I was talking to online. Now look at us. You're about to meet my kid, see my house..." She glanced at me, then returned her attention to the road. "Move me to Texas. We've made huge leaps in a very short time."

I pondered, taking in the enormity of what we were doing, and not for the first time. The speed at which we were moving compared to most couples should be a red flag. The risks involved seemed greater than ever before, but I had never been afraid to take this step with Athena.

I was only afraid that I couldn't get her to see that it was the right step to take.

"I see why our kids are throwing up flares," I said, turning to look out the window as we passed through Indiana's countryside. "But...when you know, you know."

Athena inhaled deeply, a note of caution to her tone. "And you know."

"I know."

We switched drivers in Indianapolis. The excitement at being only eight hours from home pushed us hard to drive straight through as much as possible. Just after dusk, we pulled up to a brick rancher with blue trim and attached garage. It was a cute little house, perfect for two people.

The knot in my stomach tightened as the garage door rolled up, spilling a wide swath of light across the driveway. Inside, a shiny maroon F150 truck was parked on the right side.

Athena looked over at me with a soft smile and squeezed my hand. "Ready?" she asked quietly.

I nodded, mute. I opened up the car door, stepping out into the early evening air. Our footsteps sounded through the neatly organized garage. Before Athena made it to the interior door, it swung open.

In the opening stood five feet, nine inches of grumpy, scowling man. He wore dirty, baggy jeans, a t-shirt and a bright orange SCDOT vest. His beard was disheveled, with bits of dust embedded in the hairs. His brown eyes were wide, brows hiked.

The moment hung between us for what felt like minutes before Athena finally spoke.

"Hi, Darius," she said softly while motioning toward me with a nod of her head. "I want you to meet Vance Griffin. Vance, this is my son, Darius."

"'Sup." Darius lifted his chin in a slight nod.

I moved to stand next to Athena and extended a hand to him. "Heard a lot about you. It's great to finally meet you."

He glanced down at my hand then cut his eyes at Athena. Then he stepped back into the house and walked away.

Athena glanced at me, amused. "He didn't swing on you," she said, leading me into the house.

———

DARIUS STOMPED PAST ME SEVERAL TIMES WHILE UNLOADING Athena's car, carting boxes, luggage, and bags to wherever she directed him to put them.

I followed him with my gaze, unsure of the best way to approach him. I could let it sit, but I decided against it. I would be in Columbia for a few days, so the sooner we got things out in the open, the better the visit would be.

I wanted to strike up a one-on-one conversation, but he was doing his best to ignore me. Athena left the kitchen to order dinner, so before Darius could bounce, I grabbed a stool opposite him at the island.

"So, uh...your mom said you do construction?" I asked, attempting a casual tone.

Darius leaned back against the counter, gazing across the

island with a bored, unimpressed expression. "Department of Transportation," he answered. "Road crew."

I bobbed my head as if it was the most interesting answer I'd ever heard. "Alright. A lot of manual labor, out in the elements. Good work if you can get it. What's your crew working on?"

He blurted out answers in short, angry bursts. "Highways. Street repair. Patching up potholes."

Silence hung between us for a long, uncomfortable moment before I picked up the conversation again. "So… while your mom is out of the room, it feels like you have something you want to say to me. Questions you want to ask. Shit you need to get off your chest."

Darius shrugged broad shoulders, rolling his tongue around his mouth. "I asked my mama if you was a scammin' ass motherfucker. She said no. But she probably wouldn't tell me if you were."

"What do you think? How much money has she sent me, you think?"

His expression grew dark as he pondered the question. "She ain't no punk. She ain't gave you shit." He shook his head. "Nah…maybe it's a different scam. Maybe you get her to Texas, away from her family. From her own kid," he said, seething. "Then you cut her off. You get her all to yourself, huh?"

"Do you know what Athena plans to do when she moves to Texas? Have you talked with her about the business she wants to open, the work she'll be doing? I will hardly have her to myself."

"What's that got to do with me?"

"She'll be doing work that will make her happy. Her happiness doesn't concern you?"

"And you know what makes her happy?"

"Do you?"

"I'm asking *you*," he shot back, slowly moving toward the

island. Darius wasn't close to towering over me, but he had youth and a few more muscles on his side. "I'm asking how you know from talking to her on the internet. From putting her online to do weird shit, so you can get off. Yeah, I know all about that, *Vance*."

He spat out my name as if it tasted bitter on his tongue.

"You know…" I paused, marinating in my words before I continued. "Athena won't say it, because she doesn't want her son mad at her. I don't know you, so I will. It's none of your fucking business what consenting adults do in private. What I *know* is that I am in love with Athena, and I will stand in front of anyone trying to hurt her. You included."

"You tryna roll up, play dad to a grown ass man?" His eyes narrowed so severely I could barely see the dark brown irises. "You about to teach me how to talk to my mom?"

"Nah," I answered, clasping my hands together. "You have a father, so if you need one, call him. If you're a grown ass man, then nut up and act like one, not have your mother thinking you don't give a fuck about her."

I paused, hoping my words were sinking in. When he didn't interject, I continued. "She's always going to be your mom, Darius. I can't take her from you, but you can push her away, and that'll hurt far more than anything else will. You have a bond with Athena that I'll never have. Don't destroy it by being against what clearly makes her happy."

"Everything good in here?" We both averted our eyes to the sight of Athena leaning against the wall just outside the kitchen, her phone in her hand.

"Yeah." Darius sauntered in her direction, stopping just a few feet from her. "Your boyfriend delivered your lil' speech. I guess it's time for y'all to lay down the hammer about when you're selling the house. 'Bout to tell me when I got to be out of here."

"I didn't tell Vance to say shit to you, Darius. And this is *my* house. Blood, sweat and tears bought this place. Why would I sell it? Who said I was going to?"

"Dad had some choice words when I told him you were leaving South Carolina. Talkin' about how you're so pressed to leave all of us behind now that you got a new man."

"Leave it to Kane to not know shit but always be running his mouth." Athena huffed, rolling her eyes. "You couldn't have just asked me what was happening, instead of listening to that jackass?"

She pushed off the wall and stepped into the kitchen, tossing her phone to the counter. "And since we're on the subject, I want to see a serious turnaround in your attitude and how you speak to me and to Vance if you plan to stay in this house. Rent goes into effect the first of the year. That gives you time to find a roommate or stack your money and get your own place. I'll rent this place out, but I am not selling it."

Watching him veer from roiling with anger to relieved confusion was almost comical. His shoulders visibly dropped as he sighed. "You're not selling the house? Or kicking me out?"

"No, son," she replied, her voice and tone soft. "I'm not. Now, I've been home an hour, and you haven't even hugged me. You got your mean mug on because you're mad that I got a boyfriend and you might be less important to me. Grow up, Darius. Nobody is trying to replace your ass, but Vance makes me happy. You're just going to have to be okay with sharing me."

Darius' gaze bounced between me and Athena before he exhaled a hard breath and wrapped his arms around her. The embrace lasted longer than I expected it to. When they parted, Athena sniffed and wiped a palm down her cheeks, eliminating tear streaks.

"Can't nobody replace me because I am irreplaceable," said Darius, a smirk playing at his lips before he sucked his teeth. "I ain't mean to make it sound like I don't care about you, Ma. It's not what I want, but...I want you to be happy."

Then he bent to drop a kiss on her cheek. "Sorry I look busted. I had just got home when you pulled in. I wasn't expecting you until later on—y'all must have booked it from Minnesota."

"You know I don't go anywhere without my lead foot." She let out a laugh that still had an emotional edge and gave him a light tap on the elbow. "Go change out of these dirty clothes. I ordered from Railroad Barbecue, and I need you to go pick it up. Have you been sitting on my furniture with concrete dust all over you?"

"You raised me better than that."

Darius turned to leave the kitchen, but caught me in his line of sight over Athena's head. "Don't think you're getting off easy, player. I don't have to like shit about this, but you *will* treat my mama right. I don't want to hear about no Jagged Edge ass proposal, neither. Come correct—ain't gonna be no *'we might as well get married'* bullshit."

His nostrils flared as he shot a fiery glare in my direction, then lumbered out of sight. Athena chewed her lip as she watched him go, then turned to catch my gaze. I lifted and lowered my shoulders in a shrug.

"He ruined my proposal idea. I was gonna blast that song on the beach—"

"Don't play, Vance Griffin, who claims to be descended from a fictional blood line of men that spoil their women."

"You already know I'm gonna be doing too much."

"It's what I love about you." Athena masked a laugh, stepping back and moving towards the refrigerator. "Let's see if he has anything in here but beer and protein shakes."

I followed her with my eyes as she moved away, trying not to think about everything I wanted to do with her, even if Darius was around.

Athena pulled out two water bottles, handing one to me.

Her eyes were bright, lids heavy, as if she might have been thinking the same. She smiled at me before rising onto her toes to kiss me. Her lips were soft against mine, coaxing out a groan of pleasure before we parted.

"Really? With the kid around the corner?"

"The kid is *grown*. He needs to see me love you. I'm not about to curb my joy for his benefit. If I want a kiss, I'm going to come get it."

"If that's the case, you can have more than a kiss. Say the word."

"Alright now," she said coyly, her eyebrows arching. "In a couple hours? *Word*."

A FEW DAYS LATER, WE WALKED THROUGH THE GARAGE TO Athena's car, spotless from a recent wash and full of gas. We'd spent the last few days packing boxes to ship to Houston and taking care of the house, making sure everything was in good condition. We'd made promises to return twice a year to check up on things and visit. I had a feeling that once Darius saw Black Diamond, he'd want to visit his mother regularly.

"Keep tabs on everything and stay on schedule. We can go over anything that needs repair the first of every month. Don't let things fester, alright?"

"Ma, I've been taking care of the house this whole time," said Darius, following us to the car in loose shorts and a sleeveless t-shirt.

"I want you to *keep* taking care of it. Get to work finding a roommate, someone to share the expenses. I am serious about that rent payment starting in the new year."

"I heard you the first three times you told me. How long will it take you to get to Houston?"

"It's a twelve-hour drive," I answered. "The way Athena drives, though…"

She rolled her eyes at me, then said. "We probably won't hit Houston until almost midnight."

"Text me," Darius said. "I'll be up."

"Are you okay?" Athena asked him. "Do we need to talk about anything? Are you and Vance good?"

Darius looked at me, then back to Athena. He paused for an interminably long time before answering. "Yeah. Yeah, we good."

"Okay. Well, check in with your face. Why are you scowling?"

"I'm about to send my mama off with some man she met on the internet," he said, a deep V of concern popping up between his eyes. "But...I want you to go do your thing. You're good at what you do. You should be able to do that in a spot that makes you happy. Sucks that it's not here, but..."

He shrugged his shoulders. My heart panged a little, watching the emotions cross his face.

Athena held out her arms, and Darius stepped into them. "I love you, baby. And I'm proud of you. Remember that."

"I love you too, Ma." Darius pulled back and forced a smile. "For real. Text me when you get in."

Athena nodded, hugging him again before turning to me. "You ready?"

"Let's hit it. Darius—" I held out a fist to him. "I really am glad I got to meet you."

He surprised me by bumping it with his. "Take care of my mom."

"For sure. Looking forward to seeing you in Houston in a few weeks. As soon as we have a closing date on the condo, I'll book your ticket."

Darius nodded. His gaze didn't have an edge to it anymore, and he was almost friendly. The past few days of giving him space to adjust but also not hiding from him or avoiding him had worked wonders on a friendlier relationship. I didn't see us ever being close or warm, but cordial with me and respectful of his mother was all I asked for.

The offer to fly him to Houston to help us close the house and drive Athena's car to Black Diamond didn't hurt.

"A few hours of work for a free trip to the beach? I'll be ready."

We got into the car and started the engine. Darius stood in the garage with his arms folded across his chest. I met his eyes through the windshield and detected an almost imperceptible nod of his head.

Athena slid a hand over to my lap. I glanced over at her, returning the soft smile on her lips. All the tension that had my shoulders up around my ears had dissipated. Things were falling into place.

"One kid down, three to go."

"Don't make me nervous," Athena said. "You're springing all three of your kids on me in a few days."

"They'll love you. Even Kareema."

Athena rolled her eyes, sending a frown in my direction. "Vance."

"She will *eventually* be okay. We have to get there, first. Do you think you can keep your hands to yourself while I drive us home?"

I teased her, playfully fighting the crawl of her fingers up the inside of my thigh.

"No," she replied, turning her hand over so our fingers intertwined. "Let's go home, handsome."

Nothing made me happier than hearing those words. Almost a year ago, I slid into the Instagram DMs of a woman who caught my eye. Every single moment since had been one adrenaline rush after another.

Now we were about to ride off toward a future that we had crafted together.

Athena leaned in for a kiss. Her tongue slid past my lips

and swirled around mine. I groaned, reaching for her as she pressed closer to me.

"Ay!" Darius' booming voice cut through the romantic moment. "Y'all can do that when you hit Houston!"

We pulled away while laughing. I reversed the car out of the driveway and headed west.

EPILOGUE
ATHENA

> Vance-Wanderlust Travel: Meet me on the beach in your white dress...
>
> Thena W: first of all...
>
> Vance-Wanderlust Travel: you know how the rest go!
>
> Thena W: you are so lucky you already proposed.
>
> Vance-Wanderlust Travel: I'm not scared of Darius.

"I'LL SEE YOU TOMORROW AT 10AM, SAFIYA. DON'T FORGET TO have those photos of your grandson ready. I swear, he's growing up so fast!"

My smile lingered after I ended the call, pulling my earbuds out and placing them back into their case. I plugged the case in to recharge, then pulled up my digital calendar.

I updated my monthly appointment with Safiya Otieno, a 68-year-old Kenyan woman who had retired and moved to Black Diamond. I pulled up her file in Carecenta, the software that I used to manage patient care, and added a reminder to record her blood pressure since she had been diagnosed with hypertension. I would review her medication protocol, sort her meds into easy-to-use pill organizers, and observe her for signs of potential issues.

I saved my notes and signed out, flipping back to the appointment calendar. I had a scheduled lunch with Sabrina to discuss her latest appointment with her Endocrinologist and progress with managing her Type 2 Diabetes, and a few patients at a nearby Memory Care facility to visit.

My week was rounding out to be a full one. Though I had planned to launch my business in January, I'd been busy providing comprehensive care to patients on Black Diamond and in Corpus Christi as soon as my license was granted.

Nine months had passed in the blink of an eye. Vance and I arrived on Black Diamond as the golden hues of September were fading. We breathed life into my office and our guest room, trading the stark, clinical white walls for warm earth tones, and surrounded ourselves with art, greenery, and cozy furniture. The condo didn't just look different—it felt different, like a place you'd want to kick off your shoes and relax.

It felt like home.

I savored every moment of weaving our lives together, of Vance and I moving around each other as if we'd been together for years and not mere months. Our everyday routines fostered habits that brought us together instead of catching each other in scattered video calls with miles between us.

Our mornings kicked off together, trading lonely Zoom logins for shared showers. We eased into the day on our balcony—Vance with his green tea, me with my coffee. Though we shared an office, Vance often packed up his laptop and headed down to the resort offices. Wanderlust Travel had a suite there, and he liked hanging out with Davis. Their partnership was doing wonders for The Pearl. Occupancy was up, local gigs were regular, and the resort had been booked for weddings nearly every weekend—including ours, scheduled for early fall.

I pushed back from my desk to stand, chuckling as my joints responded with a chorus of pops. I had to remind myself to move more on the desk days, where I traded home visits with clients for paperwork and calls. Shaking off the stiffness, I walked to the French doors and nudged them open, stepping out onto the balcony that skirted our condo. A gentle breeze played with my shoulder-length curls—a style I could maintain now that I didn't have to go months without a salon visit.

A knock drew me away from the view. I glanced over my shoulder and grinned at Vance framed in the doorway in his usual attire of dark shorts and a Wanderlust polo.

"Hi, gorgeous," he said, walking through my office, drawing an arm around my waist.

"Hi, handsome," I replied, leaning into his embrace. "How was the day?"

"Great. My group arrived on time, everyone's checked in and last I heard, they were already at the poolside bar." He leaned in to kiss me, then added, "Davis and I were planning to go for a ride after dinner."

I groaned, pulling back. "Don't try to butter me up with those lips, Vance. You know I get nervous about you riding around at night."

I was not a fan of Vance's new fascination with motorcycles, egged on by Davis, who was an avid rider. Vance had completed a course, and I was assured that he was a safe rider, but it made me nervous to think of him out there, vulnerable against tourist drivers.

"So I can't go?" he asked, the corners of his mouth twitching with his attempts to keep his smile at bay.

"I didn't say that. Just please be careful. I want you in one piece on two legs when we get married."

Vance chuckled, the sound reverberating through his chest. "I am always careful, baby. But I promise to take it easy."

"Thank you. Because I have plans for later." I playfully nipped at his earlobe.

"Later?" Vance turned me in his arms, stepping closer to press me against the iron railing. In his eyes, I saw sparks of something wickedly sexy. "Can I get a preview?"

"Mmmmm..." I hummed, my hands beginning to wander over his chest, my fingers trailing the stitching of the Wanderlust logo. "I don't know. If I start, I won't want to stop."

His lips captured mine in a kiss, his tongue tracing along the seam. My mouth opened and our tongues entwined, dancing in a sensuous rhythm.

"Then we should definitely start."

We kissed like we hadn't kissed in weeks or months, instead of just that morning. He moved a hand behind my head, holding me against him so he could taste me.

I already ached to be closer to him. I was still in awe that I could be with him when I wanted to be. No planes, no travel, no waiting. I moved in closer, grinding against the heavy bulge pressing into my thigh.

He broke the kiss with a hard breath. "We'd better get inside unless we're fucking on the balcony again."

I snorted a laugh at the memory of our first day at The Pearl, when we couldn't resist each other long enough to even go inside our suite. We enjoyed each other in full view of the resort, lucky that occupancy was low so we weren't caught.

Or so we thought.

Months later, Davis mentioned that he had received a call about a couple engaging in *activity* on a balcony in the Elysium Tower. Vance liked to bring it up now and again, sometimes as a challenge but mostly as a tease.

"If you weren't so irresistible, we would have never fucked on the balcony, so none of that is on me."

A smile spread across his lips before he led me back inside and locking the door behind us. He cupped my face in both hands and leaned in for another hungry kiss, then moved us through the office down the hall to the bedroom. We shed clothing along the way, murmuring between and over stolen kisses.

In the hallway, among images of our family and friends, an oversized framed print served as the focal point. It captured the moment when Vance sank to one knee at Nauyaca Waterfall in San Jose, Costa Rica, presented a glittering diamond ring to me, and asked me to spend the rest of my life with him.

I accepted before he even finished his proposal.

Our bedroom was a private paradise. Soft white linens draped the bed with cozy blankets tucked at the foot. A plush chaise lounge sat in the corner in front of the built-in bookshelves that were now full of romance books that Vance had pledged to read. We painted the walls a serene blue with black and white photographs of us from various travels on display—Vance's research trip to a boutique hotel in Cartagena, our holidays spent in Accra, Ghana, and our anniversary trip to Costa Rica the previous month.

Vance scooped me up, spilling me onto the spacious bed that we had moved from his house in Houston. It was ridiculously large but fit the room well. His warm body followed, blanketing me with his weight. My arms snaked around him, my fingers tracing the rippling muscles under his skin, more prominent since he now had access to several gyms on property.

I tipped my head back. He kissed a path along the base of my neck up to my ear. My body thrummed, wide awake. I tilted my hips, pressing against his, gasping at the heat radiating off of his body. I made room for him to move in closer, savoring the sensation of his body grinding against me, his hips rocking in rhythm with mine.

I arched into him as he took a taut nipple into his mouth. An intense, pleasured moan rolled from me as his tongue flicked over the sensitive tip. He sucked harder, then switched to the other and gave it the same treatment, following each bite with soothing kisses that set my skin on fire.

"I love this. I love you," Vance panted in my ear, beads of sweat trailing down his body as he shifted from languid, sensual strokes to forceful thrusts. His fingers and mine tightly clasped together, our bodies joined in the most delicious dance. I felt him swell and pulse as he drove deeper.

We moved together as one—I felt his every sensation reverberate through mine. I met him thrust for thrust with a need that consumed me. "You feel so good, baby," I whimpered. "I love how you feel inside me."

"Thena…." He moaned, pressing his forehead against mine as his body shuddered. "Where you at?"

I hissed, hunching my pelvis so my clit met his pubic bone. "Almost there. Take me with you!"

Vance sucked in a breath, his eyes wide open, watching me as he thrust harder, deeper, faster, our bodies smashed together, moans mingling. I moved with him, opening my legs wider, inviting him in even closer.

He cried out, his voice gruff and tight, followed by loud moans as he broke, growing stiff as his climax washed over him.

I exploded around him, my walls pulsing, clenching, throbbing. The sensation was simultaneously blissful and overwhelming, exquisite and intense.

Vance moaned, burying his head in the crook of my neck before he collapsed onto me, heaving deep, hard breaths. We laid together, our bodies still connected, our skin slick with sweat.

After a few minutes, Vance shifted, pulling out, then rolling us to the side. He sat up to pull up the light blanket we kept at the foot of the bed to cover us. We lay with him at my back as his hand caressed my skin from my breasts to my hips, down my thigh and back up. His lips brushed my cheek, then my shoulder as he rested his temple against mine.

"You know...you ain't slick," he muttered.

I smiled. "What am I not slick about?"

"You don't want me to be out there on the bike after dark. So you teased and tempted me..."

He paused when I pushed up on my elbow and shifted my body around. "Don't stop now. I need to see your face while you make up this story to blame me that you're too tired to ride tonight."

Vance laughed, pulling me close to him again. "Did I ask how your day was?"

"Changing the subject. Good tactic."

"How was your day, Nurse Wilcox?"

I tucked myself up against his chest and slid my arm over his hip. "It was great," I answered, feeling the smile take over my face. "I'm really getting into a good groove. I get calls every day to sign new clients and the medical center is interested in referring patients for postoperative care."

"If you got a few nurses to sign on as contractors, you could have a nice enterprise out here."

"I know, right? Once I get into more of a rhythm, I want to talk to Davis about providing services at the resort. I want to feel like I have my legs under me first."

"Sure. But I know you could do it when you're ready."

"I'm getting there," I said, lifting my gaze to meet his. With a smile, I brushed my fingers against his jawline. "I have you to thank, Vance. Giving me cover while I get myself situated has meant the world to me. I couldn't do this without you."

"Nah, gorgeous. That's all you. I'm just over here watching you do your thing."

The move to Black Diamond and launching my business had done exactly what I had hoped it would do—revitalize and change my life for the best. For the first time in years, I felt like I belonged somewhere. And had someone to share that with.

"I guess we should have dinner so you can meet Davis for your ride."

Vance stretched, yawning as he did so. "Sounds like a plan. You want to go down to Breakers? To Clinks?"

"Mmmm...let's cook something," I suggested, pushing myself up and throwing the blanket back. "When we toured this place, I had daydreams of casual evenings cooking together, having a glass of wine, talking about our day."

I reached for the robe that I kept near the bed and slipped my arms into it, tying it at the waist. "I love that we're together every day now. I haven't got enough of you yet today."

"You sound sufficiently spoiled. Job well done."

Vance rolled off of the bed, found his t-shirt and shorts on the way back down the hall and pulled them on. Then he joined me in the kitchen.

"You begged me to let you take me somewhere and spoil me." I rose onto my toes, hooked an arm around his neck, and kissed him. "Love you, handsome."

Vance smiled down at me, tracing the pad of his thumb over my cheek. "Being able to tell you how much I love you to your face is all I ever wanted. Love you too, gorgeous."

Meet Wade & Ameenah

Beach Thing is a charming, steamy novel set in picturesque Black Diamond Isles.

As the summer unfolds, so does a tantalizing romance between two unlikely individuals, each nursing wounds. Amid shared cocktails, laughter, and intimate secrets, they navigate personal challenges, trying to reconcile their past with a potential future together.

Turn the page to meet Wade and Ameenah, two souls on a journey where the sand meets the sea. Their love story, filled with passion, resilience, and the promise of new beginnings, is waiting to unfold.

Welcome to the Black Diamond series, where every wave brings a new tale of love.

AMEENAH

"A little more. More. *Higher*, Andrew!"

"Ameenah…"

Andrew grumbled, but lifted the sign higher. Perched on the top rung of the ladder, he held the long wooden board in place while my cousin secured it so it hung over the front entrance.

Once he had finished, we all stepped back to take in the view of the wooden building with the fresh coat of white paint and the *Tikis & Cream* sign finally hung. Satisfied, I smiled and let out a long sigh. It had been a long journey to *here*.

In the last six months I had upended my entire life to move to Black Diamond Isles, a cluster of man-made islands off the coast of Black Diamond Bay. I had found the perfect location for my coffee/smoothie/juice bar and renovated the space, doing a lot of the work myself to save money…and now I was *finally* open.

The *pièce de résistance* was a custom designed sign for the shop. My cousin, Liam, had shipped it from New York and he and my brother flew down to the island for a long weekend to hang it for me.

"Looks good, right?" Liam slung an arm over my shoulder, beaming with pride.

I stood in the middle of the sidewalk, just staring. I couldn't take my eyes off of the vibrant, beachy colors and the crisp lettering. My heartbeat sped up a little as I realized how it stood out amongst all the other shops on the boardwalk. I almost let a tear build up, but blinked it away. The long days and longer nights ahead would take care of that wistful feeling.

"It's beautiful," I told him. "I really love it. Now I'm official."

"You were always official, Meenah."

"Thanks, Liam. I mean it. For the sign, for coming down and helping me get things squared away. For…everything."

I hugged him, then stepped back to find my brother smirking, leaning his bulky frame against the counter. "You too, you big jealous fool." I gave Andrew a good heavy thump on the back, which he seemed to appreciate. "Even though all you did was hold the sign while Liam nailed it in, and stand around while he took care of my honey-do list."

"I paid for the tickets," quipped Andrew. "And I carried a couple of things from the house."

"He's a hard worker," said Liam, packing the last of the tools into a toolbox. "We'd better hit the road, though. There's an hour drive to the airport and if I miss my flight, the words Denise will use to describe me will peel the paint off of your walls."

I nodded, trying not to tear up again. This would be the last time I'd see them for a while. "I know she misses you and your help with the twins. Thank her for me, for letting you come."

"What about Kath? Should I thank her for you too?" I rolled my eyes, raising my arms to slide them around Andrew's shoulders. I squeezed him extra hard—our signature hug.

"Katherine has probably got so much done around the house without you."

"I love how you love me, Meenah." The jokey tone left his voice and his face took on a serious pallor. "You take care of yourself, alright? Don't hesitate to call, day or night. Well, not night because a man be working hard and be tired and everything..."

I giggled, appreciating the lightening of the mood before things got too heavy. "Thank you for everything you've done to support me. I know Mom and Dad think I'm crazy, but..."

I glanced back at the building, then up to my new sign, which marked the opening of my business. "This is my dream. Now go. As much as we joke, Kath will probably be happy to see you."

"Damn right," bellowed Andrew, picking up the backpack he'd toted to the shop earlier. "Man of the house comin' home!"

"He's all extra loud right now cause Kath would tell him to shut his big head up." Liam chuckled, then lifted his hand in a wave. "Ditto on what he said, though. Need us? Call us. We'll be here."

I watched them loaf down the sidewalk toward the main drag, where they would catch a cab to the small airstrip and head back to New York. Leaving me here.

In Black Diamond.

By myself.

A cold fear slithered down my spine. I shivered, trying to chase it away.

"Excuse me?"

I turned to find a middle-aged woman standing in front of my shop, holding a laminated half-sheet of paper—the *Tikis & Cream* menu. Her toasted cinnamon complexion bore a light sheen of sweat. "Are you open? I want one of these juice drinks."

I brightened, propping the door open. I flipped the

CLOSED sign to OPEN, then stepped inside and behind the counter.

"Yes ma'am, I am open. What can I get for you?"

WADE

Gage grunted while lifting the case from the back of the moving van. "I mean, you didn't have to bring the whole studio."

"I didn't." I took the case from him, then shook my head. It wasn't even heavy. "You need to hit the gym."

"I hit the gym. I wasn't expecting a workout today. Is this the last of the stuff?" Gage peered around the open rear door, inspecting the now empty interior of the van.

"That's it. Everything is out of my car."

"Let's get this in the house, then. I'll show you where you can set up."

Gage grabbed a few items and trotted from the circular driveway into the house. I was a few paces behind, trying to get used to the fact that I would live in this...*house*, if you want to call it that, all summer. With six bedrooms, eight bathrooms, a heated pool and jacuzzi, three fireplaces, a fire pit and, just over the cliff, the white sands and blue waters of Black Diamond Bay, it felt more like a mansion, but Gage shrugged that off.

"Just a house, man," he'd said when he told me about his place on an island a few weeks ago.

We'd been in the studio all day, and it had been a rough time of it. Gage thought I needed a break and offered his beach place up for the summer. "We bought it as a tax break. I thought we'd be down there all the time but according to my wife, it's not better than her parent's place, so..."

He trailed off with a shrug, miscellaneously punching buttons on the console. "You're welcome to it. Sheree and the kids will still be in Jamaica."

It took me a few days before I felt comfortable accepting his offer, only relenting after he said he'd planned on driving down with me. "May as well get some use out of the place."

I stepped into the house, still feeling a little weird about the grandiose foyer and the expensive tile floors, the spacious rooms and the air of wealth that surrounded everything from the knick knacks to the fixtures. The fireplaces had gold plated pokers. I lived a simpler existence, so the excess tripped me out, but I was grateful to have a nice place to spend the summer. I could use the time and space away from the city. Away from the studio.

Away from my father, a man I never knew, had rarely seen except through a pane of glass and a telephone handset. A man who, a few weeks ago, popped up straight out of nowhere asking to be known. I *definitely* could use some time away from him.

"So I put everything in this room back here," Gage was saying as he rounded a corner. "I had extra power runs put in because that's where I was going to put my studio. There's a nice workspace near the windows so you get a view while you're working."

Half listening, I followed Gage to the back of the house. It *was* a nice area, more like an extended sunroom with a long span of windows along one wall. Beyond the pool and the extra acreage that surrounded the house, the Bay shimmered, washing up onto the sand. I kind of couldn't wait to set up on the beach in a chair with an ice cold beer, my iPod and some earbuds.

I exhaled, feeling the weight of the world lift a little.

"You alright, man?" I turned to find Gage studying me while flipping open the black cases that held the equipment he had driven down in the van. "I mean, this place is cool, right? You gonna be okay out here by yourself?"

"Oh, yeah. It's cool. It'll be a good summer."

I set down the cases and bags I was holding and joined Gage in getting the room set up. He'd be leaving the next day, so I wanted to take advantage of having two sets of hands.

Hours later, the room was starting to resemble *Tuneage*, my Brooklyn studio. I'd opened it after Gage's first release, produced by yours truly, jumped from the mid-20's to the top ten on the Billboard hip hop charts. We were a team, always had been since back in the day. Throughout junior high and high school, Gage wrote and rapped, sang a little, too. I was the beat factory and had a lot going on in my own right. The deal was that whoever hit it big first brought the other one along.

Gage was discovered on the radio, some New York morning show where wannabe rappers would call in and freestyle over a beat. He blew everyone away, and if that wasn't amazing enough, he got a phone call later that day that a major producer wanted to talk to him. Gage turned him down. "Already got Wade on the beats. He's the only one I work with."

After orchestrating a deal that included me, he released three chart topping records. His star was bright and while it should have gone to his head, it didn't. He was the same old Gage I always knew. Married his high school sweetheart, bought a nice spot, put his kids in Catholic private school. Gage Coleman lived a real good life.

I, on the other hand...I'm not saying my life was shitty, but I spent a lot of time at the Coleman's because I didn't have much of anyone else. My mother had worked long hours at a nursing home; my dad had been...*away* since I was young. We had no real family to speak of since my mother and her family were estranged after she got with my dad against their wishes.

Gage's family became my family, and it's always been that way. When he heard about my dad getting sprung and wanting to come around, Gage understood my freakout. But since his success hinged on me doing what I do, he wanted me to get it together, and *quickly*.

I wiped a few beads of sweat from my hairline and stood from a crouching position, where I'd been running some cords under a table. I took a glance around the room to see what else needed to be unpacked and plugged in, but things were looking nice. I still had to connect my speakers, run a few auxiliary cords, and take care of some minor things, but I figured that by the following night, music would be booming from this room.

I smiled at the prospect.

"You wanna grab some beers, some wings or something? The main drag is a few blocks away. We can walk."

I checked my watch. A feeling of emptiness in the pit of my stomach reminded me I hadn't eaten in a while. "Sounds good. I want to change my shirt. I'm covered in dust."

"You think you're gonna meet someone that cares about your dirty shirt?"

I laughed, heading to the bedroom I'd claimed for the summer. "You know your mama taught us to not look like just anything in public."

"I guess you're right. I'll change, too. You can't be looking better than me."

AMEENAH

I pulled down the metal shade to obscure the open counter, flipped the OPEN sign to CLOSED on the front of the shop and stepped outside, pulling the door shut behind me.

My first full day as owner and proprietor of *Tikis & Cream* was a success. I had a steady stream of customers, hot and sweaty from being on the beach and ready for a refreshing drink. I keyed both locks and checked the door, then weaved into the stream of foot traffic along the sidewalk. I was going to have to hire some help, sooner rather than later. If every day was like today—

A bump from behind me interrupted my train of thought. I turned to mutter an apology, but the words stuck in my throat. Two broad-shouldered men were so close, I caught a whiff of spicy cologne. I saw wide smiles on handsome, smooth milk chocolate faces bearing perfectly trimmed goatees. One had gorgeous amber-colored eyes, the other's were a deep, dark espresso and he seemed...really *familiar*. Both stepped aside as they passed me, nodding in my direction as they continued their conversation.

"Excuse you," I called out to muscle-bound backs. They turned to face me, genuine surprise in both sets of eyes.

"Excuse *us*?" said the shorter one. "You came out of there and didn't even look where you were going. I almost tripped over you. So excuse *you*, miss."

"You could have said something. You bumped into me, almost knocked me over—"

"Miss," said the taller one, lifting a hand, I guess to quiet me. "We didn't see that you were coming out of the shop. Excuse us. We cool?"

I huffed, folding my arms across my chest. "Fine. We *cool* or whatever."

He smiled and pointed two fingers at me. Then I recognized him.

I was letting my smart mouth run all over Billboard's number one hip hop artist, Gage Coleman! I had his latest release on heavy rotation on iTunes and my best friend, Paige, was madly in love with him.

My eyes grew wide and I sucked in a loud breath. He placed a finger over his lips and winked, then stuck out his hand. "Gage. This is Wade."

"I'm so rude. Don't mind me. Ameenah, nice to meet you."

Gage's grip was strong, his hand soft as I shook it. Wade reluctantly offered his, and I shook it, too. Now that I looked at him instead of glaring at him, I recognized him as Gage's longtime producer.

"We're looking for beer and good wings. Does that exist out here?"

"A couple of places, yeah. But if you're looking for something close..." I pointed toward worn out shack at the end of the block with the line out the front door. "Sparky's down there has great wings. Lots of flavors. Get extra napkins, though. They're messy."

Gage nodded, rubbing his palms together. "Good lookin' out." He eyed the shop behind me, then glanced at Wade, who rolled his eyes. "Looks like you're closed up for the day. Do you want to join us?"

I *wanted* to join them, actually. I really *really* wanted to hang out with famous, handsome men that had just happened to bump into me, but it had been a long day, I still had things to do before I could go to bed, I was tired as hell and my new job had disgraceful hours.

"Thanks, but I'd better be heading home. Maybe next time!" I walked around them, making myself leave before I did or said something stupid. Again. "Enjoy your wings!"

"Gage Coleman, in the flesh! And I recognized his producer, too. Wade something."

"Wade Marshall?"

Paige's voice rose to an octave I didn't think she could reach. "Are they as fine in real life as they are in this spread for MAXIMUM? Talking about Hip Hop's Dream Team. *Mmmmph*, Gage is *everything* I want on my team."

I laughed, dropping into one end of the couch with a bowl of ice cream. "I hope a bullet in your ass is something you want, too. Sheree Coleman don't play about her man. She will cut a bitch."

"Don't I know it. I heard about one girl in a club getting too close, kept hugging him, hanging on him, grinning all in his face and wouldn't step back. Sheree took right care of that mess." I heard her tongue clicking and pages turning. "Anyway, how long do you think they're in town?"

"I don't know. I haven't seen them before and I've been here awhile. I'm guessing they just got here. And from the looks of the lights going on and off at the house on the corner, that's where they're staying."

"You mean that big house with the circular driveway and the pool and the...everything?"

"Mmmhmmm," I hummed, licking ice cream off of my spoon. I loved ice cream. It was my nightly treat—just a small bowl. To start with.

"How's everything going? You ready for me to come down there yet?"

"Actually," I said, almost choking on a too-big bite of chocolate chunk. "I'm going to need some help sooner than I thought. Not saying I can afford for you to quit your new job at that fancy law firm and move down here—"

"They won't miss me."

"Right. Does anyone else do any work? I'm sure you do everything over there."

"You're right. I am dope and they'd be lost without me." I rolled my eyes, even though she was agreeing with me. "So what are you going to do about getting some help?"

"See how long I can go before I fall over from exhaustion. Then probably place an ad in *The Bullhorn*." Black Diamond had its own newspaper for residents. If you needed to buy something, wanted to sell something, needed to announce something, it went into *The Bullhorn*.

"Please don't work yourself to the bone. At least not before I build up some vacation time and can come down there."

We chatted for a few minutes more while I scraped the bowl with my spoon—my signal that it was time to brush my teeth and crawl into bed. I set my alarm for 5:30 and I wasn't even sure that would be early enough.

"I'm turning into a pumpkin. Kiss everybody for me. Talk to you soon."

I signed off with Paige, dropped my bowl into the dishwasher and turned it on so it could work while I slept. A glint of light caught my eye as I passed the kitchen window overlooking the beach. I reached over to the wall and snapped off the overhead light, then waited for my eyes to adjust to the darkness.

I watched a figure trudge through the sand, just along the edge of the water, a mobile phone lighting up the night. Since he was walking from the direction of the house on the corner, I guessed that it was Wade.

Before I could stop myself, I opened the kitchen door and stepped out onto the deck, flipping on the porch light and walking to the edge. I leaned against the railing and waited for him to slip his phone into his pocket and make his way over.

"It's you," he said, when he got close enough for me to hear him.

"It's me, that loud mouth girl from earlier."

He chuckled. "I'm not saying all that. I was checking out the beach. I'm a city guy, so I don't get to see this often."

"This beach is great. I love the breeze off of the Bay at night." As if on cue, we both took a glance at the rolling waves, lit by the moon sitting high above. "So I guess we're neighbors."

He nodded, glancing toward the large house lit up like Christmas, then back to me. "It's Gage's place, but he's lending it out for the summer."

He paused, then the rest of the sentence rushed out of his mouth, like he was trying to beat me to some kind of finish line. "So listen, I'm sorry about earlier. I was tired and hungry."

I shrugged. "I was preoccupied. Should have watched where I was going."

"Well anyway, my mama raised me a gentleman. My apologies." He paused for a beat, then asked, "You run that little smoothie shop there?"

"I do." I nodded. "Just opened officially today."

"Yeah?" I heard the smile in his deep tenor. "No wonder you were preoccupied. That's good. I like to see people doing for themselves. Congrats."

"Thanks. You should stop by the shop tomorrow. I'll make you something on the house. If you want."

"You can't make money giving drinks away. I'll happily pay for something."

I laughed, stepping back from the railing surrounding the wood deck. "And I'll happily take your money. See you tomorrow."

WADE

"Say hey to the wife and the girls for me," I called to Gage's retreating back as he climbed the steps to board the aircraft. He lifted a hand to acknowledge me and then he was gone, swallowed up into the cavernous belly of the plane. Once the stairwell started to slowly pull up, I put the car in drive and pulled out of the private airstrip onto the main road.

Before long, I was crossing the bridge back into Black Diamond Isles. I was eager to park the car and then go find that little shake shack again.

And see Ameenah again.

We'd gotten off on the wrong foot a little. I felt like I fixed it last night, but patronizing her business would be a good move.

Not that I needed to be looking up women on the island already. Or at all. I had enough issues to deal with, enough things going on in my life that losing focus on a woman was just adding fuel to the fire.

She was pretty, though. The wild, deep brown curls that framed her face were just barely contained in a clip. Her skin was golden, probably from working on the shop. Or maybe hanging out on her back deck. I noticed her thick lips when they were pursed and scowling in my direction. *And* I noticed those thick hips when she settled her hands on them in obvious displeasure.

I strolled the main drag between the beach and the beach-side businesses. No vehicles were allowed on the street, only service carts, bicycles and foot traffic. I took my time, swinging my head from side to side, noting everything that was offered: t-shirts, beach swag, places to rent kayaks, canoes and stand up paddles, places to buy life jackets, water wings and snorkel gear. Then there were the restaurants—hot dogs, hamburgers, sausages, fries, wings, Italian ice and snow cones.

In the background, the Bay provided a regular, rhythmic soundtrack of waves rolling up onto the shore, then pulling back. I slept with my windows open last night, just to hear the sound.

I turned into the open door at *Tikis & Cream*, slipping off my shades and hooking them onto the collar of my shirt. The line was three people deep, so I stood to the side and occupied a high bar stool along the wall. Ameenah was pleasant and peppy, not showing a hint she'd been up too late investigating a creeper on the beach the night before.

Once her waiting customers had been served, she stepped around the counter, a wide smile beaming in my direction.

"You made it!"

"I had to make an airport run, see Gage off to join his family on vacation. I was checking out your menu. You think I could get one of these Frozen Sunshines you have listed here?" I pointed to an item on the menu, but she didn't need to look at it to know what it was.

"Coming right up. You want whipped cream on it?"

I shrugged. "Why not? I've already had wings and beer. My abs will be gone by the time I leave this place."

She laughed, moving behind the counter and deftly performing the tasks to make my drink. She had practiced a lot, it seemed. She knew where everything was without having to look for it, and everything she needed was in arm's reach. Whoever had designed her workspace knew what they were doing.

I had the same philosophy about the studio. No need for a huge space when I am going to use the same ten things over and over. May as well keep them near me.

"It's tempting to try *everything* when you're new to the island. Give yourself a week to explore; there really are some neat places here. And if you want, I can show you some healthier options. There's so much more to this place than the strip along the beach."

"Yeah, that'd be nice. There's a weight room in the house, but I'd like to get out every once in a while. Is there a gym nearby?"

She gestured for me to wait a moment, since the mixer was too loud to talk over. When she'd finished blending, she said, "There are two, actually. One tiny gym and one big gym, like Gold's."

"Sounds great. And like, the grocery store and a bank— which I'm sure I can find on my own, but if you're offering to be my tour guide…"

I took in the view of a bright orange, frothy concoction topped with a mound of whipped cream. "Damn! I might need to join that gym real soon if I'm going to be drinking these all summer."

"Now, this is made with fruit, ice cream and juice that have no sugar added, so I'm not giving you any unnecessary calories. Except for the whipped cream, but that's essential to finish it off."

She waited while I sucked some through the straw, then grinned at how fast my eyebrows lifted. "Yes?"

"So much yes," I swooned, sucking down more of the ice cold orange mix. "Very much yes. This is good."

"Thanks. I created it myself."

"Oh yeah? Well, you outdid yourself with this one."

She whipped a white towel from where it had been tucked into the back pocket of her khaki shorts, grabbed a bottle with a spray nozzle from behind the counter, and began wiping down surfaces.

"My family owns a restaurant group back in New York. One of the spots we own is a storefront near Long Beach. I worked a lot of summers there, and in the down time I would experiment with different combinations. I'm always trying something new with ice cream and fruit and juice…it's pretty interesting."

She'd been talking and wiping, making her way across the room. I'd been sipping and listening, watching her. Finding herself at the table next to mine, she set the spray bottle and the towel down and climbed up onto a stool. "At least…I think it's interesting."

"No, it is. It is. I mean, it's recipes, right? A little of this, a little of that, something to hold it together. I can relate."

"Yeah. A lot like that."

A small group piled into the shop, laughing and talking loudly, toting beach bags and towels. "That's my sign to get back to work. Let me know when you want that tour. Happy to do it."

I gave her a wave as I left, slurping the rest of my drink and headed back to the house, set to get my room ready for work. I'd been off my game seriously since I'd heard from my father three months ago. It was coming out in everything I put my hands to. My work and my relationship with my mother were both strained. I couldn't afford to mess up either. Ruth Marshall was everything I had in the world. And without music, I may as well not exist.

As soon as I stepped into the house, my phone vibrated in my pocket. I pulled it out to glance at the display, but I already knew it would be her. Like always, exactly when my mind drifted to her, there she was on my phone. We had a crazy connection that way.

"Hey Ma," I greeted her, pressing the phone to my ear as I made my way through the house. I strolled through the kitchen and grabbed a bottle of water from the stash Gage had left in the refrigerator.

"So you're alive," she responded, dryly. Truth be told, it was her regular tone. She only perked up for company. "Good to hear your voice, son."

"Thanks, Ma. We made it yesterday, then had to get unpacked and everything before Gage flew back out this morning. Just now getting back to the house. What's going on up there?"

I listened to my mother give me a rundown of the boring things happening in Astoria. I'd offered to buy her a brown-stone, something in Westchester or even out in the country upstate, but all she wanted was a nice place in the city she'd lived in for most of her life. She loved the upscale condo I bought her...updated interior, stainless steel appliances and the rooftop terrace. She and her girlfriends—The Biddies, they called themselves, liked to sit up there, drink and play cards with a view of Queens in every direction. Every once in a while she talked me into showing up so The Biddies could fawn over me.

"So you're really going to hide out on some island all summer, then? Leave your poor, destitute mother back in New York with no one to take care of her?"

I was laughing before she'd finished her sentence. I knew how much money I deposited into her account every month. She was nowhere near destitute, and she'd made friends with every resident in her building. I couldn't even stop by to take her to dinner nowadays. She was always rushing off to one thing or another.

"Stop, Ma. Don't make me feel guilty. You know I need this."

"Yeah." She heaved a deep, long sigh. I knew the feeling. "Yes, you sure do. Over the years, there were a lot of times I wished I could disappear. Have you heard from him?"

"I saw him a few days before I left town. I won't give him my number, so he doesn't call, but he found out where *Tuneage* is, so he'd been dropping by every few weeks."

I leaned my shoulder against the entryway to my temporary studio, watching the waves through the enormous windows. "I have nothing to say to him. You know?"

"Neither do I."

"Has he been in touch with you?" I pushed off of the wall and listened hard. If that man was bothering my mother I would be on the first thing smoking back to New York to let him know what was up. He'd been gone for a long time, far too long to mend broken fences.

"No, I haven't seen him since the last time I took you to visit him and you said you didn't want to go anymore. He stopped calling a bit after that. And then I moved and changed my number."

"Okay. Good. Let me know if you see him or hear from him. You hear me, Ma?"

"Don't worry, I will let you know. How's everything down in...where are you?"

"Black Diamond. You're welcome to come and check it out. Stay a few days. I'm right on the beach."

"Oh, you know I'm not really a beach person. It sounds nice though. Maybe later in the—" She paused at an electronic beep, then continued. "Hey, Neeta is calling me. She's supposed to come over and play Bid Whist. You take care of yourself, son."

"I will, Ma. Love you and say hey to Aunt Neet for me."

I slid the phone back into my pocket and headed to my studio, turned on some music, and got to work.

Continue your trip to the sugar white sands and emerald waters of Black Diamond in Beach Thing, A Black Diamond Romance at booksbydlwhite.com/beachthing.

Acknowledgments

I'm probably going to forget someone. As the old saying goes, charge it to my head and not my heart.

First to the fam I was born into, the fam I chose and chose me: **I love you all the most and then some**. I thank you so much for your support and enthusiasm for me and these books I write.

Specifically to my Wordmakers, the PDubs, the Trollops, my GirlTime pals, the Guncles, and all my pockets of friends —you make life fun and worth living. Thanks for entertaining my 11PM bursts of *"what if I wrote this?!"*

So many thanks to everyone who read early copies and offered fun reaction emojis and supportive comments. It's good for my feels and my ego.

Special thanks to Johanna Olaitan from **<u>Neptune Travel Group</u>** and Enecia Miller at **<u>Awaken Your Soul Travel LLC</u>,** whose work I brazenly borrowed as inspiration for Vance.

Special thanks to all of the nurses in my life, specifically my friend Toni G, whose life as a travel nurse was an inspiration for Athena. Hope I did you proud.

Thank you to KWM, the best Beta in this hemisphere and *AdotK Edits* for getting. me. *together.* My goodness.

Shout out to me for this *perfect* cover. I do spectacular work—the image is courtesy depositphotos.com.

Also by DL White

Pick up my titles in eBook, print or audio at Booksbydlwhite.com/books

Brunch at Ruby's, a Ruby's novel

Dinner at Sam's, a Ruby's novel

Unexpected, a holiday short

Beach Thing, a Black Diamond Romance

Leslie's Curl & Dye, a Potter Lake Small Town Romance

Second Time Around, a Potter Lake holiday short

The Guy Next Door, a Potter Lake Small Town Romance

The Kwanzaa Brunch, a holiday short

A Thin Line

The Never List

Hey, Lover

www.ingramcontent.com/pod-product-compliance
Lightning Source LLC
Chambersburg PA
CBHW020318200626
46814CB00006BA/2313